Vanished

A BLACKPOOL MYSTERY

Jordan Gray

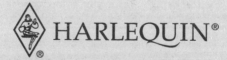

HARLEQUIN®

TORONTO • NEW YORK • LONDON
AMSTERDAM • PARIS • SYDNEY • HAMBURG
STOCKHOLM • ATHENS • TOKYO • MILAN • MADRID
PRAGUE • WARSAW • BUDAPEST • AUCKLAND

Special thanks and acknowledgment to
Lillian Stewart Carl for her contribution
to this work.

Recycling programs
for this product may
not exist in your area.

ISBN-13: 978-0-373-83752-6

VANISHED

CHAPTER ONE

BLACKPOOL'S RED TILE roofs gleamed in the sunshine. Boats dotted the sparkling water of the bay and blooming heather streaked the hills beyond. Even the sinister shape of Ravenhearst Manor, its ruined walls and chimneys like the edge of a serrated knife atop the cliff southeast of town, seemed merely picturesque. What better day for a festival? Michael Graham asked himself.

He wove his way through the people thronging Dockside Avenue and entered what passed for a town square, a cobblestoned rectangle between the old town hall and the longest of the piers—the Magic Lantern Theatre on one side, the seawall bandstand on the other. Murmuring, "I beg your pardon, excuse me, sorry," he dodged a World War II commando and narrowly avoided bouncing off a cavalier dripping lace. The students in shorts and T-shirts who evaded him seemed positively underdressed.

Beside him, Rohan Wallace's dreadlocks bounced up and down as he nodded at a Napoleonic officer wearing a hat the size of a schooner under sail. Beside Rohan, their friend Dylan Stewart collided with a woman garbed in a Victorian gown, knocking her parasol to the ground. He mumbled an apology, retrieved the parasol and handed it back.

Michael swallowed the last bite of his Scotch egg and licked the savory bits of crumb and sausage from his fingertips. Last year, he and his wife, Molly, had wandered through Blackpool's Seafaring Days celebration like children through a toy shop. This year they were participants. Michael had even put together a sort of costume out of an old turtleneck and pea jacket. Molly, on the other hand…

Where was she? He'd last seen her near the stall that was selling strawberries and cream.

Alice Coffey walked by without even a glance his way, her nose high above the cloud of powder-scented perfume emanating from her black clothes. Michael got the message: To some of the locals, he and Molly were still no more than glorified tourists. Newcomers. Outsiders. How long did you have to live in Blackpool, he wondered, and how much did you have to go through to be completely accepted?

Never mind. He and Molly had plenty of friends here. He'd gotten to know native Blackpooler Dylan because of their shared interest in mountain biking, and he'd met Rohan, who was an even more recent arrival, during the terrible events surrounding the theatre murder last spring. That first gruesome murder—the night Molly planned to introduce plans for a documentary on the 1939 Blackpool train robbery—had led to several others that Michael and Molly helped solve. All of Blackpool was both intrigued and appalled, especially when stolen artwork from the train seemed to bear the fingerprints of the Crowe family ancestors.

The tall Jamaican nudged Michael now and pointed to a group of local teenagers. Michael recognized them as part of the tunnel rats, a group devoted to exploring the maze of tunnels and caves beneath Blackpool. The Abercrombie boys and one of the Norton girls were dressed in pirate costumes, while the older Norton girl wore a serving wench outfit. All four were in high spirits, while tossing coconuts at targets that had been set up.

"Smart kids, the tunnel rats," Rohan said. "And afraid of nothin'."

The tiny form of Barbara Norton pushed past them, her rhinestone tiara glittering. "Hannah!" she called.

The serving wench looked around. "Hullo, Mum."

Barbara held out a scarf. "Goodness, Hannah, didn't you look at yourself? Tuck this into your bodice."

Hannah's bodice was a little too authentic for a teen-ager—and her mother. Did Barbara know her daughters were tunnel rats? Afraid of nothing was right. Some of the tunnels beneath the town had been prettied up as tour-ist attractions and rooms for paying guests, but others, like those beneath Ravenhearst Manor, were dark and dangerous—and said to be haunted by ghostly apparitions from many a local legend.

"I'm thinking of doing something with the smuggler's tunnels in my next game," Michael said to Rohan. "A cave-in, an old gravestone, a set of rusty tools, pirate's treasure or someone bent on mischief lurking in the dark-ness—it all gets your adrenaline racing. And better to have it racing from imagined rather than real danger."

"Mon, you don't need to be findin' pirate treasure," Rohan teased, "not with your video game business."

"Well, no. But I'd like to find out if the rumors of gold hidden in those tunnels are true."

Rohan smiled, his white teeth flashing against his dark skin. "Dylan, do you think they're true? Dylan?"

Their friend had been pensive and inattentive all af-ternoon. Now Michael saw why. Dylan's blue eyes were focused on the slight figure of his wife.

Naomi stood in the shadow of the old town hall's outer wall, speaking urgently to Willie Myners. Michael didn't

count Naomi's Goth clothing as a costume—she always
dressed that way—and Willie's sweater and jeans were
nothing out of the ordinary. With their pale, nervous
faces, the duo looked like ghosts hovering around the
fringes of the celebration.

Every one of Dylan's impressive muscles was clenched,
so that even his Robot Chicken tattoo bulged with tension. He took a giant step forward just as Naomi glanced
around. Her red lips thinned. Her own step toward Dylan
allowed Willie to slide quickly as a snake into the alley
running between the town hall and the Artist's Gallery.

"Here," she called to her husband. "You've closed
the bicycle shop, have you? All these day trippers and
students—you could be making loads of money. But
no, you're spying on me. Give it a rest, Dylan." And she
slipped away into the crowd.

Dylan sputtered, his broad face twisted into a scowl,
his hands making fists at his sides.

The jaunty music of a brass band echoed off the old
stone buildings and out over the harbor. Sharing a wary if
sympathetic glance, Michael and Rohan said simultaneously, "The band's playin'," and "Look, there's a group
forming up for a country dance."

Michael added, "Molly and I learned country dancing
when she was writing a grant for a heritage society in
York."

Molly wasn't among the couples, though. Lydia Crowe
was. Her vacuous, candy-box prettiness made her seem
younger than her twenties, and Michael's gaze, sweeping
the area for Molly's familiar form, didn't linger. But that
brief glance was enough to attract Lydia's attention. She
hurried forward. "Hullo, Michael. Let's dance!"

Lydia might be a tunnel rat, too, but today she wasn't
dressed like one. Her Jane Austen-style dress was so sheer

Michael could almost see the goose bumps raised by the cool ocean breeze.

She seized first one hand, then both.

"Half a tick, Lydia, I…" Too late. Lydia was in his arms, gripping him like a boa constrictor, pulling him toward the dancers. His booted ankles twisting on the cobblestones, Michael had no choice but to hang on, face the music and dance.

MOLLY GRAHAM SMOOTHED the skirt of the 1920s flapper dress that Angela Ogbourne at the Style Shop had found for her, its satin a shade of purple that matched her favorite amethyst necklace. She gave a wriggle that set its fringes to dancing flirtatiously. But Michael wasn't there to show his appreciation. Where was he, anyway? Somehow they'd gotten separated when she'd gone for a snack of strawberries and thick yellow cream.

"Molly!" called a voice that was not Michael's.

Licking the last of her sweet treat from the corners of her mouth, Molly looked around to see Tim Jenkins beckoning with his microphone. She'd first met the ITV reporter at a fund-raiser in London, and now he'd taken her suggestion to do a story about Seafaring Days.

The reporter's height, long neck and prominent teeth reminded her of a giraffe, one that could use more leaves. Tim was working, interviewing Rebecca Hislop in front of the Havers Customs House while his camera operator panned from them to Blackpool's scenic waterfront and back again.

Swathed in a vintage ruffled gown that made her look like one of the chrysanthemums for sale at her gift and flower shop, Rebecca was saying, "Besides salvaging the goods on a wrecked ship, some of the locals would light fires atop the cliffs opposite Glower Lighthouse, luring ships onto the rocks, among them one belonging to the king himself... ."

"Which king?" asked Tim.

"One of the Georges. No matter, the soldiers came, and the judges, and they say the dead still haunt the lighthouse. That's why the lens is changed to red on All Hallow's Eve, to keep the ghosts away. But that's not all. Folk in the olden days were smugglers and worse, pirates and slave traders, as well. Now they're gone—perhaps—but their tunnels are still here. So are their old buildings, and their dark spirits—or so the story goes."

Tim glanced at Molly. She shrugged and smiled. Today, baskets of flowers hung from the quaint old buildings along Dockside Avenue and from the shops opening onto the narrow, deeply shadowed lanes behind. Contemporary Blackpool's picture-postcard appearance only hinted at the drama of its seafaring past. At least she hoped the drama was in the past.

She and Michael had already discovered that here, memories were long and secrets plentiful, secrets that could turn deadly. But she could no more quell her husband's curiosity about those secrets than he could hers.

Tim's eyes and the lens of the camera followed Rebecca's gesture to the classical elegance of the Customs House. "That building's designed by Charles Crowe," she said, "one of Blackpool's local heroes. And one of its villains, as well. He turned his hand to a variety of employments, some more ethical than others, and had the money to prove it. Story goes, he buried a priceless treasure somewhere in town!"

From behind Molly, Aleister Crowe's smooth voice said, "Surely the ITV audience would be much more interested in facts, not sailor's tales and gossip."

"There's often more history than fantasy in such

persistent tales," Molly told him, even as she took a step farther away from him.

Turning his back on Rebecca and sending Molly a thin smile, Aleister informed Tim, "My ancestor Charles Crowe was quite the Renaissance man, served in Nelson's navy, traveled, traded—many of the local folk were jealous of his achievements. They still are. They spread scurrilous tales about him. What can you do when you're the object of such envy?"

Rebecca rolled her eyes. Tim hadn't yet blinked.

"Charles was a brilliant architect," Aleister went on. "He designed not only this building, but also many of Blackpool's finest structures, such as the church and the town hall. Your cameraman should be filming important historical landmarks like those, not recording all of her, her…"

Gossip, Molly finished in her head.

Aleister's rather stuffy dark blue double-breasted suit wasn't a costume, she thought. He meant it to evoke the rather formal clothing of the Prince of Wales, and had no doubt bought it from the same tailor, Gieves and Hawkes of Savile Row.

Aleister wasn't an unattractive man—his clothing was impeccable, whether provided by Savile Row or Armani, and his dark hair with its widow's peak was tidily groomed. It was his condescending manner and smug smile that grated. He even carried a cane, its handle fashioned into a silver crow.

With a sympathetic glance at Tim's bewildered expression as Aleister cornered him, Molly slipped off to starboard while Rebecca made her escape to port and her own vendor's stall.

"Enjoy the festival, Molly," she called. "The turnout is great this year! My assistant back at the shop's run off her feet, and I'm shifting loads of stock here. Tell Michael I'm keeping the new season of *Heroes* back for him, eh?"

"Sure will. Thanks." Yes, Molly thought as she headed toward the harbor, keeping an eye out for Michael—he had to be here somewhere—not only was Blackpool burgeoning with tourists buying goods and services from the local merchants, those same tourists were feeding coins into the buckets of charities that she'd written grants for… *Oh!*

Molly caromed off something large and soft. Even as she excused herself, she recognized Detective Chief Inspector Maurice Paddington, a large, rumpled man whose name was laughably appropriate. Though today instead of the affable smile of the children's storybook bear, his face was set in a gargoyle's scowl. He popped the last bite of his Scotch egg into his mouth and then wiped his hands and mopped his moustache with a handkerchief the size of a pillowcase.

"The television crew's your doing, is it?" he asked Molly, saying "crew" as though it was synonymous with "rats."

"Guilty as charged, Inspector."

"Those stories of lost treasure have caused a lot of trouble for Blackpool over the years. Townsfolk have died searching for it. Outsiders, students, beachcombers, tourists—they've killed for it."

"Which is why the Crowe family pretends it doesn't exist. Unless they want it all for themselves." Molly looked to see Tim Jenkins beating a hasty retreat from Aleister and his lecture-pointer cane.

"Surely you don't believe it exists," said Paddington.

"We've been through this before, Inspector. You know I like to keep an open mind."

"You and your husband and your open minds—and

them, as well," Paddington added, turning a baleful gaze toward Liam McKenna.

Liam's usual appearance—bristling beard, earrings, mystical tattoos—was so piratical that today he'd merely needed to add a tricorn hat to his bald head. He was walking backward, guiding an unusually large entourage on one of his Other Syde tours. "Tormented spirits of Emma Ravenhearst and Charles Dalimar crying out for revenge in the ruins of Ravenhearst Manor. And there's buried treasure, as well. Pirate's loot or gold stolen from gypsies in Romania, home of Dracula—who may not be all legend, eh? Gypsies, the Romany, placed a curse on the gold, so that generations of treasure-hunters have met dreadful fates…"

"Gypsies!" exclaimed Paddington. "*Tchah!* What nonsense! We've got quite enough ridiculous legends without fancies of that sort!"

With his attitude Paddington seemed like the scion of generations of Blackpoolers like Aleister, when he was almost as recent an arrival as Molly and Michael. But the inspector's glare was already focused on someone else. Willie Myners.

The man had done an odd job or two around the Graham household, called in by either their housekeeper, Iris, or their caretaker, Irwin. But Rohan Wallace did better work. He'd become a friend of Michael's along with Dylan Stewart, and Molly hadn't seen Willie recently.

Now he was shrinking away from a young, very angry man. "That's Robbie Glennison, isn't it?" Molly asked.

"The very same," Paddington answered. "He works for Callum at the Smokehouse. When he works at all. He's not quite right in the head."

Robbie looked like something dredged up out of the harbor, eyes bulging and lips flapping. Between the noise of the crowd and the band, Molly couldn't hear what he was telling Willie, but there was no mistaking his rage.

Willie raised a hand protectively and took a step back that almost sent him into the gutter. As usual, he was casually dressed to the point of sloppiness, but his shaggy head of dark hair and his pale, intense face gave him the rakish charm of a romance novel's bad boy. Not that Molly cared for bad boys. Michael could occasionally have a devil-may-care air, but Molly had quickly learned that came from his childlike curiosity, a trait she now loved about him. Most of the time.

Paddington started toward Willie and Robbie. For once, Molly hung back. She could believe Robbie was unstable. He certainly looked it now, leaning into Willie's face, jabbing a bony forefinger into the chest of his sweater.

Then Police Constable Luann Krebs cut in from the side. Her glasses gleaming with zeal, her broad shoulders set beneath their epaulettes, she demanded of the two men in a voice loud enough for Molly to hear, "What's this, then, Robbie? Willie? Have you got a problem I can sort for you? Or are you just making trouble?"

Neither man answered. Robbie glared one last time at Willie then shambled up Compass Rose Avenue, kicking petulantly at a rack of newspapers outside the offices of the *Blackpool Journal* and earning a dirty look from Fred Purnell, editor, reporter and publisher, who was just coming out of the front door.

Willie melted into a second guided tour, this one conducted by Liam McKenna's sister, Holly. She was as beautiful as Liam was grotesque, her long, black hair hanging to her waist like a silk curtain, her off-the-shoulder blouse, flowing skirt and necklace of fake gold coins suggesting campfires and gypsy wagons. She greeted Willie with a smile and a wink. The other members of her group, mostly men, did not.

Shaking his head, Paddington made a creditable about-face and stalked off.

Molly and Michael suspected that Paddington had been assigned to Blackpool to while away time until his retirement without getting in the way of the productive members of the North Yorkshire Police Authority.

Krebs had arrived last spring and taken part in the investigation of the murder outside the Red Lantern Theatre. Krebs made no bones about having been sent by her superintendent-father to play a big fish in a small pond—she intended to advance rapidly. And right now she was staring after Willie Myners, her eyes calculating.

Molly didn't try to fathom what was on Krebs's mind. Instead, she smiled at Fred Purnell—his inquisitive nature had also placed him on Paddington's handle-with-care list—and turned toward the bandstand just as the music stopped.

There was Michael, trying to pry Lydia Crowe off his chest. No problem if he'd danced with her. Big problem that she was claiming more than a dance.

Her fringes shaking with indignation, Molly arrived at the scene just as Michael finally extricated himself from Lydia's tentacles. He had barely sent Molly a grin of mingled relief and embarrassment when two more male figures converged on the scene.

Aleister in his dark suit really did look like a crow, Molly thought. She should have dressed as a scarecrow. But this time he ignored Molly. He grasped Lydia's arm, shook his head reprovingly and opened his mouth.

He stood there without speaking as a twentyish, red-haired and freckled young man dressed in a dark blue Austen-era frock coat appeared on Lydia's other side.

Addison Headerly's gaze was fixed on her face with the open adoration of a puppy for a bowl of kibble.

Molly's eyes met Michael's, two minds with one thought: *Addison's in love with Lydia. Poor Addison.* The Headerlys were as old a Blackpool family as the Crowes, but Molly sincerely doubted Aleister would consider them in the same league.

Aleister tried to shoo Addison away, his patrician nose turned up. The youngest Crowe, Aubrey, stopped and then reversed course. Addison held his ground. Lydia stood with her arms folded and her lower lip protruding, but the sparkle in her eyes betrayed her pleasure at being the center of attention.

The Grahams backed away from the scene, Michael stooping low enough to bring his mouth close to Molly's ear, seizing the opportunity to take a tiny nibble of it. "Here's us, love, thinking small towns are peaceful places. Blackpool's proved us wrong."

"There's more drama here than at the Actor's Studio." Molly spoke more lightly than she felt—drama sometimes devolved to tragedy.

He imitated her light tone. "You've got plenty of opportunities to meddle in other people's business."

"There you go, Mr. Pot, calling Mrs. Kettle black." Beyond Michael's arm, Molly saw Tim Jenkins and his camera operator starting toward Holly's tour group. The comfortably padded form of Fred Purnell crossed his path, either intending to suggest an alliance or defend his territory. A gull squawked, making a sound like a rusty screen door. The sea lapped gently at the concrete seawall as they got closer. The band started up again.

Then the music trailed away into a ragged blare. People shouted, pointed then surged toward the seawall. "Whoa,"

Molly exclaimed, even as Michael asked, "What the hell is that?"

A magnificent pirate ship sailed past the lighthouse and into the harbor. A Jolly Roger snapped from the top of its tallest mast, and its tightly-reefed sails shuddered. With a rolling rumble and succession of flashes, the cannons ranged along its railing fired. Smoke filled the docks and gulls hurled themselves shrieking into the sky. All the people who had rushed forward now ducked for cover.

"It's the pirate's curse!" a woman—Holly?—screamed.

Coughing in the acrid smoke, Molly didn't protest as Michael's strong arm wrapped around her waist and pulled her down behind a concrete planter teeming with flowers. Still, she managed to peer out from one side as he peeked out from the other.

Neither would miss a moment of this. Whatever this was....

CHAPTER TWO

NO CANNONBALLS PLOWED through the docks. No grape-shot swept the street. No one, Molly realized, was hurt.

Michael was helping her to her feet when a plummy voice rang out, channeled through a bullhorn. "My apologies for the dramatic entrance. The cannons are film props, not real. No harm was intended."

"Maybe it wasn't *intended*," Molly said.

Michael coughed. Still tasting the pungent smoke herself, Molly pounded him on the back even as her eyes turned toward the ship.

The sea breeze dissipated the smoke. With one last rumble of its engine, the ship glided to a stop beside the long pier extending into the Blackpool Harbor and Marina. Sailors dressed in traditional striped tops and red neckerchiefs tied up the vessel and, when everything was secure, ran out a gangplank.

Paddington hurried up, muttering about nerve, public nuisance and permission from Blackpool Council. But with an excited buzz, the entire crowd rushed the dock and he was pushed aside, leaving him to stand chewing his moustache beside Krebs. Her hand opened and closed at the side seam of her navy blue uniform, as though searching for a truncheon that wasn't there.

Michael and Molly were swept forward with everyone else. They found themselves standing at the end of the gangplank as a man in a beautifully tailored blue yachtsman's jacket and white peaked cap set down his bullhorn, then stepped onto the dock with the nonchalance of either an actor or a lord.

Molly's internal social Rolodex spun and produced an ID. She whispered in Michael's direction, "That's Trevor Hopewell of Hopewell Transport PLC, one of those octopus corporations that own everything from airlines and shipping companies to motorway garages...." Her voice trailed away. She'd seen photos, but they didn't do justice to the man's dashing good looks. In his mid-thirties, blond hair, square jaw and lean build, he was the kind of guy who turned every woman's head. Even Molly felt her eyes glaze over and her mouth drop open.

Behind and above her, Michael snickered. All she heard was, "He's a pretty one, yes..." She elbowed him into silence as the man stopped in front of them.

"Trevor Hopewell," he announced to them. "I've been hearing about Blackpool's Seafaring Days—thought I'd have a look, being something of a seafarer myself."

"Molly Graham. My husband, Michael." She got a grip on herself, and on Hopewell's hand, which she then passed on to Michael. He offered the man a slightly off-center grin as well as his and Molly's business bona fides—her grant-writing, his video game design.

"Quite impressive," Hopewell said, but his eyes, not the piercing blue of Michael's but a more ambiguous shade, focused on Tim Jenkins's microphone and camera operator and Fred Purnell's camera and notebook. Every one of his teeth gleamed in a smile. "Members of the press, I see. Please, come aboard the *Black Sea Pearl,* my lads. Mr. and Mrs. Graham, you, too—anyone else? Ah, yes, the local constabulary." He regarded a baldheaded man in oil-stained overalls at the base of the gangplank. "And you are...?"

"Owen Montcalm," he replied. Montcalm gestured with his scrimshaw pipe, its arc taking in all the fishing and pleasure boats bobbing nearby. "I run this marina. Thought you might like to discuss a docking fee."

"Of course, of course," Hopewell told him, and began waving all and sundry up the gangplank. The sundry— including Paddington, Krebs and another constable, Fotherby—joined the procession, as did Addison Headerly and Aubrey Crowe.

Michael pressed forward. As though the gleam in his eye and the furrow in his brow wasn't enough to tip Molly off to his racing thoughts, the camera he produced from his pocket revealed all. He was always contemplating new video games, and had just this morning said something about one involving pirates. Here was his chance to do research.

Singing just loud enough for him to hear, "Fifteen men on a dead man's chest, yo ho ho and a bottle of rum," she trailed him up the gangplank and onto the ship.

She thought he replied, "Thank you, no, I'd prefer single malt," but his response was lost amid the other voices.

Hopewell snapped his fingers, summoning a man dressed in a first mate's outfit. The navy blue jacket and dashing red neckerchief were worn over an open-necked shirt so dazzlingly white it emphasized his swarthy face and drooping jowls, his crisply gelled black hair, and discolored teeth bared in a stiff smile.

"My personal assistant, Martin Dunhill," Hopewell asserted, and added to Owen Montcalm, "Name your fee. Martin will see to it."

Owen cited a generous price. Dunhill replied in a voice that was less plummy than lemony, "When I've seen your invoice, I'll pay up."

Leaving them to it, Hopewell urged his visitors down a hatchway.

Molly expected period reproduction furniture, gleaming brass lanterns, hammocks for the sailors. But no. The pirate ship was no more than a shell around a modern yacht outfitted in casual, comfortable elegance. This wasn't the first expensively appointed yacht she'd seen, but that didn't mean she wasn't amazed by it.

Some of the visitors fanned out into other areas. Michael and Molly stayed with Hopewell, who walked a small group through living rooms, a professional galley, a dining area with a table so glossy Molly could have ice-skated on it. From the corridor where Molly stood, she could see the glass-and-steel desk that dominated his office. It was similar to the glass cases ranged along the corridor outside that held a variety of historical artifacts.

"These are just some of my collections." Hopewell pointed to one of the cases, indicating a gold ear-pick salvaged from a sunken ship of the Spanish Armada, a curved gypsy knife inlaid with silver and a Scottish Highlander's dirk carried at the battle of Waterloo. Michael stepped between Molly and the showcase, camera flashing.

No matter. Here was her chance to dart into Hopewell's office and inspect what she'd thought was an old pocket watch displayed on his desk. She slipped away from the group and through the doorway.

Papers and folders were stacked rather than scattered on the desktop, and what looked like a map of Blackpool was half-covered by a pleated nautical chart of the Yorkshire coast. But Molly's eyes went to the Victorian timepiece protected by a glass dome. Perhaps it had belonged to one of Hopewell's ancestors. She would ask, except his voice was fading away behind her, talking about engines and accompanied by multiple footsteps.

Another voice approached from the opposite direction—Dunhill again, speaking in a rapid mumble. He was still negotiating with Owen, Molly supposed. She started for the door, then stopped when Dunhill's voice rose. "Hopewell's got no need of the likes of you."

As soon as she heard the second man, Molly realized it wasn't Owen. "Well, well, well, if little Martin Dunghill hasn't come a long way, fetching and carrying for a man with more silver than sense. How's the family, Marty?"

Dunghill? Clearly the two men knew each other, and there was no love lost between them.

"The boss has got sense enough not to want your drugs."

"You just tell him what I've got here. He'll see me, right enough."

Quickly, Molly stepped behind the open door and peeked through the crack between it and the frame.

The second man was Willie Myners—like a bad penny, he kept turning up. But it wasn't a penny he held in the protective curve of his fingers. Gold glinted, then vanished as he thrust the object into the pocket of his worn corduroy trousers.

Was it a piece of jewelry? Fine jewelry wasn't the sort of thing Molly expected Willie to be carrying— his odd jobs were hardly actual employment. And what was that about drugs? Was Willie dealing, right here in Blackpool?

Dunhill sneered. "I know a confidence trick when I see one, Sunshine. Off you go."

Willie stood with his hand on his pocket, his stance combative. "This is a pirate ship. Pirates have treasure. What's all this in the display cases, if not treas—?"

Hopewell's voice echoed down the passageway. Willie started toward it, but Dunhill shoved him in the opposite direction so brusquely he almost lost his footing. "Here!" he protested. "Be a pal, Marty, let me talk to the boss!"

"Push off," Dunhill said. "Now."

Molly stepped into the corridor as the two men disappeared around the corner. Should she tell Hopewell what she'd overheard? But Michael had just been teasing her about meddling in other people's business. Hopewell obviously trusted Dunhill to oversee matters on his yacht, and Dunhill was doing just that.

"There you are, Mrs. Graham," called Hopewell. "I've been talking to your husband about the history of the area."

"I'm sure you have." Molly walked up beside Michael with a smile of indulgence for both men—a doubtful glance back to where Willie had showed Dunhill something that gleamed like gold.

MICHAEL WONDERED WHY Molly's pink cheeks were rosier than usual. Then he noticed the watch on Hopewell's desk, and deduced that she'd nipped into his office for a closer look. She could tell the time on her iPhone, but no, she loved watches.

Hopewell led the way back up to the deck, where they found Jenkins's camera operator peering down a hatchway like an anteater nosing into an anthill. But it was Fred Purnell who asked, "How long are you planning to stop in Blackpool, Mr. Hopewell?"

"Trevor, please. I've never visited this lovely little town before, sad to say, but I'm planning to rectify my mistake and stay for a while. Pirates, smugglers, wreckers—what a treasure trove of legends!"

Michael could swear that Hopewell's teeth sparkled in the sunlight as he spoke. No wonder Molly had struggled to conceal her amusement when he'd first introduced himself. The man had a lot to offer in the way of entertainment.

"Thank you very much for the tour," Molly told Hopewell.

Finding a bit of paper in his pocket, Michael jotted down his and Molly's phone numbers. "Please let us know when you can join us for dinner. I'd enjoy discussing pirates, smugglers and wreckers—I'm working on a new video game…"

Michael was interrupted by Jenkins jostling him and Purnell aside. Purnell in turn bumped up against Addison Headerly. Leaving the men to sort themselves out, the Grahams waved a final time to Hopewell and headed for the pier behind the official trio of Paddington, Krebs and Fotherby.

Martin Dunhill stood at the railing next to a dark-haired, heavy-jowled man in civilian garb, whose black beads of eyes considered the crowd and the town beyond. Molly's face flushed an even deeper pink, one of the many shades of her soft complexion, which complemented her shoulder-length auburn hair and amber-brown eyes. "What is it?" Michael asked, placing a protective arm around her shoulders.

She seemed not to hear him over the splash of water against the pier, the rattle of ships' rigging, the music of the band. Then, spotting Rohan Wallace coming toward them, she shrugged. "I overheard something. I'll tell you about it later. Would you like to get a bite to eat at the Café?"

Michael considered the dockside eatery. He could see even from here that people were queued out the door and along the pavement. Those who had gotten inside were probably packed so tightly onto the balconies the pressure could launch the bright table-umbrellas like rockets. He made a counteroffer. "I'll bring home a takeaway from the Jade Dragon."

"Good idea. Make mine moo shu tofu with a side of curry chips, okay? Hi, Rohan."

"Hello, Molly," Rohan replied with an affable nod. "Have you been visitin' the ship?"

"I'll let Michael fill you in. I promised to stop by the Style Shop, show Angela my dress in action. See you at home at six?" Rising on her toes, she kissed Michael's cheek.

"Right, love." Michael allowed himself a moment's appreciation of her dress's action as she walked away. Then he looked around at Rohan's half smile. "What happened to Dylan? Have we lost him?"

"Yeah, mon. He said he was goin' back to the shop. I'm thinkin' Naomi's comment about missin' customers got to him. Still, there's no harm in askin' if he's got time for a beer at the Dockside." Rohan started back along the pier.

"Yes, mate, the sun *is* over the yardarm—no pun intended," Michael said with a last look at the *Black Sea Pearl*'s useless but dramatic masts and yards rising high above the other boats. Dunhill no longer stood at the railing, but Hopewell was posing for both sets of cameras beside one of the mock cannons.

Michael and Rohan dodged and ducked toward Dylan's Bicycle Shop, which was tucked into the hillside just below Dockside Head. The tall white-painted cylinder of Glower Lighthouse atop the Head seemed innocent enough in the afternoon sunshine, but as with so many places in Blackpool it concealed dark secrets—like an entrance to the town's catacombs.

Michael said, "Naomi's certain the shop's haunted by ghosts from the lighthouse—wreckers and plunderers and their victims, as well. She and Dylan should organize tours of their own, give the McKennas some competition."

"They could hold seances on mopeds," Rohan suggested with a laugh.

The men rounded the corner of the Mariner's Museum. There was Dylan Stewart just outside his shop, his massive hands wrapped around Willie Myners's throat. Dylan's red hair and angry red face made him look like a Viking berserker, a far cry from his usual good-natured, gentle-giant temperament.

In contrast, if Dylan was a Viking, Willie was a mop. His legs and feet slipped and slid on the cobblestones while his hands grappled with Dylan's mighty grip.

Michael and Rohan ran up to the shop. Between them they pulled Dylan off the smaller man, and Michael helped Willie to his feet. Hadn't he just glimpsed the man scuttling around a corner on Hopewell's yacht? He seemed to be everywhere today.

Dylan trembled with rage, his hands knotted at his sides. "I'll kill him, the dirty, rotten…"

"I'll have the law on you, Stewart. You've got no right knocking me about. If you can't keep your wife happy, then losers weepers." Willie staggered away down the street.

"Stay away from her," Dylan bellowed at the other man's retreating back, but his bellow broke into something more like a sob.

Rohan looked at Michael. Michael looked at Rohan. Michael turned the sign hanging in the shop window from Open to Closed, shut the door and took Dylan's arm. The faint smell of beer emanated from his friend's jacket. He must have gulped down a pint after seeing Naomi with Willie earlier. Maybe another one would help him to calm down.

Rohan and Michael marched Dylan into the Dockside and found a settle that had just been vacated. Despite the rough-and-ready appearance of the ancient building, the pub, too, was filled with tourists.

"Hullo, Chuck." Michael leaned across the bar to place their order. "Three pints of Sommerset Stout, please."

Charles—Chuck—Greeley simultaneously pulled the pints for Michael and cast a sharp eye at a boisterous group of youths playing a slot machine in the corner. Feeling his gaze on them, they quieted.

Chuck arranged the glasses on a tray. "Has Molly given any thought yet to writing me a grant request? Such a fine old historic building as this shouldn't be allowed to fall into ruin. I reckon English Heritage or the like could help renovate the place."

"She's taking a bit of a sabbatical just now," Michael replied, without going into detail about her grant-writing work being so successful she could afford to pick and choose her projects. "I wouldn't get my hopes up, though. Most grants are for nonprofits."

"Alice Coffey and her ilk, they'd have me running a nonprofit museum, not a going concern. Many thanks to your missus and Fred Purnell and all those trying to bring trade to the town." Chuck palmed Michael's money and turned to another customer.

Michael distributed the pints and sat down beside Dylan. His friend stared into his dark ale as though for inspiration, then took a huge swig that left foam clinging to his upper lip. "Willie Myners is a nasty piece of work," Dylan stated.

"He is that, mon," Rohan agreed. "But what's he to you?"

"There he was outside the Mariner's Museum getting up Alfie Lochridge's nose, and Alfie looking down at him through those priggish eyeglasses of his—a pince-nez. Who wears a pince-nez these days? Anyway, Alfie was giving him a piece of his mind, far as I could tell."

"Alfie gives everyone a piece of his mind, except for Michael here," Rohan said.

"He says my video games are disgraceful though he appreciates their historical accuracy," Michael explained. "I have a suspicion he's embarrassed to admit he plays them himself. Willie must have gone straight to the museum from Hopewell's yacht. Did you hear what he was on about with Alfie?"

Dylan shook his head. "Not a bit of it. Willie looked round, saw me and grinned like a jackal. I knew what he was thinking, the filthy…" He swigged again.

Michael swallowed a drink of his own ale, letting the complex flavors linger in his throat, before he asked what he had to ask. "What *was* he thinking, Dylan?"

"About Naomi. You saw them together. You heard what she said to me. She's not happy here, she's not happy with the shop, she's constantly on edge. Willie's promised her—God, what *hasn't* Willie promised her? I know she's gotten tranquilizer tablets from him. Now she tells me he's been dealing—uppers, downers, oddments of prescription drugs. And that's not all." Dylan's speech was growing more slurred by the word, and Michael regretted buying him another drink. Usually, Dylan didn't allow himself to get drunk, but then, usually he wasn't this upset.

It was Rohan who answered the next question, saving

Michael from having to voice it. "You mean she's, uh, havin' an affair with Willie?"

He shrugged. "She spends a lot of time with him. Although maybe that's because of the pills. Or to hear more about how she and her artwork are too good for Blackpool."

His glass was empty. So were his eyes, staring blankly at a wizened and weathered local fisherman just entering the pub. For a long moment, the newcomer's bloodshot eyes fixed on Dylan. He swayed forward, then he turned around and stepped up to the bar.

Pills, Michael thought. Even in Blackpool there would be people looking for a quick high or an easy low—and not just among the tourists and visiting students. There was no escaping human nature.

And that was one of the problems with the Stewarts' marriage. But just because Michael knew a good relationship took the ongoing commitment of both parties didn't make him a marriage counselor. Still, Dylan was his friend—for better or worse.

Dylan slumped in the corner of the settle. "Naomi's not a bad sort, not like Willie. She's just—she's not happy here. What do I do? I can't afford to take her away from this town. From him."

Rohan finished his own pint. "Let's get him back to his flat, Michael—let him sleep it off."

"Naomi might be there. I'm not sure he needs to talk to her just now, not in this mood. I'll take him home with me."

Rohan helped Michael dig Dylan out of the settle and walk him to the door under the gaze of various tourists and Chuck Greeley, and also that of the fisherman, who again leaned forward, then again thought better of it and went back to his drink. Maybe he wanted a bicycle, Michael told himself.

Dylan muttered, "Blackpool'd be better off without Willie Myners. Naomi would be better off without him."

Neither Michael nor Rohan could deny that.

CHAPTER THREE

MOLLY CUT THE SANDWICH IN HALF, causing watercress to spill from one side and a slice of tomato from the other. She didn't even attempt to halve the second one, a pile of bread, ham and cheese. Michael could eat it whole. When she'd offered to throw together some sandwiches, she'd meant "throw"—cooking wasn't one of her skills.

Michael's voice on her iPhone hadn't minced words: Dylan was sleeping off a pint of ale too many in one of their spare rooms and he didn't want to leave his friend alone. She'd stopped by the Jade Dragon, but there, too, a line of customers extended out the door, not least because it was a cyber-café as well as a restaurant. Never mind, then. She'd run into Coffey's Grocers and bought a few basics, which was all Coffey's carried anyway. Then she'd retrieved her MINI Cooper from the parking lot outside the abandoned train station and hurried the twenty minutes or so home to Thorne-Shower Mansion, where she'd changed into boot-cut jeans and an Oxford shirt.

Now she carried a tray onto the balcony. Despite the glorious view in the distance of Blackpool's tiers of pantiled roofs and narrow streets, Michael's face was set in a frown. Molly poured him a cup of tea, something she'd learned from their housekeeper, Iris, to prepare in proper British style.

Silently they ate and drank, until at last Michael drained the teapot into his cup, added more milk and sugar, and leaned back. "Rohan offered to help with Dylan, but I told him to enjoy his holiday weekend, so he went off for a tour of the *Black Sea Pearl*. Good job he's come to town—Blackpool needs someone with his skills. And he's a fine sportsman, as well." Michael considered the expanse of the sea, more of a thoroughfare than the solitary road that led over moorland and past forest into Blackpool.

"So what's up with Dylan?" Molly asked. "It's not like him to get drunk. You'd think he was drowning his sorrows."

"He is. We saw Naomi with Willie Myners." In as few words as possible, Michael told Molly about the young couple's troubles.

Molly made a wry face. "Poor Dylan. Poor Naomi. I noticed her myself this afternoon, in the churchyard, looking like death warmed over. As for Willie, I saw—and heard—him on the yacht arguing with Hopewell's assistant, Martin Dunhill. That's what I wanted to talk to you about."

Michael listened to her story, his frown returning. When Molly held out her hand, he took it in his, closing his strong, warm fingers around hers and gently teasing her palm with his thumb.

Even as she enjoyed the delicate shivers tingling along her arm, she said, "It sounds as if Willie's the local drug dealer. Paddington was giving him the evil eye, but short of catching him red-handed, what can he do?"

"Willie sounds to be up to more than drugs."

"You mean the gold object in his pocket? That sure wasn't drug paraphernalia."

"Dylan said Willie was talking to Alfie Lochridge earlier. Maybe he meant to ask Alfie about whatever he has but Alfie would have none of it. Then Willie tangled with Dylan and here we are."

Molly looked at her lovely Victorian mansion, at the view to die for, at her husband and best friend. "Yes, here we are. Are we lucky or what?"

"We've struck lucky, love." Michael raised her hand to his lips, kissed it back and front, then delicately nibbled on her forefinger.

Caught between giggling and melting, she at first didn't notice the sound of the doorbell from the far side of the house—not until it was followed by a series of thuds. Someone was getting much too enthusiastic with Thorne-Shower's sea serpent–shaped brass knocker.

With a wink and a promise, Michael released Molly's hand and stepped into the house. They made it to the front hall just as Irwin answered the door.

On the porch stood Police Constable Douglas Fotherby, a heavyset man with a perennial dark stubble shading his lantern jaw. Without so much as a "hullo," Fotherby asked, "Dylan Stewart's here, is he?"

So which of the good citizens of Blackpool had reported Dylan leaving town with Michael? Molly wondered. The town had big eyes and even bigger ears.

Irwin's muddy brown eyes, already enlarged by his glasses, widened even further. "I beg your pardon?" he said to Fotherby.

"You heard me well enough, Jaeger. Dylan Stewart. Someone's filed a complaint against him."

"I can guess who," Molly muttered under her breath.

Michael said, "Dylan's sleeping. You'd best come back—"

Fotherby pushed Irwin aside, strode into the house and demanded, "Where is he? This way?"

"Hey!" Molly exclaimed, just as Irwin, his iron-gray moustache quivering, shouted, "Here, you!"

They hurried after Fotherby as he galloped up the stairs and started opening doors. "Aha! There you are!" He dived into the bedroom, strode over to the bed and started shaking Dylan awake. "Stewart! Open your eyes! Sit yourself up!"

Awkwardly pushing himself off the mattress, Dylan stared at Fotherby and then around the room, until his gaze settled on the Grahams. "Michael, Molly, I'm sorry to cause trouble."

"That's what you do best, is it?" demanded Fotherby. "Cause trouble? Listen here, Stewart, if you raise a hand to Willie Myners again…"

"Willie Myners?" Dylan's face flushed. "Why are you taking after me, you fool? Myners is the one causing trouble in Blackpool."

"That's not what I hear," Fotherby retorted.

Dylan tried to rise to his feet and fell back, the color draining from his face. "Ow, my head."

"If I get another report of you bothering Myners, it's off to the lock-up with you. You hear me?" Fotherby shook his finger under Dylan's nose. Molly wished Dylan would bite it off.

"All right, enough of this." Michael stepped forward.

Dylan gazed up at the constable, his expression partly resentful, partly nauseated. "Go harass someone else."

As if taking him at his word, Fotherby turned on Michael. "And you, Graham. Stay well out of it or I'll be arresting you for, for…" He searched for something, his fleshy features creasing with the effort. "For perverting the course of justice."

"I doubt it," said Molly.

Fotherby included her in his glare. "Thought you were a proper clever-clogs, did you, interfering with the murder behind the theatre when you'd barely arrived in town."

"We didn't interfere with anything. It interfered with us." Which wasn't strictly the truth, Molly told herself, but still…

"You came poncing into Blackpool, telling us our own business," Fotherby went on. "You'd better watch your step, the pair of you. Things happen to curious people here."

"What sort of things?" Molly demanded, even though she knew very well what happened. They ran a very real risk of being killed themselves.

Michael pulled her back a step. "Is that a threat, Fotherby?"

The man smiled with his lips, not with his eyes. "Just keep on meddling, you'll find out." And, settling his hat more firmly on his head—he hadn't bothered to remove it when he came inside—he swiveled to glare at Dylan. "You hear me?"

"I hear you, I hear you," Dylan said, his hands loosening and contracting in his lap but not going for Fotherby's throat the way they had for Willie's.

"I'll show you out, Constable." Irwin's gesture toward the door was more of a command.

His smile spreading into a sneer, Fotherby allowed himself to be escorted away.

"Well!" Molly said.

Dylan's comment was longer and ruder.

Shaking his head, Michael said only, "Let's get some food into you, Dylan. And an aspirin or two, as well."

By the time Molly heated a can of soup, arranged a few crackers on a plate and made another pot of tea,

Dylan had washed his face and combed his hair. He sat at the breakfast nook table next to Michael and slurped his soup, his color improving by the moment. Or, Molly noted, it *was* improving until the quiet room erupted with an electronic version of "Sympathy for the Devil."

Dylan hauled out his cell phone and looked at the screen. "Hullo, Naomi."

Naomi's voice, compressed into a mosquito whine, emanated from the tiny speaker.

"I'm on my way. Half a tick." Dylan shoved the phone back into his pocket. "Michael, thank you kindly for looking after me. Molly, thank you for putting up with me, but I'd best be getting on now. Naomi's apologized. She wants to make it all up."

Molly could tell by Michael's fixed smile that he was thinking the same thing she was: the odds against Naomi and Dylan fixing their relationship were long indeed. But kudos to them for trying.

The Grahams detailed Irwin to return Dylan to town, and stood side by side watching the estate car vanish down the driveway and into the shadow of the trees.

They stood there in contented silence for several minutes. Molly considered the slowly fading sunlight—evenings lingered, this time of year—and remembered the golden gleam in Willie's hand. "What did Willie want to show Hopewell?"

"We've asked ourselves that already," Michael said, "to no result."

"What's this about Trevor Hopewell?" The strong female voice behind them was British, but inflected by a lengthy stay in America.

Molly glanced around to see the tall, spare figure of their housekeeper approaching from the small cottage she and Irwin shared—in separate quarters. "Hello, Iris. Did you have a good day out?"

"Quite nice, thank you, though I had words with Holly McKenna over the codswallop she was feeding a group of tourists. There are loads of references for Yorkshire's history, so no need to make things up out of whole cloth, I don't care if she and Liam did originally come from Cumbria." Iris's sharp features beneath her shock of white hair twisted in distaste. As the widow of an American history professor and the author of several historical romances, she had little patience with people who failed to do their research. Molly counted herself lucky that Iris was content to help out at Thorne-Shower, where her mother had once been housekeeper, as well.

With a few interjected comments from Michael, Molly filled Iris in on their day, starting with Lydia ignoring Addison in order to dance with Michael, and Aleister being upstaged by Hopewell's dramatic arrival.

"The *Black Sea Pearl*," said Iris. "That caused a sensation, and no mistake. There was Aleister almost flinging Lydia into Hopewell's arms, while Addison stood by looking as grim as a rejected suitor in an Austen novel. But then, Lydia was quite happy to flutter her lashes at Hopewell and prattle on about her adventures as a tunnel rat."

"And Aleister didn't stop her?"

"Aleister looked very pleased with himself, as usual."

"Hmm, sounds like Aleister is doing a little matchmaking," Molly said with a grin.

"Most likely he's doing business with Hopewell Transport," Michael told her.

"Where's your sense of romance?" she replied.

"Excuse me?" he countered. "I thought we were doing quite well when it came to romance."

Grinning, Molly went on, "No surprise Hopewell would be interested in the tunnels—we've already seen that he's interested in treasure. So has Willie Myners." She told Iris about the conversation she'd overheard on the *Black Sea Pearl,* and Willie's further adventures with Naomi and Dylan.

The estate car returned up the driveway and stopped in the parking area. Jingling the keys in his hand, Irwin greeted Iris and gave his own account of Fotherby's intrusion into the house. "Willie's a layabout and a sneak," he added, "with a criminal record to boot. Dylan's not the only Blackpooler who'd be happy to see him walking Hopewell's plank."

"Metaphorically speaking," added Iris.

"So we hope." Irwin's caterpillarlike gray eyebrows drew together.

Molly's wasn't the only face that went tight. The Blackpool murders of last spring were still too vivid a memory.

Michael's iPhone suddenly emitted Bollywood star Shahrukh Khan's version of "Pretty Woman." "Hullo—Dylan?"

Dylan's agitated voice was so loud it escaped past Michael's ear. Molly leaned forward. So did Iris and Irwin. "Naomi said she'd be home, but she wasn't. So I went round to Willie's flat at the Oceanview—thought she might be there after all. I heard someone running down the back steps as I knocked at the door, so I tried the knob. That's when I saw the lock was broken. The door opened right up. There's no one here now, but the place is a mess. Someone turned it over and then took to their heels when they heard me."

"Stay there, Dylan," Michael told him. "I'll be right with you."

"*We'll* be right with you," corrected Molly.

Dylan's voice rose in panic. "I don't know where Naomi is. She's gone. She's vanished."

CHAPTER FOUR

MICHAEL AND MOLLY hurried from the car park behind the boarded-up station toward the Oceanview. He heard her boots pattering along just behind the thump of his—it wasn't her fault he had a longer stride—and slowed his pace. "You were saying you saw Naomi at the church?"

"Yes," she replied, "right after we left the *Black Sea Pearl.* You remember, I wanted to show Angela at the Style Shop how well my dress fit."

He smiled reminiscently at the "fit" of the dress.

"I was turning into Pelican Lane," Molly continued, "and I noticed several tourists taking photos of the church. Aleister would love that, since old Charles renovated the place. Typical Crowe, taking what was probably a very nice medieval building and ramming Georgian windows through the walls and raising the steeple until it's out of proportion."

Michael's eye strayed toward the foursquare steeple of St. Mary's, or Calm Seas as it was known to Blackpoolers, after one of the most frequent prayers uttered there. The spire rose above the roofs of town like an exclamation point.

"Naomi was sitting on the bench beneath the old yew tree, sketching the Crowe mausoleum. The row of columns can cast some interesting shadows. Although, judging by her Goth look, she was imagining the spooky stuff inside—coffins, cobwebs, a crypt."

"It wouldn't be Blackpool without the spooky stuff. Here we are."

The Oceanview apartment block was a slab-sided stucco building that clashed with every other structure in town. It had been erected by the town council in the 1950s, a decade not known for architectural sensitivity. But the inexpensive flats were homes, just as much as Thorne-Shower Mansion was home.

Dylan's anxious face peered over the concrete balcony that formed a gallery running in front of half a dozen doors. Michael and Molly raced up the steps toward him. With a wordless gesture of frustration, he led the way past the peeling paint into Willie's flat.

A short hallway, a living room, a kitchen, a bedroom and bathroom, all sparsely furnished and smelling of stale food and mildew—the tour took only a moment. Drawers were turned out, couch pillows upended, cabinet doors opened. Molly focused on the food-crusted dishes piled in the kitchen sink. "Yeah, it sure seems as if someone searched the place. Or vandalized it. But then, it wasn't very neat to begin with, was it?"

"I've never been inside before," conceded Dylan. "Willie's never struck me as a tidy sort, no, and Naomi's got other things on her mind."

"You mean her artwork?"

"She's good at it, talks about working as an illustrator. But that cow Temperance Collins at the gallery won't exhibit any of her work, and won't represent her to the Tyne and Wear Arts Council in Newcastle. Just about broke Naomi's heart, that did."

As far as Michael was concerned, the work Temperance did exhibit was rubbish—but then, she'd made it clear that video and anime art was beneath her notice.

Dylan ran his hands through his hair, so that it stood

on end like ginger-colored antennae. He pointed toward an open door at one side of the kitchen. "I thought I heard someone legging it down the steps as I came in the front. But when I looked out, the yard was empty."

Michael eyed a steep stairway leading down into a concrete yard dark with shadow. "We'll have to ask the other tenants if they saw anyone, although with the festival underway, I doubt anyone's here."

"Liam and Holly McKenna certainly aren't," said Molly. When Michael and Dylan regarded her with confusion she said, "Didn't you see the poster downstairs advertising Holly's fortune-telling sessions and seances? The number given is the apartment right below this one."

"I'll talk to them. I'll talk to everyone in town if I have to." Dylan plucked a yellowed copy of the *Blackpool Journal* from the kitchen table and threw it on the floor. Beside his thick shoes, a headline read, "Henry Humboldt Passes Away. Norrington Reveals Ownership of the Magic Lantern Theatre."

That was an old newspaper, Michael thought. Archie Norrington had owned the theatre ever since he and Molly had lived in Blackpool.

"So who trashed the place?" Molly peered into a small closet that held little more than a broom and a dustpan, themselves in need of a cleaning. "A burglar searching for valuables in all the wrong places?"

"Willie himself," suggested Michael, "packing up in a rush? No offense, Dylan, but if you tried to mop the cobblestones with me, I'd be getting out of town."

"Willie's not afraid of me. Not so much as he should be, leastways."

"Was it Naomi?" asked Molly. "Maybe she was trying to get back at Willie for causing her trouble."

"She went looking for trouble." Dylan braced himself

against the sink, his muscular shoulders quivering like jelly.

"Maybe we should call the police," suggested Molly.

Dylan shook his head. "We don't know that this isn't exactly the way Willie left his flat. As for Naomi...I don't think they'd be overly concerned for her.... Our best bet is finding Willie."

Sharing a sympathetic glance, Michael and Molly left him to collect himself and went back into the living room. "If only we had an idea what to look for," she said. "Neither Naomi or Willie left a forwarding address."

"Not as such, no." Michael walked on into the bedroom. He considered the unmade bed, the gaping wardrobe, a chair loaded with clothes. Surely if Willie was planning to leave town, with or without Naomi, he'd have packed a suitcase.

Michael peered under the bed and saw nothing but dust kittens accumulating into dust lions. He inspected the wardrobe and found only odd bits of clothing and a jumbled pile of shoes. Perhaps Willie *had* packed a suitcase, then. Or a duffel or rucksack.

Dylan's heavy tread crossed the room. His voice steady, he asked, "Anything?"

"His shoes," Michael began.

Molly's voice came from the living room. "Michael, I think I've got something."

"Hold on, Molly." Michael pulled out two athletic trainers and placed them side by side, then set two leather shoes next to each other, trying to ignore their smell. There was one bit of footwear left over, a wellie boot, its green rubber sides so battered it might have come out of a rubbish bin or even washed up on the beach. "Why would he keep one boot?" he asked Dylan.

"The other one's probably around. Maybe that's where

he keeps his drug stash. I'll have a look," Dylan replied, and headed back to the kitchen.

Still clutching the boot, Michael walked into the living room to find Molly standing by a fiberboard desk. It was cluttered with odds and ends, from dirty cups to DVDs to a sleazy magazine and a dead plant. She pointed at several sheets of blank paper. "Those are pages torn from a spiral-bound notebook of drawing paper. I didn't notice if this was what Naomi was using when I saw her drawing by the church, but then, we're not trying to find out whether she was here, just where she's gone."

Michael glanced toward the kitchen, where a thud indicated Dylan was eviscerating any remaining cupboards. "Is that your big discovery, then?"

"No. Look here." She indicated the bracket clamping the lamp to the desk. From its protruding edge hung a long, thin, ragged strip of dark cloth, swaying in the draft from the partially open front door. "Maybe it's from a costume or coat worn by whoever was searching the flat but was startled away when Dylan knocked."

"Or maybe it's from one of Willie's coats."

"He wasn't wearing a dark blue coat or jacket when I saw him earlier today—he was wearing a Fair Isle sweater."

"A what?"

"A Fair Isle sweater. One of those with lots of intricate colored stitching around the yoke. The top. This part." Molly patted the area beneath her throat.

"Ah. Yes, that's what he was wearing, right enough. And there's no dark blue coat in the wardrobe, though that doesn't prove anything. For all we know, that thread's been there for months."

"I doubt that. It's just about the only thing on this desk that isn't dusty, greasy or both." She noticed the boot in his hand. "I think I saw the mate to that under the couch."

Michael squatted down to peer beneath the settee. Aha, there *was* a lump of battered green vinyl there.

He reached warily under a sagging spring, past a rancid fish and chips wrapper, and pulled out the second boot. It weighed a lot more than the first. Some of Willie's drugs?

Dylan emerged from the kitchen, using a dishtowel to mop a brown stain from the hem of his Motocross sweatshirt. "He left an open can of beans in the fridge... What's that?"

Michael sat down on the chesterfield, Dylan and Molly on either side. All three heads bent together as Michael pulled away the ragged T-shirt stopping the mouth of the boot. He tipped it up. Into his hand fell four coins, so heavy that he almost dropped them. Instead he let go of the boot, and turned the four coins over and over.

Each was polished to a shine that dazzled even in the gloom of the apartment. Three were gold with Latin and Cyrillic inscriptions—Michael could make out only the word *Transalpina*. The fourth coin was a huge silver disc stamped with a lion's head.

"That's it," hissed Molly. "Willie was trying to show Trevor Hopewell one of those gold coins."

Dylan whistled. "So where'd a bloke like Willie get those? No one woulda ever given him those for drugs."

"Maybe we were right when we thought the place'd been sacked. Maybe they were searching for these?" Michael asked. "Who knew they were here?"

Before she could react, the front door slammed open. They all jumped, startled, and instinctively Michael clutched the coins to his chest.

Down the hall and into the living room came Douglas

Fotherby, his fleshy shoulders coiled beneath their epaulettes like a bull entering a china shop. "Making yourselves at home, are you? Stewart, I thought I told you to leave Willie alone."

This time Dylan was steady enough to stand up and lean into Fotherby's face. "Willie's not here. I'm looking for my wife."

"Ah," said Fotherby, puffing himself up. "Churchay la femme, is it?"

Wincing at Fotherby's French, Michael stood up, as well. Fotherby turned on him. "Graham, don't you know better than to interfere with the scene of a crime? Looks to be a burglary in progress."

"What makes you think this is a crime scene, Constable? Did Willie complain to you again?"

"I've not heard from Willie," Fotherby said.

Molly, too, rose to her full height, such as it was, and demanded, "So on what basis are you accusing us of a crime? Can you tell if anything is missing?"

"You just said, Stewart, that your *wife* was missing. Gone away with Willie, has she? Thought you'd turn the place over, like she was hiding under the bed?" Fotherby's eyes grew so large they reflected the glitter of the coins in Michael's hands. "Well, well, well. She's not the only thing walking off, hmm? Good job one of the neighbors reported your break-in."

"We didn't break in," said Dylan. "The door was open."

"Hand over those coins," Fotherby ordered.

With a sigh of frustration, Michael did as he asked. "Here you are. Evidence. Of something."

"There's a bit of cloth caught in the desk lamp, too," Molly told him.

Fotherby held the coins against his navy blue uniform

coat, not sparing one glance for the desk. "Off you go, the lot of you. I'm securing the crime scene."

"It's not a crime scene," insisted Dylan, even more anxiety creeping into his voice. "I'm looking for Naomi is all. Just 'cause I don't know where she is doesn't mean there's been a crime!"

"Oh, so Willie invited you here? Push off!"

Michael steered Dylan toward the hallway. Beside him, Molly's lips twitched—she was no doubt trying to come up with a crushing retort.

Outside, on the balcony, an older woman in a pinafore apron and pincurls backed hastily away from the open door. Dylan pounced. "Daisy Coffey, isn't it?"

"That's me, yes."

She was another member of the Coffey clan, then. Margaret and Randall Coffey ran the grocer, Alice Coffey ran the Historical Society and Daisy ran the rumor mill. Her distended nostrils reminded Michael of Alice.

"Have you seen a girl in black clothes, black spiky hair, red lipstick?" Dylan asked.

"The scraggy vampire lass? She was here this morning, right enough—had a row with Willie that set my crockery to rattling. Screeching like a gull, she was. So was the round blond one last night."

Willie had more than one girlfriend? Michael wasn't sure whether Dylan's wince registered that fact or if his reaction was to "scraggy vampire."

"Although," Daisy added, her pale eyes above her plump cheeks narrowing in reminiscence, "the women's voices were never so loud as the man's. 'You've got no choice,' he was shouting, and there's Willie saying, 'Hush, the walls have ears.' The walls don't need ears, not with that sort of to-do."

"A man?" asked Dylan. "When was this?"

Daisy shrugged. "This afternoon. I'd just come in from the shop—I help Margaret at the grocer's, don't I, when there's a crowd in town—and I'd had me a look at that posh yacht of Trevor Hopewell's. Could be a film star with that face, though not one of those going about with the dirty hair and whiskers…"

"Did you see who was arguing with Willie this afternoon?" Molly asked.

"No. I heard the door slam and steps going down the stairs, is all."

Michael and Molly exchanged glances. Had someone confronted Willie, then come back after he left?

Dylan asked, "When was the last time you saw Willie?"

"Not long after the row," Daisy answered. "Just happened to be adjusting my lace curtains at the exact moment he was leaving."

Michael said, "Thank you," even as he and Molly urged Dylan down the stairs.

"You can't comb your hair in Blackpool without someone noticing," Molly said.

Michael nodded. "Even so, Fotherby got here very quickly."

"He's just doing his duty. Isn't he?"

"Does his duty involve dancing attendance on Willie Myners?" Dylan asked.

Michael had barely said, "No," when Molly pointed toward a garish poster at the bottom of the stairs.

"Other Syde Tours of haunted Blackpool," she read. "Fortunes told and seances conducted by Mademoiselle Fate."

"Mademoiselle Fate?" Michael repeated. "Where do they get these names?"

"Margaret Coffey gives the McKennas a break on the

rent for that room over the grocery store," Molly went on, "and in return Holly reads her fortune."

"How do you know that?"

"She was talking about it with Betsy Sewell when I ran into the grocery store to buy a bottle of balsamic vinegar and some buffalo mozzarella. Items Margaret didn't have, by the way, and seemed to think were some sort of big-city affectation. Betsy made some comment about crossing Holly's palm with gold, but then, Betsy's into occult history, New Age items, that stuff."

Michael knew. Betsy Sewell's Curio Shop was a cuckoo's nest, if ever there was one. But Molly found her amusing.

"Crossing Holly's palm with silver and paper," said Dylan, "never mind that the film version of gypsies are always saying gold."

"The McKennas don't half go on about gypsies," Michael added. "Gypsy curses…that's part of their spiel."

"Holly dresses the part," said Molly. "She was wearing a necklace of fake coins earlier today. I wonder if they knew about Willie's coins? Was he arguing with Liam this afternoon? Liam's got a loud voice, but I can't imagine why he'd tell Willie he had no choice."

Dylan tried to peer in the McKennas' front window, but the curtains were shut tight. "To hell with Willie's coins. It's Naomi who matters. I'll start asking about. Someone has to have seen her this afternoon. Or Willie. If I ever get my hands on him again…" His words trailed away.

"If she doesn't turn up soon," Michael cautioned, "you'll be obliged to file a formal missing persons report with Paddington."

"Let us know what else we can do to help," added Molly.

"Yeah, thanks." Dylan was already making tracks

toward Dockside Avenue. As he hurried past the narrow aperture of Bell Street, a slender shape stirred in the shadows, then slipped away. But not before Michael caught a quick reflection from a pair of glasses, and an even quicker sparkle of police insignia. Luann Krebs.

He looked at Molly. Molly looked at him. With a mutual shrug, they closed ranks, linked their arms around one another, and turned for home.

As soon as they stepped back into the house, Molly said, "It's been a long day. I'm going to treat myself to a bubble bath."

"I'm going to my office," Michael replied. "Do a bit of research on those coins."

"Iris would be proud." Molly blew him a kiss and went on her way to the spacious master bath, one of the first renovations she'd insisted on Michael and Irwin making after moving to the decaying Victorian pile that was Thorne-Shower Mansion.

Michael's long legs took the steps to the third floor two at a time. In his office, he switched on the largest of his computers, and while it booted up, he gazed around the room at his collections of action figures, movie posters, books. What he saw, though, was Willie on board the *Black Sea Pearl,* a gold coin in his pocket. A gold coin with Latin letters spelling out *Transalpina,* and Cyrillic letters, as well. Surely that mix of writing styles indicated an origin in Eastern Europe.

He sat down at his keyboard, and within moments established that *Transalpina* was an alternative name for Wallachia. Which was where? He was soon following links that led him all over the world—and then, surprisingly, back to Blackpool itself.

"Still at it?" asked Molly from behind him.

Michael swam up from the depths of his research. The digital clock on his desk couldn't be right—had he been sitting there for an hour? Rubbing his eyes, he turned around to see Molly in her favorite pink bathrobe, the one that made her auburn hair glow. Her feet were encased in the slippers he'd given her. They were shaped like furry white rabbits, long ears perked forward, open red mouths exposing felt fangs.

With a smile at her slippers, and another at her lovely face, he said, "The gold coins are from Wallachia, today part of Romania. Wallachian coins were originally made of silver, until the supply of silver dried up. Then they started using coins brought in from other countries. Willie's big silver coin, the one with the lion—that's a Dutch thaler."

"Thaler? I bet that's where dollar comes from."

"Could well be, yes. There's no way of telling whether Willie's thaler came here by way of Wallachia."

"But the other coins are Wallachian, even though they're gold, not silver?"

"Apparently so," Michael replied. "One ruler during the sixteenth century minted gold coins that were copies of the older silver ones, but there are very few of those."

"If they're rare, then they're extra valuable. And yet a shady character like Willie has three. That's quite a nest egg for him."

"They're only valuable if he can find someone to buy them."

Molly nodded. "That's why he wanted to see Trevor Hopewell."

"There's more to it than that. I found an article from the *Blackpool Journal* about two boys exploring the passageways beneath the town back in the 1840s. One of them was named Abercrombie."

"Tunnel ratting must run in the family—you explore the Blackpool tunnels with the modern-day Abercrombie, right?"

"Yes, and I'm wondering what else has been handed down in the family," said Michael. "The boys found several Wallachian coins, but the story doesn't say what happened to them."

"Ooooh!" Molly's eyes lit up.

"That's not all. Do you remember the copy of the *Blackpool Journal* that Dylan threw on the floor in Willie's kitchen?"

"With a headline about the Magic Lantern Theatre, yes."

"I found it on the *Journal*'s Web site. The article about the coins was in the same issue. A good thing I set up that Web site for Fred, isn't it, even though all I wanted was to test a new Web platform."

"No good deed goes unpunished," said Molly with a grin. Her voice turned cautious. "Maybe Willie having a copy of that paper is just coincidence. Maybe the paper was lining a kitchen cabinet or—no. One cabinet was lined with a 70s-style yellow-and-green flowered paper. The other ones weren't lined at all."

Only Molly would have noticed that. "There were no other newspapers in the flat. I expect Willie saved this one for a reason."

"You'll have to ask Rohan and the others if they've ever seen Willie scrounging around the tunnels. And where he might have found the coins. One reason people keep exploring and mapping those tunnels is because of the rumors of treasure. Pirate treasure, smuggler's goods, and there was Liam McKenna telling one of his tour groups about gold stolen from gypsies in Romania. Gold that was cursed." Molly raised her hands and waggled her fingers in a "woo-woo" motion.

"Rumors of treasure. Oh, yes." Michael switched off his computer. "I'll ask Rohan, but if the rats knew where Willie found the coins—where the lads in the 1840s found the coins, come to that—the spot would already be over-run. As soon as word spreads that Willie has those coins, the tunnels will be flooded."

"The coins are Willie's, I guess, unless the police can prove otherwise. I hope Fotherby locked them up at the police station. I don't exactly trust him." Molly strolled over to the window.

"Nor do I." Turning off the desk lamp, Michael joined her.

Night had at last fallen. Toward the bay they could make out the converted Victorian gas lamps along Dock-side Avenue, illuminating the scene for people still eating and dancing. Hopewell's yacht was lit with tiny fairy lights outlining the masts and yards. The lights of other boats in the marina and out the harbor rose and fell with the waves.

Beyond the town, over the sea and the land alike, darkness ruled. There wasn't even any dim glow from the grounds of Ravenhearst Manor beyond the harbor, an islet in the midst of encroaching peat bogs. "No tunnel rats or ghost hunters are running the Ravenhearst gauntlet tonight," Michael said. "No tourists, either, despite all the ones stopping in town."

"Most of the stories you hear about ghosts at Raven-hearst are caused by a wall collapsing or an owl hoot-ing…"

"Or by one too many pints at the pub." Michael always told himself that any dim lights they saw at the charred ruins of the manor were those of torches, not of restless spirits better suited to Other Syde tours. And he intended to keep right on telling himself that.

Molly leaned back against him. "Wallachia's in Romania? So is Transylvania, right?"

"Right." Michael inhaled her scent, that of fall woods and spring flowers, wafting upward from her warm body. He slipped his cold hands into the front of her robe. Ah, yes.

"Dracula's from Transylvania," Molly went on, even as she snuggled her arms around his. "The fictional vampire, at least. But the historical figure—Vlad the Impaler—really is from that area. I thought Liam McKenna was just blowing smoke with all that about Dracula's gold, but… maybe there is an actual connection. Rebecca says the rumors have been going around Blackpool for years. No reason Liam and Holly didn't pick them up when they got here, especially since they make their living from what Aleister calls gossip and sailor's tales."

"They're not the only ones."

"I bet Willie went looking for more coins and Naomi went with him—she wants out of town, after all. But people get lost in those tunnels. People die…" Molly's voice drifted away into the darkness.

"Naomi's out there somewhere, love," Michael stated. He didn't need to add the corollary: *We will help Dylan find her.*

CHAPTER FIVE

MOLLY ADDED AN EXTRA teaspoon of sugar to her cup of tea. Funny, when she lived in the U.S., she almost never drank hot tea, preferring it iced and her hot drinks made with coffee. But now that she lived in the U.K., the cuppa was a given, like driving on the left. "I've got nothing," she said.

Iris's reading glasses rode low on her nose. A pencil poised in her hand, she peered at the newspaper lying in the space between tea cozy and toast rack. "When I lived in the States, I'd do the *New York Times*'s weekend puzzles, but they're quite undemanding compared to these British puzzles."

"Sorry, I can't concentrate. I'm worried about Dylan and Naomi."

"Michael's phoning him, is he?"

"That's what he said." Molly glanced at her watch. It was past ten Sunday morning—but then, she and Michael had slept late. Or remained in bed, rather, if not exactly sleeping.

Now he bounded down the stairs and into the breakfast nook, so quickly the hanging plants swayed behind him. "Dylan's not answering. Either he's switched off his phone because he's found Naomi, or he's fallen down exhausted in the attempt. I've asked Rohan to meet us at the bicycle shop at half past eleven."

Molly rushed to finish dressing. Within half an hour

she and Michael were walking toward the Stewarts'
small apartment above the bicycle shop. The sun shone as
brightly as though Molly had special-ordered it to provide
maximum publicity for Seafaring Days. A fresh breeze
frilled the harbor with delicate whitecaps and already several small power and sailboats crisscrossed the water.

The peal of St. Mary's bells signaled that it was almost
time for the 11:00 a.m. worship service. Along Dockside
Avenue, seagulls picked their way through yesterday's
litter. An ice cream van squeezed down the street and
found a place to stop. The other vendors were doing a
brisk business, the aromas of cooking food overcoming
the usual fish-and-mold smell of the harbor.

Martin Dunhill, in his first mate's blue coat, white
shirt and red neckerchief, was eating a meat pie in front
of Clough's butcher's stall, a baseball cap shading his
eyes. Addison Headerly, today's jeans and sweater con-
siderably less dashing than yesterday's frock coat, stood
beside Peggy Hartwick's booth, drowning his sorrows in
scones, cream and jam. Rebecca Hislop wove flowers and
ribbons into a crown for a child, while the child's mother
fingered the sun-catchers dancing and glittering around
her stall.

Molly glimpsed another man in nautical garb before
the tall doors of Havers Customs House, made a quick
right-angle turn and ran up the steps. "Good morning!"

Trevor Hopewell was reading the plaque fixed to the
tidy Georgian front of the building, its raised letters relat-
ing the achievements of Charles Crowe. Small letters at
the bottom said Donated by Ophelia Crowe.

Hopewell swept off his cap, tucked it beneath his arm
and eyed Molly from her denim jacket to her cropped
jeans. "Mrs. Graham. Molly, if you don't mind. And Michael, as well! What a pleasure."

"Good morning," said Michael at Molly's elbow. He pulled off his aviator sunglasses and hung them by the earpiece from his black T-shirt, the better to fix Hopewell with a steady gaze.

"Are you having a good time at Seafaring Days?" Molly asked Trevor.

"Fine festival. Top hole."

"Are you planning to do some research here at the Customs House? It's the place to come, with old log books, research papers, maps."

"Maps of sunken ships in the area, I'm told."

"I was reading an article about sunken Spanish treasure ships off Florida," said Molly. "The archaeologists found lots of gold and silver, some of it as coins. Do you collect coins as well as all the other fascinating things you showed us yesterday?"

"Oh, yes! I've got quite a number of rare and priceless coins."

With a mutter of "Aha!" Michael chimed in, "Have you ever seen any gold coins with the Latin inscription *Transalpina,* and a Cyrillic inscription, as well?"

Trevor stepped from the shadow of the portico into the light, his eyes widening, his brows rising. "Sixteenth century Wallachian coins of Vladislav III? No, I've never seen any, more's the pity. They're legendary among the collectors in my numismatics club."

So Trevor probably would have bought Willie's coins, if his reputation for dealing drugs hadn't preceded him. Molly wondered where Willie and Dunhill had met.

Here came Fred Purnell, his camera slung around his neck, his nose for news quivering. "Good morning, Mr. Hopewell. Having a chat with our local sleuths, are you? Michael and Molly helped solve a murder at the theatre, and now I hear them talking about Wallachian coins, another of our local mysteries."

"We're not sleuths," Molly protested.

"We got caught up in some bad business is all," Michael added.

"Have Wallachian coins turned up here in Blackpool?" Trevor asked.

Michael seized his opportunity. "Fred, you published an article several years ago about two lads in the 1840s finding Wallachian coins in the old tunnels."

Martin Dunhill hurried up the steps, the very unnautical baseball cap pulled low over his forehead, shielding his eyes from the bright sun behind them. He swiped his throat beneath the open collar with the neckerchief from his uniform then stuffed it into his pocket and said, "Boss, you've got that phone interview in half an hour with the BBC's legal department."

Trevor barely even glanced at Dunhill, giving him a "down, boy" gesture and focused again on Fred. "Coins? Tunnels?" Molly could have read a newspaper by the light shining from his eyes. With a shrug, Dunhill slipped away.

Fred replied to Trevor, "Supposedly, Charles Crowe brought gypsy gold back from Romania, gold he came by dishonestly, and so, out of guilt and fear of reprisal, he hid it in the tunnels running beneath the town."

"Indeed," breathed Trevor. "The Charles Crowe on the plaque there? Any relation to Aleister Crowe and his siblings?"

"They and their great-aunt Ophelia are Charles's descendants," answered Michael. "Keepers of the family flame."

"Crowe was a remarkable man," Fred said, "although 'remarkable' cuts both ways. He dominated a generation of Blackpoolers, despite being away for long stretches. Fought with Nelson, did business in Eastern Europe, engaged in the opium trade—that was quite lawful at the time, mind you. Charles was also a bit of a blackguard, greedy and secretive."

"He dug out these tunnels, then? They're not mine workings or something similar?"

"Crowe built half the town, so likely he improved the mining tunnels and built new ones. They're smugglers' dens, pirates' lairs and more going back for centuries. The local people still explore them and turn up interesting items—which brings us round to the coins, which may or may not be part of Crowe's secret gold that vanished so many years ago."

"Gold that has a curse on it," murmured Molly.

"You don't need a curse to explain people cheating, robbing, even murdering for wealth of all descriptions," Fred told her. To Trevor he said, "An interview with the BBC?"

Taking a step back, Trevor glanced at his watch. It was a pricey Patek Philippe, Molly noted. "Corporate law. Always a fascinating topic, eh? Mr. Purnell, I'm looking forward to hearing more about the town's hidden treasures. Molly, Michael, I'll have Martin phone about that dinner date. I'm looking forward to learning more about your detective work, as well." He set his hat firmly on his head and glided down the steps.

"Wallachian coins," Fred said, half to himself. "You won't believe this, Molly, Michael, but Daisy Coffey's saying that Willie Myners has a bag full of them. Willie Myners? That layabout? Pull the other one!"

Molly smiled. Ironic that Fred would be skeptical about something that was true. Sort of. Then her smile faded. "Daisy must have been listening at Willie's door while we talked to Fotherby yesterday. I bet she even looked inside."

"Ah, yes," Fred said with a nod. "I wanted to ask you about that. Daisy says you and the lad from the bicycle shop were involved in a break-in."

"We weren't involved," Michael stated. "And to be accurate, Willie has four coins, not a bag of them—three gold Wallachian and one silver Dutch thaler."

"Willie's found himself the pot of gold at the end of the rainbow, has he? Cripes!" Fred's eyes lit up almost as brightly as Hopewell's had earlier.

Gold, Molly thought, did tend to cast quite a glow. "All we know is that P.C. Fotherby took the coins."

"Did he, now? I'll ask Paddington for a photo or two, then."

"Good luck with that," Molly told him.

Suddenly, the distinctive rhythms of Bollywood echoed off the portico. Michael dived for the pocket of his cargo pants. "Hello? Dylan? I phoned but you didn't... What? I'll be right there."

"What is it?" Molly and Fred both asked simultaneously, but Michael was already running down the steps.

"Naomi phoned Dylan," he shouted over his shoulder. "She's on Willie Myners's boat. It's drifting out into the harbor—she can't operate it and Willie's badly hurt."

"Willie's hurt?" Molly repeated, even as she fell farther behind Michael, with Fred huffing and puffing behind her. "He has a boat? I suppose that makes sense. He must use it to smuggle drugs into town. There are always boats coming and going from the marina."

There was Rohan, galloping through the crowd on Dockside Avenue in an admirable display of broken-field running. He and Michael almost collided outside the Bait and Tackle Shop. They exchanged a few terse words, then Michael called to Molly, "I'll be back soon as may be!"

Side by side, Michael and Rohan disappeared toward the marina.

Molly stopped dead. "Michael! Don't..." *Get involved in anything dangerous,* she wanted to finish, but danger had a way of sneaking up on you.

Wheezing, Fred caught up with her. "Smuggling? Drugs? The illegal sort, you mean?"

"Or maybe legal ones used illegally," she told him. Knowing that it was too late to protect Naomi now, she added, "I'll fill you in on the way to the marina."

MICHAEL AND ROHAN CUT THROUGH the crowd and onto the pier. Their shoes thudded on the wooden planks. Lines banged among the maze of pleasure craft and fishing boats. Water sloshed, gulls called.

His broad chest heaving, the whites of his eyes glinting, Dylan stood with Owen Montcalm beside the Grahams' small cabin cruiser. "An old banger of a boat," Owen was saying, "but Willie had the money so I sold it to him. No affair of mine where that money came from." Using his pipe as a pointer, he indicated a gray shape bobbing in the harbor. "That's it. Looks to have been drifting for half an hour or thereabouts—it'll be running aground on the sandbar before long."

Digging through his pockets for the keys, Michael leaped onto his boat.

Dylan followed, Rohan on his heels, and Owen cast off the lines. It took only a moment for Michael to start the engine and maneuver away from the crowded pier. Once in the open water of the harbor, he accelerated. The salt breeze combed through his close-cropped hair, but it wasn't the breeze that chilled him to the bone.

Dylan's voice blended with the throbbing rumble of the engine. "My phone went dead. I had to recharge it—had to recharge myself. Didn't catch a wink last night. Good job I'd just turned the phone back on when she called—she can't drive a moped, let alone a boat. She's not mechanical, she's artistic. She's in trouble, she said. Terrible trouble."

Poor Naomi, Michael thought.

Rohan asked, "Willie's hurt?"

"So she said. No more than he deserves."

Willie's boat, a cabin cruiser even smaller than the Grahams' and much the worse for wear, bobbed up and down like a cork. Naomi clung to the strut supporting the half roof. Her face, turned toward them, was more than ashen, it was almost green. The circle of darkness that was her mouth emitted jagged part-sobs, part-shrieks, that resolved themselves into words as the men grew closer. "Help me, Dylan. I'm so sorry. Help me…"

Skillfully, Michael guided his boat next to the peeling paint of the cruiser. Rohan scrambled over the side and tied the boats together while Dylan followed. He embraced Naomi, muffling her cries in his denim jacket.

Michael vaulted onto Willie's cruiser. Beneath his boots, the deck was flecked with rust-red droplets that spread into splotches, forming a trail that led into the shadow of the half roof. He wanted nothing more than to climb back onto his own boat and leave. But he couldn't do that.

"Where's Willie?" Rohan asked Naomi.

She could only shake her head against Dylan's chest. Over the crushed spikes of her black hair, Dylan focused on the rusty smears and winced.

Grateful for Rohan at his side, Michael ducked beneath the roof.

Willie Myners lay curled below the wheel. His sweater, his jeans, his hands—all were stained rust-red, burnt umber, crimson. How many shades of red did blood come in? Kneeling, Michael pressed his fingertips into the clammy flesh of Willie's throat. He detected the slightest of pulses, faint and uneven. "He's alive, just. We need to get him back to town."

"Sorry, mon." Leaning over Willie and Michael both, Rohan turned the cruiser's starting key. The engine coughed, but didn't catch. He inspected the gauges behind the wheel and announced, "There's no petrol."

"It's no good dragging him into the other boat," said Michael. "The police…"

"I'll phone them." Rohan returned to the deck. Michael heard the three beeps of 999 and then Rohan's voice. "Man hurt—boat—Blackpool Harbor."

His stomach knotted, Michael stood and walked out onto the deck. Naomi was still clinging like a barnacle to Dylan's chest.

"What happened?" Dylan asked her. "You phoned me, said you wanted to make it all up, but then you vanished."

Her fingers with their shiny purple nails opened and shut against Dylan's jacket. Clean fingers, Michael noted, not stained with blood.

He looked away, hoping Dylan hadn't noticed his friend inspecting his wife's hands for traces of murder.

"Yeah, I did," she said, her words coming in ragged spurts. "I meant to give Willie up as a bad business—there was no way forward, not with him. But then, yesterday afternoon, he called and said his ship had come in and he was leaving Blackpool for good, and if ever I wanted to leave, start over again, this was the time. You've been away, Dylan. You've had your sports tours in the U.S.

and all, but I've never been farther than Scarborough or Darlington. I've asked you to go somewhere else, to Newcastle, maybe even London, not this little…"

"I've got to mind the shop, Naomi. We can't afford to give that up and start over."

She shook her head. "And I couldn't afford to stay and give up my dreams. So I came to the boat, this boat, yesterday evening. Willie was waiting. Said he had to run back to his flat for the coins and we'd leave this morning after the petrol dock opened."

"And?" Michael asked, in as gentle a tone as he could muster, while Rohan roamed the deck behind him.

"He was nervy then, looking over his shoulder, but when he returned he was downright demented, in a fury one moment and a misery the next. He said the coins were gone. He'd been robbed. His ship had come in and then sank like the *Titanic*."

Looking over his shoulder, Michael repeated silently. Had someone threatened him, or had the scene at his flat scared him? Or both?

Dylan's eyes were bleak. Michael knew his friend was thinking the same thing he was. Willie had found his gold coins, his nest egg, gone. Michael felt a pang of guilt. If Dylan hadn't called him and Molly to the flat, if he himself hadn't found the coins, if Fotherby hadn't taken them… Then Willie's attacker would have.

"It wasn't fair," Naomi went on. "He wanted to make an honest sale of honest goods. Leastways they were honest by the time they reached him."

"The coins he wanted to sell to Hopewell," Michael said.

Naomi peered at him, her makeup so smudged her eyes reminded him of a badger's. "Yeah. That prat Hopewell was going to make him a rich man. Save he couldn't get to Hopewell, could he? That's Willie for you, all bark and no bite."

"Where did he find the coins?" Rohan asked.

"I don't know," said Naomi. "He'd only had them a few days."

The boat rocked and rolled. The sound of the band came faintly over the water. Above the town rose cliffs honeycombed with secrets, and beyond them the peat bogs that isolated Blackpool from the rest of Britain. No surprise its inhabitants would dig into the hillsides like prisoners trying to escape a dungeon.

"There was no reasoning with Willie," Naomi finally said. "There was no reasoning with you, Dylan. But I'm sorry I didn't phone."

Dylan didn't point out that reason had very little to do with the situation. "Thomas Clough told me you'd bought two bacon rolls and two cans of lager last night, but he didn't know where you'd gone with it."

"Back here. I was afraid to go home, Dylan."

Dylan flinched at that.

"We ate and drank the beer, and I had me a Valium or two and went below deck. I fell asleep and dreamed, really strange dreams, Dylan. I thought I heard you calling for me—"

"I *was* calling for you." Dylan tightened his grasp of her slender shoulders.

"—and then it wasn't your voice at all, but Willie's and another one. I could barely hear them from where I was in the cabin, and they weren't shouting but talking low and urgent like, with a sort of snarl. Then it was quiet, and when I woke up again I wondered why the boat was rocking so bad, being at the dock and all, and I came up here. It was an accident, wasn't it? The boat lurched and he hit himself on something…"

Once again she buried her face in Dylan's jacket. It was Rohan who looked over at Willie, curled into a fetal position, beyond all hope and care. "I don't know how he was hurt, Naomi, but it was no accident."

Michael checked Willie's vital signs again. They were even fainter now, but his wounds were so extensive, Michael had no idea how to help him. By the looks of it, Willie had probably been stabbed or shot. He'd bet on the former, since the sound of a shot would have carried across and someone would have noticed.

Whatever it was had happened on the deck where the bloodstains started. Willie had staggered to the wheel and collapsed, his life's blood leaking, pooling, draining away, leaving his eyes sunken, his complexion gray and his breath shallow as Blackpool's beach at high tide.

Or… Michael followed the blood droplets to the railing of the boat. Perhaps Willie had collapsed where he was wounded, and his attacker's *weapon* had left the trail of gore. "The boat was tied up at the pier when you went to sleep?" he asked Naomi.

Rohan stepped forward, leaned over the railing and pulled a rope on board. He held it up. "It's been cut, not untied."

"Any blood on it?"

"The end's been dragging in the water… What's this?" Rohan reached into a metal crevice in the boat and pulled out an open pocket knife. "There's blood on this."

"Put it down, Rohan. That's probably the murder weapon."

Rohan dropped it instantly.

Naomi's muffled voice said, "Willie used that to cut our bacon rolls. That's all I know. I didn't see anything. I didn't hear anything."

Well, no, Michael thought, she wouldn't have, would

she, sleeping off the effects of the drugs in the cabin below deck?

Then he remembered Daisy Coffey's voice saying, "She had a row with Willie that set my crockery to rattling." Although that might not have been Naomi at all, but the mystery blonde woman. And even if it had been Naomi, it didn't mean she'd killed the man.

"I'm sorry," she said. "Dylan, I'm so sorry."

CHAPTER SIX

MICHAEL AND MOLLY SAT side by side on the blue plastic chairs of the hospital's casualty department waiting room. Even though this was hardly the time and place to be angry, she couldn't resist a mild, "You didn't have to rush off to a crime scene like that."

"Dylan needed my help. So did Naomi. It was just the scene of the crime, not a crime in progress."

"I know," she said. "I'm glad for that much."

"I suppose Fred's running with the story, as he always does?"

"Oh, yeah." Fred had been waiting at the pier when the Blackpool constabulary, for once working with commendable efficiency, brought Willie in and transported him to St. Theresa's hospital. "I figured if I didn't tell him about poor Naomi, he'd get a twisted version from Daisy or Rebecca Hislop or someone."

"A little bit of spin, is that it?" While Michael's words were teasing, his tone was grim.

With a sigh of both affection and aggravation, Molly massaged the tight tendons in the back of his neck. "I know, I know, we didn't intend for any of this to happen. Maybe the person who attacked Willie didn't intend for it to happen, either."

"I wouldn't bet on that," said Michael.

The door labeled Staff Only Past This Point swung open, and a man clad in a white coat and wearing a stethoscope plodded through. His thick glasses turned from side to side, and his high forehead furrowed beneath thinning strands of gray-blond hair. "Michael Graham, is it? And Molly? I'm Dr. Harvey Parker."

Michael and Molly stood up and shook Dr. Parker's hand, which was dry and squeaky-dusty—he'd just removed latex gloves. "Ah, yes, we met at the library," Michael said, "when Mrs. Hirschfield opened the miniatures exhibition. You made several of the ships in bottles that are displayed next to Charles Crowe's miniature of Blackpool. Well done!"

"Thank you." Parker's smile flashed like the beam of a lighthouse and then vanished. "I thought D.C.I. Paddington was here…"

"I am here." Paddington walked down the hall from the main entrance as though he was marching to his own band. "Reporters! That Jenkins fellow and Purnell are lying in wait at the porte-cochere, along with visitors who think this disturbance is a jolly good show, and even townspeople who ought to know better."

At that moment, Molly agreed with Michael that Paddington resembled a cross between Charlie Brown and Adolf Hitler.

Before Molly could add her two cents—or two pence, depending—Paddington started grilling Parker. "What about Myners?"

"He died a few minutes ago. He never came round. He'd lost too much blood—there was nothing we could do."

Molly closed her eyes. Death. Sudden death. Another murder. She and Michael had already seen enough. She opened her eyes to find Michael's face pale but composed.

Paddington's expression was set like concrete. He pulled out a little notebook and pen. "Was he stabbed?"

"Yes," Parker replied. "A long, narrow blade perforated his abdomen."

"How long a blade?" asked Michael. "Three or four inches, about the length of a pocket knife?"

"Larger, I expect. But I'm not a trained medical examiner. I'll sign the body over to the forensics team, Inspector, and they can sort the matter out."

"Fotherby says there are no knives on the boat, save that small one your friend found, Graham."

Molly suspected Paddington wasn't going to thank Michael for his part in alerting the town to a new murder case, and she was right. His moustache twitching, he stepped closer to Parker.

"When was Willie attacked?"

"At a guess, at about a quarter to eleven."

Michael chimed in, "Owen Montcalm said that he gave up trying to keep people out of the marina so he decided to go and enjoy the festival. He left around ten and everything was in order."

"I have officers on the case, thank you, Graham." Paddington's pen scratched across the notebook.

A nurse held the swinging door open. "Doctor?"

"If you'll excuse me." Parker hurried past her and the door closed behind him.

"Well then," said Paddington, "what's all this about Dylan Stewart and his wife?"

Michael's words came reluctantly. "Naomi meant to run away with Willie."

Paddington tutted. "Hell hath no fury like a man betrayed, eh? Dylan's a sizeable chap. If he took to violence there'd be no stopping him."

Michael said nothing.

"Or Naomi herself stabbed Willie. Lover's quarrel."

Molly waded in. "There are a lot of people in Blackpool with grudges against Willie," countered Molly. "You yourself saw Robbie Glennison arguing with him. Not fifteen minutes later, I overheard Willie on the *Black Sea Pearl* trying to get past Martin Dunhill so he could show Trevor Hopewell a gold coin."

"A gold coin?" Paddington asked. "Oh, please, not that rubbish about treasure again."

"It's not rubbish. We found three gold coins and a silver one in Willie's flat."

"Didn't Fotherby hand them in?" Michael asked.

"Fotherby?" demanded Paddington. "He reported a spot of bother with the pair of you and Stewart at Willie's flat. Stewart broke in searching for his wife."

"Dylan didn't break in," Michael pointed out. "The door was open."

"Fotherby was watching the place," Molly said.

"Willie needed watching," said Paddington.

"And now Fotherby's got his coins."

"He's police, isn't he? What makes you think these coins were Willie's?"

"What makes you think they weren't?" Molly retorted. "He may have found them in the tunnels, just like a couple of boys did in the 1840s… Oh! Maybe they're even the same coins!"

"Where did Willie get them, then?" asked Michael.

"Good question." Molly made a mental note to research where the 1840 coins had gone.

Paddington raised his voice to override both of theirs. "That's what I'm asking—where did Willie get any coins? Douglas—P.C. Fotherby—was very wise to take custody of them. I'll have a word with him, soon as the Scene of Crimes team from headquarters in Ripon arrives."

Raised voices and quick footsteps sounded from the entrance hall. A heavily pregnant teenager burst into the room. Her plump cheeks streaked with tears, her blond curls sagging, she gasped, "Rebecca saw Willie being carried up from the pier. Krebs said he'd been hurt. Where is he?"

"Who are you?" demanded Paddington.

"I'm Michelle Crookshank. I'm Willie's fiancée."

"Fiancée?" Paddington repeated.

Michael said, "How do you do, Michelle. I'm Michael Graham and this is my wife, Molly."

At least someone was worried about the man, Molly thought. Darting a quelling look at Paddington to give the girl a few minutes before dumping the bad news on her, Molly headed to a counter that held an electric kettle and an array of cups and tea bags. If she'd learned nothing else from Iris it was that here in Britain, anything from a broken heart to a cracked foundation could be helped by a good strong cup of tea.

Michelle sat down and sniffled like a drain in need of Drano. With a put-upon sigh, Paddington handed over his huge handkerchief and the girl buried her face in it. Molly's eyes met Michael's. *A round, blonde lass.* Was this the woman Daisy had heard arguing with Willie on Friday?

The kettle whistled. Molly dunked a tea bag in the hot water, laced the black brew with several lumps of sugar and a dollop of milk from a nearby carton, and pressed the resulting medication into Michelle's unoccupied hand.

Paddington sat down, the chair creaking beneath his weight, and turned toward the girl. "Michelle, is it?"

She raised her mottled face. "That's me name."

"You heard Willie had been hurt?"

"Been stabbed, Krebs was saying. I reckon my dad done it, because of the kid here." She pointed to her rounded abdomen.

"Your dad... Krebs!" Paddington produced his walkie-talkie and bellowed into it. "Find a man named Crook-shank, first name—what?"

"Geoffrey," Michelle said.

"Geoffrey," Paddington repeated.

"Michelle," Molly asked gently, "were you buying drugs from Willie?"

"Drugs?" Paddington's round face flushed with frustration. "I could never prove that's what he was up to."

"What else is there to do in a dump like this?" Michelle retorted with a thin, defiant smile. "Booze, pills, smokes, a few giggles at the old train station, that's about it. Lessen you're after digging about in the old tunnels, but not me. There's a bad smell in there, and bats."

Paddington prodded, "Had a special relationship with Willie, did you?"

"Are you deaf? We're engaged. We're getting married."

Molly cast a sympathetic look at Michelle's belly, bulging against the confines of her blouse. Yeah, that line about marriage had been working for unscrupulous men since the Stone Age.

"Did you argue with Willie at his flat about caring for the child?" asked Michael.

"Yeah. But that's when he told me he'd been waiting all this time for his ship to come in, and it finally had. We don't have to wait no longer. We're gonna get married at a registry office, and we're gonna find us a nice flat in Newcastle with room for the baby."

Waiting for his ship to come in. There was a metaphor used often in Blackpool, Molly thought. Michael had said that Naomi had used it, too. Sometimes it was more than a metaphor, like when Trevor Hopewell's *Black Sea Pearl* came sailing in.

Paddington leaned closer to Michelle. "Did Willie threaten you? Were you carrying a knife, by any chance?"

"You think I stuck him? Are you daft? Willie's gonna take me away from here."

"Now, now," Paddington began, but was interrupted by more footsteps. This time it was Krebs and a weathered older man dressed in well-used fisherman's garb.

"He was just outside," Krebs announced, "looking for the lass, here."

Michael recognized the older man. "I know you. You were at the pub yesterday afternoon. I thought you wanted to have a word with Dylan, but you never spoke."

"Yeah, that was me." Geoffrey Crookshank sat down on Michelle's other side. "I seen Dylan slapping Willie around, and you and the Jamaican lad stopping him. Pity, that. I'd have let Dylan dig that bloke six feet under, then I'd have shaken his hand and bought him a pint for doing Blackpool a public service."

Michelle set up another wail. "Dad, how can you say that?"

"Dylan Stewart actually knocked Willie about? And here's me, talking about him being such a sizeable chap." Paddington smiled, no doubt feeling he was on top of the situation.

"Made more than a few threats, as well," Geoffrey said. "Ask Chuck at the Dockside. Ask anyone."

Paddington turned to Michael. "Is this true, Graham?"

Between his teeth, Michael said, "Yes. But didn't you already know that? Fotherby seemed to."

Paddington mumbled something that sounded like, "Of course." Dylan hadn't been mincing words.

"Everyone had heard the rumors that Willie and Naomi Stewart was—" Geoffrey stopped in midsentence and glanced over at Michelle.

"Naomi didn't mean anything to him," Michelle protested. "They had a row and she walked out."

So both women had fought with Willie? Interesting, Molly thought.

"I've got both Stewarts at the station, along with the Jamaican lad," Krebs told Paddington, and regarded Michael. "We'll be needing your statement, Mr. Graham."

"Yeah," Michael said, and extended his hand to Molly.

She took it, thinking how warm living flesh was, how reassuring. How fragile.

"Well now, Crookshank," Paddington said, "We'll be obliged to interview you and your daughter about hurting Willie, since he did Michelle here wrong."

"He didn't do me wrong!" Michelle insisted. "He loves me! We're gonna get married!"

Geoffrey pulled Michelle against his side. "It's all right, pet. None of this is the little one's fault. I'll see to the pair of you, never you worry." And his red-rimmed eyes glared up at Paddington. "How could she have stabbed the man. Look at her!"

"Who said anything about Willie being stabbed?" Paddington demanded with a glint of triumph.

"Who *hasn't* said it? Fotherby's standing just outside describing the crime scene to Fred and that skinny telly reporter. By now everyone in town knows all about it."

Paddington rolled his eyes heavenward. "Where were you between half past ten and eleven this morning?"

"We was together at home," Michelle replied. "I was making the sandwiches."

Geoffrey added, "I've got a couple of sports signed on for a fishing trip this afternoon. They always expect me to feed them as well as bait the hooks and reel in the fish. No worries, though, I charge extra for the sandwiches and the flask of tea, and double charter rates during the festival."

"Of course, publicity for the festival hasn't helped anyone in town," Molly told Paddington from the door, then hurried out into the hall.

Behind them, Michelle screamed. "Dead! No, no!"

"There, there." Geoffrey sounded desperate. Paddington must have just broken the news about Willie. "Think of the little one."

Michael at her side, Molly outpaced Krebs from the antiseptic-tinged, gloom-ridden air of the hospital into the sunshine of Mariner Street.

Yes, quite a few people stood along the sidewalk and around the corner onto Leaning Cross Street. Henry Marley was working his way through the crowd with a tray of samples from his nearby chocolate shop.

She and Michael held back, letting Krebs clear a path past Fred Purnell and Tim Jenkins, who now had a sound person with a boom microphone as well as his camera operator in tow. They were close to tearing P.C. Fotherby limb from limb in their eagerness to get an interview. "Now, now," said Fotherby, simpering with self-importance, "I'll have a few words for the national media first."

Molly looked from Krebs's solemn face back to Michael. "There's one woman not trying to get away from Blackpool, not until she's made her mark, anyway."

"How soon before we see her footprints on Paddington's forehead?" Michael asked.

"Not long. I just hope she doesn't decide to make her reputation on Dylan's or Naomi's heads."

"Ah," was all Michael said, but Molly could tell that her remark had hit home.

Krebs led the way to the police station, a converted Victorian house on Walnut Grove Street a block from Dockside Avenue, and ushered Michael and Molly through the sturdy door and past the vestibule. "Wait here," she instructed, and strode on past the front counter.

Dylan, Naomi and Rohan occupied a row of plastic chairs to one side. Rohan's rich mahogany complexion looked as if it had been dusted with ash and Dylan was pasty. With heavy makeup smeared over her stark white face, Naomi could have passed for a zombie risen from its grave.

They looked up as the Grahams walked in. Molly shook her head and Naomi began to cry into Dylan's shoulder. "Thanks for going to the hospital," he said to them. "They told us to come here and not to leave."

Michael nodded and they perched in the nearby bay window. After a long moment in which the only sounds were the bleeps of electronic equipment, low voices and shuffling footsteps from the rear of the building, Michael asked Dylan, "Where were you this morning when I phoned?"

"At home. Asleep. I'd been up all night searching for Naomi. I stirred up some teenagers at the train station—Blackpool Council needs to either clean the place out or tear it down—and I poked about in the tunnels a bit, then I went back to Willie's flat. After that I gave up and went home. If I'd known Willie had bought himself a boat, I'd have looked there."

Naomi peered down at her hands, which she was twisting like a hangman's noose in her lap.

Michael rephrased his question. "Where were you between half past ten and eleven this morning? That's when the doctor thought Willie was stabbed and the boat was set adrift."

Dylan's crest of red hair drooped and his massive shoulders slouched. "Michael, we're mates. You're not implying— It wasn't me Daisy heard arguing with Willie yesterday. I was sleeping off that pint at your house…"

"I know. The killer had to be out and about around ten-thirty this morning, that's all."

"I wasn't, not then. I was asleep in the apartment. I switched my phone back on at eleven, and Naomi called within five minutes. I called you and Rohan, and here we are."

"I was walkin' around then," Rohan said. "So were a lot of other people. The vendors were workin', Hopewell's sailors were on and off the yacht, the band was tunin' up. Mon, whoever stabbed Willie and set the boat adrift could have walked right past me, and I wouldn't have noticed a thing."

"Surely he…" Molly stopped. "He or she" would be more correct, but less diplomatic. "Surely the attacker got blood on his hands."

"So he tucked his hands into his pockets," said Michael, his brow furrowed. He loved working through scenarios—that's why he wrote games. "He'd washed them long since and checked himself for bloodstains. Likely he's either cleaned the knife or hidden it, as well— unless that pocket knife's the murder weapon. Paddington's chances of catching the attacker with any evidence still on him are well and.truly…"

The word *gone* hung in the stale air as Paddington

slammed through the outside door, with Fotherby at his heels, and Krebs emerged from the back.

All three faces reflected a dour self-importance, but it was Paddington who spoke. "Dylan Stewart, I arrest you in connection with the murder of Willie Myners. You do not have to say anything, but it may, it may—ah, damn, what's the wording…"

Krebs picked up the script. "It may harm your defense if you do not mention, when questioned, something which you later rely on in court. Anything you do say may be given in evidence. I'll lock him up, guv'nor." She grabbed one of Dylan's arms.

"Inspector Paddington," Michael protested, "you've got the wrong person!"

"He didn't do it!" cried Naomi.

"That's just not fair!" Molly said indignantly. "You're jumping to conclusions!"

And Rohan finished the chorus with, "Trust the police to get everything wrong."

Shaking his head, Dylan looked pleadingly at each face in turn, and then shambled behind Krebs toward the station's small holding cell.

CHAPTER SEVEN

MICHAEL STOOD OUTSIDE the police station, shoulders braced, chin thrust out, anger simmering. Paddington and Krebs, with Fotherby making flanking movements, had interviewed him, Rohan and Naomi—separately, so as to winkle out any discrepancies in testimony—while Molly paced back and forth in the waiting room.

Now, on the front steps beside him, she tucked her iPhone into her pocket. "There. Your sister Robin suggested I call the solicitor she introduced us to at the Fund for Children's Christmas party in London. So I did. He's going to do whatever it takes to get Dylan out on bail. Paddington doesn't have a real case, just circumstantial evidence."

Michael watched Rohan and Naomi disappear down the street toward the bicycle shop, Rohan having promised Dylan to help her run the business in his absence. Hopefully a very short absence. "A murder case," he said. "We should leave well enough alone, let Paddington and Krebs and even Fotherby deal with it."

"No kidding." A flash of memory of the theatre murders—and fear—glanced across Molly's eyes.

Michael felt that same memory and fear ooze through his own mind. He drew Molly close against his side and for a moment she clung to him. Then she drew herself up stubbornly. "But it's all going wrong. If Paddington thinks Dylan's the killer, he won't investigate any further."

"No. He won't."

"Did you see the way Dylan looked at us? He knows we've had some experience in detective work, whether we wanted to or not. He knows we don't like leaving well enough alone. He needs our help."

"Yes." Again Michael squared his shoulders and raised his chin, using his anger to tamp down that ever-recurring fear, a fear less for himself than for Molly. "Let's have a meal and talk it over."

"Good idea. It's too late for lunch, and too early for tea, but with this crowd in town, Emily's shop will be open."

Walking shoulder-to-shoulder, they took off toward Dockside Avenue.

Tim Jenkins and his expanding crew crossed their path, hurrying in the direction of the marina. Two police cars now blocked the end of the pier, and several overall-clad figures climbed in and out of a panel van like invading aliens. The activity was orchestrated by a man with a suit, a tie and a beak of a nose. His sandy red hair glinting in the sunlight, he intercepted Jenkins and designated a spot for him at one side of the gawping crowd. The Scene of Crimes team from Ripon had arrived.

The Grahams lingered a moment, but when the technicians disappeared behind the screens erected around Willie's boat, Molly and Michael pressed on around the corner into Bell Street. They walked up the steep, narrow lane below overhanging eaves and dangling baskets of flowers and opened the door of the Delightful Tea Shop.

"Michael! Molly!" Every gray hair straying from Emily Crowder's bun stood on end with static electricity and curiosity. "What's this I hear about Willie Myners?

He's found Charles Crowe's lost treasure and someone's murdered him for it?"

The Internet didn't move as quickly as news in Blackpool, Michael thought. Molly filled Emily in while she seated them at the only vacant table, a small one near the elegant stone fireplace.

"You don't say!" Emily exclaimed.

"I'm afraid I do say," Molly replied, and placed their usual order. "Tea, toasted ham and cheese sandwiches, chips and Peggy's apple tarts with cream, please."

"Right you are," said Emily, and walked off toward the kitchen.

As Michael sat down, he caught a movement beyond the open door of a small private room.

"What are you looking at?" Molly asked.

A waitress exited the room and shut the door behind her. Michael leaned back in his chair. "Aleister Crowe's in there, with Lydia and Aubrey. They appear to be having a serious conference."

"About Willie's gold, what do you want to bet? They're planning what to tell both Ophelia and the media. Damage control."

"Spin doctoring," said Michael. "We've seen Aleister at work. The paintings his family helped steal, his father's activities during the war, the lot. We learned his MO during the murder investigation last spring."

"What's the collective noun for a gathering of crows, like a parliament of owls or an unkindness of ravens? A murder? A murder of Crowes-with-an-*E*. Not that I think Aleister killed Willie to keep him from spilling the beans on the location of Charles Crowe's treasure. He's more subtle than that, as we know from experience." Her face puckered with yet more memory.

Don't dwell on it, Michael told himself. "I can't see

either Lydia or Aubrey having a go with a knife—they're the lightweights in the family."

"Lydia's a tunnel rat, isn't she?" Molly asked. "Maybe she knows something about Willie's coins… Oh, thanks, Emily."

Emily set down a teapot and cups. Molly poured for Michael, then herself, the fragrant steam wavering upward. She pitched her voice to blend with the buzz of other conversation and the clatter of utensils against crockery, asking, "So are the old Blackpool legends of Charles Crowe stealing and hiding a gold treasure really true?"

"I doubt even the Crowes have an answer to that," Michael said. "Unless they've got Charles Crowe's secret diaries or the like."

"Charles doesn't strike me as the kind to write down his secrets. And even if he had, Ophelia would have burned them long ago." Molly sipped warily at her steaming cup, then pulled out her iPhone and set it to take notes. "Okay. We need to list the prime suspects, the people with motive, means and opportunity."

"You've paid close attention to working with your uncle at the Mystery Case Files agency, haven't you now?"

"Of course I have. If I wasn't so good at writing grants, I'd be a detective, like him."

"All right then," Michael replied with an indulgent if wry smile. "Aleister might have a motive, of a sort, but what about means?"

"The Crowes probably have everything from Cro-Magnon skinning flints to broadswords tucked away at the Crowe's Nest. All of these old country homes do. And rumor has it that cane of his is really a sword stick."

"But what about the knives available to everyone in Blackpool?" Michael nodded toward the waitress, advancing toward their table with two plates. "How many does Emily have in her kitchen? How many does Iris have at our own house, come to that?"

"Thank you," Molly said again, as the girl set the plates on the table.

The delicious odor of golden-brown fried potatoes distracted them, and for a few moments he and Molly did nothing but eat.

At last she patted her lips with her napkin and said, "Yes, everyone in town has the means to have committed Willie's murder. As for opportunity, well, that's why the police ask around and establish who was where when."

Trying to keep his objectivity, Michael replied, "Just because Dylan says he was home asleep at half past ten doesn't mean he actually was. If he was down by the pier just then, no matter how many people were coming and going, someone would have seen him. He's a hard chap to miss, with the hair and the tattoos and all."

Brisk and businesslike, Molly patted out notes on her tiny screen with her fingertips. "Then there's Naomi. If she'd had blood on her hands, literal blood, wouldn't you have noticed?"

Suddenly, Michael was again bobbing in the harbor. "Her hands were clean—I remember her purple nail enamel. But there was plenty of water to wash in."

"What was her body language, her tone of voice on the boat…?"

"She was upset."

"Of course she was, but maybe it was because, say, she'd argued with Willie over Michelle, or she'd told him she no longer had any use for him and she was going back to Dylan. Either way, he turned violent and she stabbed him in self-defense."

"She just happened to be carrying a knife about with

her? The doctor thought the blade was longer than the one we found."

Molly nodded. "You're right. The murderer must have deliberately taken the knife on board with him. Her. The question is, would Naomi, well, not exactly *frame* Dylan, but let him be accused, even convicted, in her place? Especially if that freed her from Blackpool?"

"I don't think so," said Michael. "She doesn't seem nearly hard enough for that."

The inner door opened and the three Crowes trooped through the crowded main room. Lydia brushed crumbs from her clothing—a saucy blouse, a tight skirt, high-heeled shoes. Aubrey adjusted the collar of his striped shirt. Aleister held his cane like a croquet mallet. Spotting the Grahams, he let his siblings go on ahead and detoured to their table.

"Well now," he said, his deep, resonant voice lowered to a husky whisper, "are our local amateur sleuths back at work?"

"Define 'work'," Michael asked.

"Don't play the innocent with me." Aleister's lips tightened in a thin smile. "I suggest you remember, the pair of you, what happens when you take it upon yourself to ask questions."

Molly's cheeks flushed. "Are you trying to tell us you have a stake in Willie Myners's murder, Aleister? What are you trying to hide this time?"

His smile petrifying, Aleister bowed and strolled away after Aubrey and Lydia.

She muttered, "When he looks at me I feel like I've just walked into a giant spiderweb."

"Quite." A giant spiderweb. There was a hazard for his game... Michael pushed down his irritation at Aleister and went on. "Michelle Crookshank and her father. She was afraid he'd murdered Willie. And then they alibied each other."

"Which pretty much cancels out both alibis, especially since Geoffrey's got a great motive—what Willie did to his daughter."

"With his daughter."

"Yeah, she's young and in love with love, and Willie played on her romantic fantasies, not that I can see him as the romantic lead." Molly pulled a face. "Looking for love in all the wrong places. It's an old story, but that doesn't make it a good one—especially when there's a child involved. At least Geoffrey doesn't want to throw her and the baby out onto the street, although if he ends up in prison, things will be rough for her."

"What if she ends up in prison?" asked Michael. "Perhaps she decided her child would be better off with no father, rather than the wrong one."

"Or what if she heard about Willie and Naomi and killed him out of jealousy—if I can't have him, then no one can. I agree with Geoffrey, though. She can hardly walk. It wouldn't have been easy for her to climb onto the boat. And Willie could have outrun her."

"She might have waited until he turned his back."

Emily arrived with two slices of apple tart, each swimming in a pool of thick yellow cream. "Everything's all right for you, is it?" she asked them.

"Everything's great, as usual," said Molly.

They dug into the sweet apple, golden pastry and rich, smooth cream.

When Molly picked up her phone again, Michael said, "Robbie Glennison. You mentioned you and Paddington saw him arguing with Willie?"

"Oh, yeah. He might have punched Willie out right there if Krebs hadn't intervened. Paddington said that when Robbie works at all, he works for Callum at the Smokehouse, though he made some remark about him not being right in the head. Considering Paddington thinks you and I aren't exactly right in the head, I'd take that with a grain of salt, except Robbie really did seem, well, off."

"Were they arguing over drugs, do you suppose?"

"I wouldn't be surprised. He could have wanted Willie to keep quiet about his habit, or he could have been asking Willie to give him a discount or forgive a debt. Maybe, in his own twisted fashion, he thought killing Willie would be the equivalent of entering detox."

"Twisted. Oh, yes." Michael set down his fork.

"Should we put Fotherby on our list?" Molly asked. "He's taken his own sweet time telling Paddington about the coins. And he was awfully quick to protect Willie's interests. You don't think Fotherby had any private deals going with Willie, do you? A profit-sharing plan?"

"Maybe so, but Willie can't have made much in the way of profit, not in such a small town. Those coins, though, they were another matter. Obliging of me to turn them up, wasn't it?"

"You didn't know Fotherby was lurking outside," Molly said.

"Yes, but in an odd sort of way, I feel I owe Willie for sinking that ship he was expecting. If I hadn't found his coins, maybe he'd have been able to get away with Naomi, and there's no saying how that would have ended."

"Not with him selling the coins to Trevor Hopewell, although maybe Willie was planning to catch up with him later, when Martin Dunhill wasn't around."

"What about Dunhill as the killer, then? Or Hopewell, come to that? What if he killed Willie for the coins? He has an impressive display of cutlery on his yacht."

"But Trevor only heard about the coins this morning, after Willie had already been attacked."

"Or so he pretended."

"Hmm, yes," Molly said reluctantly.

Michael's lips tightened—could she be blinded by Hopewell's looks?

"Maybe he doesn't just have the face of a movie star," she went on, "maybe he can act, too. But if he killed Willie, he cleaned up and got to the Customs House awfully fast."

"Hopewell reminds me of Aleister. He'd find murder to be a bit messy."

"So, like Aleister, he'd have his valet or butler do the dirty work for him. Or his first mate. Martin was no friend of Willie's. They knew each other from somewhere, and he saw the coin.… Or maybe he didn't. Willie was holding it in his fist. In any case, I saw Martin at the festival this morning, before we saw Trevor."

"Anyone else?"

"Daisy Coffey? Is she telling the truth about hearing him argue with both Naomi and Michelle and the unidentified man—who might have been Liam McKenna? He and Holly are certainly profiting from the whole gypsy gold story." Molly pushed her plate away so briskly the knife and fork clanked together. "It's always possible Willie was killed by someone we don't know. Dealing drugs is risky business, even if it's just the penny-ante stuff Willie was in."

"It's because his business was so small that I think there's more to it than drugs."

"Yeah. Like gold."

Michael stared at Molly across the table. "There we are, then."

She stared back at him. "No, here we are. Asking questions."

"Aleister's right, damn him. We don't want to attract the wrong sort of attention."

"And yet…" Once again Molly drew herself up. She saved the notes on her phone, tucked it away, and said, "A man's dead. There are people in trouble—especially Dylan. If there's no new evidence, Michael, he'll be on trial for his life."

"Not his life. The U.K. abolished the death penalty fifty years ago. He'll be on trial for his freedom."

"Being locked away for decades to come, for something you didn't do—that's not a life."

"No. It's not." With a firm nod of his own, Michael stood up.

Molly got to her feet, then to her tiptoes to kiss her husband's cheek. "We'll be careful, okay?"

"We'll be all right," he said, even as he reminded himself about those good intentions paving the road to hell.

CHAPTER EIGHT

THE GRAHAMS FOUND EMILY and settled the bill just as she opened the door of the shop for Alice Coffey. Unlike Naomi's black clothing, which projected hipster attitude, Alice's soot-colored skirt and cardigan simply seemed stodgy. She swept by Molly, Michael and Emily, using her giant handbag like a locomotive's cow-catcher.

"She's called an emergency meeting of the Historical Preservation Society," Emily explained.

"They're not meeting about my getting them conservation grants," Molly told Michael as they dodged yet more customers to emerge onto the street.

"Is it Willie's death that's set the cat among so many pigeons, or his gold coins?" Michael replied.

"Both."

A delivery van filled the street from curb to curb in front of Creighton's Antiques, and two men maneuvered a Chippendale sideboard through the door of the shop. "I think I'll go check that out," Molly said.

"If that sideboard's genuine it will cost a packet."

"Not the sideboard. I want to ask Charlotte about the Abercrombie boy and the 1840 coins. What if she and Winston have had those coins all this time? Willie could have stolen them when he was doing repairs for the Abercrombies. I mean, finding out where Willie got the treasure might point to his killer."

"That's working backward. I'd rather have a word with

Callum at the Smokehouse, see what he knows about Robbie Glennison. Mind how you go, love."

"You, too," Molly said, and watched appreciatively as Michael strode away—he did wonderful things for a pair of cargo pants, a black T-shirt and a light leather jacket. Then the delivery men climbed into their van and drove off, and Molly hurried across the street.

The bow window of the antique shop was piled like Ali Baba's cave with relics from the past: books, toys, dishes, boxes spilling jewelry. Today Molly's eye was caught by a necklace of semiprecious heart-shaped stones. The price printed on its tag was quite reasonable. When Charlotte Abercrombie herself looked out of the door with a friendly, "Hullo there," Molly pointed.

"Is that from an estate sale?" she asked.

"Sort of." Charlotte's hazel eyes, set deeply in her thin face, widened. "My boy Connor found it in one of the tunnels near Ravenhearst and I cleaned it up. I told him I'd put the sale price toward his school fees."

"Connor's brave. Michael says the tunnels below Ravenhearst are really dangerous."

"I worry all the time. Worrying, it's like gripping the armrests of your seat on the airplane, right? Keeps you flying?" Only half of Charlotte's mouth smiled. "Winston says every Abercrombie for generations has explored the tunnels, back before even Ravenhearst was built."

Good. Charlotte herself had introduced the topic of the tunnels. Molly joined her on the front step of the shop, beside a rack holding colorful paisley shawls similar to the one Charlotte was wearing. "There was an article in the *Journal* reporting that a boy named Abercrombie found some Wallachian gold coins in those tunnels in the 1840s."

"Oh, yes," said Charlotte. "The lad was Winston's—I'm

not sure, great-great-great grandfather? An ancestor-in-law, leastways."

"Where are the coins now? Still in the family?"

"No. One of the multiple great-grandmothers said the coins were cursed and sold them to a Crowe—Hugh, I think it was. They've not been seen since."

"Locked in a vault at the Crowe's Nest," surmised Molly, adding to herself that the 1840 coins might as well be in Fort Knox for all the likelihood of Willie getting his hands on them. So much for her bright idea of his coins being the 1840 ones.

"Alfie at the Mariner's Museum borrowed a similar gold coin from the British Museum and put it on display three years ago when the town council was trying to drum up interest in the Seafaring Days festival. That's when Fred Purnell wrote his article—loves legends and scandals, does Fred. Of course, others of the local folk were trying to nip Seafaring Days in the bud. Ophelia Crowe, for example, wasn't best pleased with Fred's article, or Alfie's display. Out of sight, out of mind, I suppose, when it comes to Charles Crowe's gypsy gold."

The Mariner's Museum—something teetered at the edge of Molly's thoughts, but she couldn't grasp it. "Do you think the coins were cursed?"

"The ones Willie Myners turned up were cursed, weren't they?" Crossing her arms, Charlotte peered suspiciously toward Dockside Avenue and through the slit between the buildings that afforded a glimpse of the sea.

So intense was Charlotte's stare that Molly glanced over her shoulder, half expecting to see pirates rushing up from the harbor. But she saw only visitors. "Well, yes, Willie was murdered. But to quote Fred Purnell, gold tends to create its own curse. There may have been other factors involved, though, like jealousy, and, well—someone wanted to get rid of him," she concluded.

"Quite," said Charlotte. Despite the warm afternoon, by British standards, at least, she pulled the shawl even tighter around her shoulders. The faint odor of mothballs emanated from it, mingling uneasily with the scents from the tea shop across the street.

"How did you find out about Willie's coins?" Molly asked.

"He stopped by just two days ago, asking what they might be worth. I was gobsmacked to see more Wallachian coins, and a thaler, as well. When I asked where he'd found them, he smirked and said, 'Wouldn't you like to know,' then wrinkled his nose, made an odd little squeaking sound, and clicked his teeth together."

"Sort of imitating a rat? A tunnel rat?"

"No surprise there are more coins in those tunnels. Every time there's rain or a landslip, people go right back to searching. You'll not catch me in there."

"Me, either," said Molly, a tickle of claustrophobia tightening her shoulder blades.

"I gave him a fair estimate for the coins," Charlotte went on, "but he wouldn't sell them to me, or even leave them on commission. He said he wanted to cut out the middleman. Or woman."

Across the street, several older ladies, including Daisy Coffey and Rachel Donner, walked into the Delightful Tea Shop. "Emily says Alice called an emergency get-together."

"I should think so," retorted Charlotte. "First there's all the strangers in town for Seafaring Days, then mysterious and suspicious treasure, then yet another murder—she's having a hard time keeping Blackpool's reputation tidy."

"If it had a tidy reputation, then it wouldn't be Black-pool," Molly said.

"Miss?" called someone from inside the shop. "What's the provenance of this moon medallion?"

Charlotte went to attention. "Excuse me, Molly."

"Of course." She pointed to the necklace that she'd eyed in the shop's window. "Set that aside for me, would you please?"

"I certainly will," Charlotte told her. "Ta-ta."

Molly turned away from the window, her mind ticking. Alice wanted to protect the town's reputation. Aleister wanted to protect his family's. Willie's discovery of the coins had reminded everyone of the unflattering rumors about Charles…. Molly snapped her fingers. *That's right!* Michael had told her Dylan had seen Willie talking to Alfie at the Museum. Maybe Willie had gone there with his coins after he spoke to Charlotte.

Molly pulled her phone from her pocket and tapped Michael's icon, even as she headed toward Dockside Avenue.

MICHAEL SKIRTED THE VERANDA filled with diners and strode down the alley at the back of the Smokehouse, taking a deep breath of the delectable smoke emanating from the curing shed.

But he caught no more than a glimpse of the racks of herring glistening with an oily, sooty sheen before Callum Wyn-Rodgers stepped out of the door, shut it and wiped his hands. "Well, hullo there, Michael. Good to see you. I'm afraid I'll not have time for a round of golf until next week."

"Not to worry, Callum. I didn't stop in to ask about a game. I'm planning out the next part of my renovation work at the house, and wondered if you could recommend my hiring on Robbie Glennison."

Callum snorted. "I think not. Just sacked the man myself on Friday."

"Did you now?"

Callum led Michael into the rear of the restaurant, past a long stainless-steel table glinting with the odd fish scale. "Robbie came in late once too often and botched the filleting and trimming twice too often. When I told him he was no longer working for me, he shouted and threatened me with the knife he was holding. One of the other lads rang the police, and P.C. Fotherby escorted him out… Damn!"

Michael strolled as casually as he could to Callum's side. His friend was inspecting several long, flexible boning knives hanging along the wall like the teeth in a shark's jaw. "I should have noticed before. A knife's gone missing. In the fuss, Robbie probably never handed his in. I'd sooner let it go than ask for its return."

"Has a temper, has he?"

"He's got a temper, right enough. He was sent to anger-management courses some months ago, after he started fights at the Dockside and the Café, but I can't see as they've done him any good. He needs medication—and not the medication he's been buying from Willie."

"Willie Myners?" Michael's casual, innocent air was wearing very thin, but Callum didn't seem to notice. "You've heard about him, I suppose."

"I've heard he was stabbed to death trying to leave town with a chest of gold doubloons, and that the coins have gone missing."

"I've heard there were only four coins, three Walla-chian ones and a thaler."

"Where's Wallachia?" asked Callum.

"Eastern Europe. Romania."

"Ah, that's the gypsy treasure, then."

Michael couldn't pretend he hadn't heard about that. He tried another angle. "Thanks for warning me about Robbie. I've seen him about town, thought he might be available for odd renos and repairs."

"He is, yes. But you're running the risk of him leaving the job half-finished, or leaving you with a bigger job than you had to begin with. Rohan Wallace, now, he's right dependable."

"Yes, he is…" The sound of "Pretty Woman" had Michael diving into his pocket. "Molly?"

Her trans-Atlantic accent filled his ear. "Charlotte says Willie brought his coins to her to evaluate two days ago, but wouldn't tell her where he found them and wouldn't leave them with her to sell. The coins that the Abercrombie boy found in the 1800s went to the Crowes, who weren't happy when Alfie Lochridge displayed one from the British Museum three years ago."

"Alfie!" Michael exclaimed. "Dylan saw Willie talking to Alfie!"

"Bingo," said Molly. "He seems to have taken a shine to you. Why don't you speak to him?"

"Sure. I'll try. Where are you now?"

"Walking past the Customs House, heading for the festival. Alice Coffey might have a—well, let's say informant, not gossip—in her cousin Daisy, but I've got Rebecca Hislop. Her booth is right there in the square, at the end of the pier, and she was already making sales when we walked by at eleven. She had to have been setting up at ten-thirty or so."

Michael remembered the church bells had been signaling that it was almost eleven, but when Molly had been checking over the vendors, he'd been eyeing the *Black*

Sea Pearl and trying to decide whether to model the hero of his new game on Errol Flynn's classic swashbuckler or Johnny Depp's more contemporary one, who swished as much as he swashed.

"Well done, Molly—ah, I'm getting another call. Cheers." Michael eyed the screen of his phone, hit a button then put it back to his ear. "Rohan. Is anything happening at the bicycle shop?"

"Naomi's heard from your sister's solicitor friend. He'll have Dylan out of jail by teatime."

"That's good news."

"In the meantime, Paddington's sent Krebs to close the shop and ransack it. She's puttin' screwdrivers in evidence bags, along with the knives from the kitchen and..." Michael heard Naomi's tired voice in the background. "And she's takin' Naomi's nail scissors. Coppers, they don't know when to quit."

Michael had wondered more than once why Rohan had such a negative opinion of the police. "I'm on my way to the Mariner's Museum. Wait for me there, and I'll catch you up."

"Sure, mon, no problem."

Slipping his phone back in his pocket, Michael turned to Callum. "Thank you."

Callum had his own phone in his hand. "Thank *you*. I'd never have noticed that missing knife if you hadn't stopped by. I'll pass it along to Paddington—Robbie needs interviewing, doesn't he?"

"He does that," Michael agreed.

"Keep your clubs polished, eh?"

"I will." Michael told himself that a round of golf at one of the courses near Darlington would be a welcome distraction. So would parasailing, or scuba diving or some other activity. But work came before play.

He left Bell Street for Compass Rose Avenue, a street almost wide enough for two cars to pass as long as they folded in their wing mirrors. The wood-and-plaster facade of Betsy Sewell's Curio Shop looked like something from a fairy tale, appropriately enough. Its front window sported an Other Syde poster, as well as incense burners, New Age books, souvenirs of Blackpool and assorted gimcracks.

Betsy herself stood on the front step, holding an elephant-shaped watering can over a pot of nasturtiums. "Hullo. You're Molly's husband, are you?"

"Yes, I am. Michael Graham." He stepped closer to the window, wondering what the paper posted below the Other Syde notice was.

"You collected her after she came to the book signing last month. That went well, didn't it?"

Michael tried to hide his smile. The event had gone well for Betsy.

"The old guard, the Coffeys, the Crowes and all—who knew they'd get the wind up over a simple book?"

Betsy had known very well that hosting an author who claimed a conspiracy of witches and Freemasons had manipulated Yorkshire's history would create controversy. She'd sold a lot of books to people who came to see what the fuss was about, including Molly. The book itself turned out to be unreadable, but no matter—Betsy had giggled all the way to the bank.

Now the shop owner glanced demurely at her flowers. "I heard about poor Willie and his chest of Turkish gold coins. No surprise—he had a very dark aura."

Daisy had made a meal out of her glimpse of the coins, Michael thought. Peering at the smaller poster, he saw that it was a very nicely drawn and lettered map of Blackpool.

Who was the artist? Ah, there in the lower corner was the name: Naomi S.

"Lovely map, isn't it?" Betsy asked. "Hand-lettered, with bonus insets of Ravenhearst Manor and a harbor view, printed on acid-free archival paper with a deckled edge to make it look old. Naomi Stewart did the original sketch—quite nice, really, although I had to ask her to erase some of the skulls and tombstones and such before I had it printed up."

"You've been working with Naomi, then?"

"Well, Willie contacted me to begin, then brought Naomi round for a conference. He was telling her she had a bright future, only needed to get away from Blackpool, is all."

Willie was acting as Naomi's agent? *What cheek!*

"I crossed their palms with some folded paper for that—I'm not the one with gold coins, am I? A shame about Naomi's husband being arrested. But you can hardly blame him."

"Blame Dylan?" Michael asked. "For what?"

"For Willie's karma catching up with him." Betsy opened the door of the shop, setting wind chimes to tinkling. "I'd be glad to help you look for the rest of the treasure—it's got to be there in the tunnels. I've had a lot of success with my dark crystal."

"Your crystal? You, ah, you gaze into it?"

"Silly man," Betsy said with an airy laugh. "Of course not. You dangle the crystal, letting it swing to and fro. If you hold it over a map, it will stop swinging over the site of the treasure. Or whatever else you're searching for."

"I see," Michael said cautiously.

"That's what Willie was doing with the original of Naomi's map, I expect—searching for the rest of the treasure. He must have had his own crystal. Strange, though…" Betsy's forehead crumpled.

Michael wondered what she could possibly consider strange.

"He stopped in yesterday evening to collect his commission for last week's map sales. He would have been better off waiting until after the festival—I'm selling loads of maps—but he's always short of money. You'd think if he had a chest of Turkish coins, he wouldn't need a few pounds from the maps. But he wasn't half-upset, as though someone had snatched the coins right away!"

Someone had, Michael told himself.

"I suppose the police have his treasure chest now." Betsy sighed heavily. "About that crystal, Michael…"

"Some other time, thank you." Michael hurried on up the street. He zigged around the rack of newspapers in front of the *Journal*'s office, then stopped dead before completing his zag. Hand-printed on the front of the rack, in stark black letters on white paper, were the words Crowe Treasure to be Revealed at Last?

Quickly, Michael fished in his pocket for a coin—one stamped with the profile of Queen Elizabeth II—and bought a newspaper. Oh, yes, Fred Purnell had printed up a new front page to wrap around this morning's edition, one with an article less about Willie Myners's murder as about the notorious lost gypsy gold, complete with a grainy photo of a Wallachian coin, "Transalpina" and all.

Michael speed-read the story, which began with a perfunctory tribute to Charles Crowe's architectural and historical legacies and continued with a much longer, lovingly detailed account of the rumor. Or nest of rumors, rather, about how one of Crowe's multiple fortunes had come from a rich duchy in Eastern Europe, one he bested in a business deal. Or perhaps worsted, since Crowe hardly had a reputation for honest dealing.

Or perhaps the treasure had originally belonged not to Wallachian or Romanian nobility, but to a gypsy family, one that swore a blood oath to get it back, an oath that had presumably been passed down the generations and transmuted to a curse in the popular mind.

Trust Fred, Michael thought, to get both Dracula—Romanian nobility—and Romany curses into the same paragraph.

Crowe had then hauled the treasure home on one of his ships and buried it somewhere in town. Because of the oath, or curse, he never spent it or allowed his family access to it. By now, it would be worth millions.

"Right," Michael said. He made a hard left up the steps and through the doorway of Fred's office.

Usually, he enjoyed visiting the *Journal* office, with its inspiring odors of paper and coffee and the faintest afterglow of mildew, as befit the stolid Victorian building. Today, though, he had no time for the framed copies of major headlines—wars ending, prime ministers elected, and, of course, the mystery of Emma Ravenhearst—or the antique typewriter with several keys missing.

Fred looked up from his computer keyboard and grinned a slightly giddy welcome. "What do you think?"

"I think Aleister Crowe is going to have your guts for garters."

"That would be a great story, wouldn't it? Crusading newspaper editor and local hero persecuted by local nob. Local snob, come to that."

Michael pulled up an old wooden chair, spun it around and straddled it. "These rumors have been going about for years now…"

"Centuries."

"But is there any basis in them?"

"They turn up repeatedly in old issues of the paper. I've heard them from the older people in town. Winston Abercrombie's grandmother, for example. I interviewed her just before she passed away at the age of one hundred. Sharp as a tack, she was."

"But…"

"And there's James Norton—not the son who runs the hardware shop, the father. He's known several generations of Crowes and believes there's something to the story."

"Yes, but…"

"Give it up, Michael. You yourself saw Willie's coins."

Michael gave it up. "Did Fotherby ever hand the coins in to Paddington? Or is Paddington speaking to you at all?"

"He's barely giving me the time of day, but then, he's not seen this page yet." Fred chuckled. "Yes, Paddington has the coins locked up. Now. He let me have one quick glimpse. No photos, but I'd already pulled one off the Net. Sixteenth century Wallachian coins of Vladislav III, in gold yet, are the Holy Grail of some coin collectors."

"Trevor Hopewell mentioned something of the sort."

"With his money, he can afford them," said Fred. "Whether Fotherby would have handed in the coins without Daisy Coffey going on about them, and without Willie himself being murdered, I can't say. It's not as though Paddington would have put any credit in Willie claiming he'd been robbed, eh?"

"Not a bit of it," Michael said.

"The Ripon team will be taking Willie's body away for a postmortem exam. Their detective inspector is a closemouthed sort—if the team is turning up anything on

Willie's boat other than bloodstains and fingerprints and such, like the murder weapon, he's not telling Tim."

"Tim Jenkins?"

"I'm giving him the story of Crowe and the gold in exchange for him keeping an eye on the police." Fred spun his chair back around to his keyboard. "Sorry, Michael, I've got to work on getting out a whole new edition."

"Yeah. And I've got to work on clearing Dylan's name."

"Good luck with that. Paddington seems quite sure he's got his man, it's all over, and he can get back to alphabetizing the traffic manual or whatever it is he does with his time."

Michael stood up and replaced his chair. "Wait until he sees your new front page."

But Fred's fingers were already flying over the keys, the lines of letters expanding across his screen to form the provocative words, *murder* and *long-vanished treasure*.

CHAPTER NINE

"CHEERS," MOLLY SAID to Michael, but he'd already switched to his other call.

Tucking her phone away, Molly glanced toward the stately classical facade of Havers Customs House. It felt like several days, not just one, since she and Michael had stood there talking to Trevor Hopewell, right before the load had hit the fan.

Right before the rest of the load had hit the fan, she corrected, and walked on toward the pier.

Just beyond the *Black Sea Pearl*'s mooring, Tim Jenkins and his two crew members waited with several other reporters, all of them jousting with a variety of cameras, microphones and recorders. It was hard to tell the pros from the amateurs—quite a few of the festival attendees were also standing by with their own electronic paraphernalia at the ready, from digital cameras to cell phones.

Molly stopped beside Tim. "How's it going?"

"Typical crime scene investigation," Tim answered. "They put up screens so there's nothing to see, and no one's telling us anything, save that the dive team's on its way."

"Assuming there's any evidence to dive for."

"That's the thing about a murder case, isn't it? You don't know what you're looking for until you find it." Tim peered again at the boat. "Ah, the screens are coming down. They're finished for the moment, then. Thanks for giving me a head start on the case, Molly—and for inviting me to Blackpool for the festival."

"Thanks to you, Molly," mimicked Douglas Fotherby, from just inside the police-taped line of demarcation across the pier. Luann Krebs, several paces farther in, frowned at him, then fixed her gaze hungrily on the Ripon team.

Molly drew herself up to her full five-foot-four and shot Fotherby her worst glare. But there was no point in doing verbal battle with someone who was pretty much unarmed.

Turning his back, Fotherby took up a stance that would have been parade-rest, if his bull-like neck hadn't been thrust forward to see what was happening. All Molly saw was the red-haired, suit-clad man with the aquiline—and then some—nose talking to a man who was now peeling off his overalls.

"He's in charge, right?" Molly asked Tim.

"That he is. Chap named Ross, Detective Inspector. I once interviewed him in connection with a robbery in York. Good man."

That was comforting, Molly thought. She dragged herself away from the scene and went on toward the vendor's stalls. At first glance, Rebecca Hislop seemed to be merely arranging her cellophane-wrapped flowers and assorted gift items, from soaps to shortbread to DVDs. At second glance, Molly saw that Rebecca's cornflower-blue eyes were fixed on the scene at the pier.

"There you are." Rebecca turned to Molly. "You and Michael will have the case solved by now, I expect."

Molly's smile stiffened. "We're not detectives."

"You're not innocent bystanders, either," Rebecca countered.

Molly couldn't disagree with that. Fortunately, Rebecca

went prattling on, which was exactly why Molly had paid her a visit to begin with.

"Fred says that poor Willie was killed between half past ten and eleven. I started setting my things out just then. I might well have witnessed the murderer walking about red-handed." She shivered. "I mean to say, Dylan Stewart didn't kill the man, did he? Never mind what Naomi was up to with Willie. There's no accounting for taste, is there?"

Before Molly could reply, Rebecca kept going, "It must have been almost half past eleven when first Dylan, then Rohan and Michael came running down the street and onto the pier. Naomi called for help from the boat, didn't she? I didn't see either her or Dylan before that—not till all hell broke loose."

As far as clearing Dylan went, so far, no good. Molly sniffed at a bouquet of miniature roses, but they had very little scent.

"Aleister Crowe has to be upset about Willie bringing those coins to light," Rebecca continued.

"I wonder if he knew yesterday evening that Willie had them," Molly said, "or whether he learned about them today, after Willie's death."

"Of course he knew yesterday. It was Daisy Coffey—she's a gossip, that one…"

Molly smiled, but made no comparison between pots and black kettles.

"She was telling Margaret Coffey about Michael at Willie's flat and the bag of gold coins, every one with Count Dracula's profile on it, and Margaret told Randall Coffey at the garage, and Randall was repairing the thermostat on Aleister's Alfa Romeo—just got the latest model, of course."

"Of course." Molly stepped aside while a visitor bought

a pirate doll and several postcards. She reminded herself that Aleister hearing about Willie's coins in plenty of time to commit the murder meant nothing. The world was about to hear about Willie's coins. Aboriginal people in the Australian outback would soon be chatting about Blackpool and its lost treasure.

Rebecca slipped several ordinary British pound coins into her money box and turned back to Molly. "I didn't see Aleister out and about this morning, but Sandy Mason said that Lydia and Aubrey were at Calm Seas when the service began—texting rather than reading their prayer books. And Addison Headerly arrived in good time to sit down with them—poor lad, he'd do better to forget Lydia—but Aleister came in late and out of breath."

"He did, did he?" Making a mental note to check that out, Molly abandoned the pretense that she and Michael weren't interested in the case. "What about Robbie Glennison?"

Rebecca's eyes widened. "There's a suspect for you. Willie was cheating Robbie, giving him oregano instead of marijuana and sugar pills instead of tranquilizers, or so Daisy's saying. She'd heard them arguing outside Willie's flat."

Outside? More likely inside, Molly thought to herself. "I saw them having words, too. So did Paddington. He wasn't particularly shocked today when he heard about a drug problem in Blackpool."

"Why should he be? Even Fotherby knew what was going on, not that he seemed particularly concerned about it." Rebecca's voice took on a sarcastic edge. "But then, Blackpool's finest was making his rounds this morning claiming tribute, a free pie from Thomas Clough's stall and scones from Peggy Hartwick's. You should have seen the look Daisy Coffey gave him when he walked straight to the head of the line."

"I can imagine."

"Who else was out and about?" Rebecca asked the air. "Ah. Trevor Hopewell. I noticed him leaving the pier, shining in the sunlight like a new penny. Or a new pound." She emitted a sigh of admiration. "If Willie was killed closer to half past ten than eleven, Trevor might just have had time to do it, stop in at the yacht for a wash and brush-up, then come to the festival."

Molly raked back through her memory. Hopewell hadn't been breathing hard when she and Michael met him at the Customs House. He'd looked freshly washed and brushed, but that didn't prove anything. She moved along. "We passed Martin Dunhill eating a pie at Clough's about five minutes before we met up with Trevor. Then he came up to us to give Trevor a message—he hardly seemed like someone who'd just committed murder."

"The first mate chap from the yacht? Yes, he was also here whilst I was setting up, just larking about. He and Trevor, they're night and day, eh? Though Dunhill's never so off-putting as Robbie… Well, speak of the devil."

Molly spun around to see Robbie Glennison ambling toward the area. Nothing suspicious in that; everyone in town was stopping by the crime scene. Especially now that another van had pulled up and a dive team was clambering down into the Blackpool police department's orange inflatable boat.

Molly turned back to Rebecca. "Was Robbie here this morning?"

Rebecca's brow furrowed. "No. I don't think so. I saw Michelle Crookshank, though. Willie's the father of her child, isn't he? Wasn't he, rather. Poor lass."

"Yes. Poor lass is right."

"Michelle was mooning about here when I arrived to set up. She would start down the pier, get as far as the *Pearl,* then stop and wander back up this way."

"Maybe she was trying to make up her mind whether to go on to Willie's boat or not. I bet she suspected Naomi was with him." And that's why, Molly added to herself, Michelle had told Paddington she was home making sandwiches for her father. She'd lied. That wasn't good.

Rebecca unfolded and then refolded a couple of tea towels. "Mind you, Michelle could have been searching for her father. He walked by just about the same time, heading for his boat, I expect—he gets quite a bit of charter business during the festival. Or he could have been going to the Bait and Tackle Shop. He's often there if he's not on the water."

Molly's brows rose and fell. Geoffrey had lied, too, then, saying he was home with Michelle.

"Geoffrey's been very protective of Michelle since her mother died. In fact, if you'll excuse my saying so, I'd not be surprised if *he* killed Willie."

"It's not for me to excuse anyone. Or accuse anyone, for that matter. Michael and I would like to, to…" Molly was saved from finding an end to that sentence that was anything other than *clear Dylan's name* when Rebecca pounced on a plump woman and a plumper child.

"I've got ever so many soaps," she told them. "They're handmade here in Blackpool. Jasmine, sandalwood, there's the freesia and rose."

With a friendly nod at Rebecca, Molly stepped away from the stall. The Scene of Crimes team was pulling out, the van and one of the police cars moving at less than a walking pace through the onlookers and along the narrow street. Krebs was rewinding the police tape, contracting the circumference of the crime scene to just around Willie's boat and the van that had disgorged the dive team. Ross stood at the side of the pier, arms crossed, looking down. From where she stood, though, there was no sign of the inflatable, let alone the divers.

What she could see was the peaked roof of Grandage's Bait and Tackle Shop, its tiles so old and so damp they wore a patchwork of moss. The small building sat on the pier only a few paces from its end at the harbor wall. Molly picked her way through the gathered crowd and behind Fotherby, and pushed through Grandage's battered door. She wrinkled her nose at the odor of dead fish and stale beer, then assumed a smile when she caught the attention of a sun-bronzed man in his forties. "Hullo there. You're Michael's missus, are you now?"

"Yes, I am. Molly Graham."

"Jamey Grandage." He shook her hand, his own scarred and hardened by years of hauling nets and mending tackle.

Three elderly fishermen occupied a small table, each nursing a bottle of beer. Several tourists of the outdoorsy male variety sat before them like an audience at a variety show. "And when the fret cleared and the fog finally lifted," said one of the fishermen, "we realized we'd never cast off the lines when we set out. We'd spent the entire night tied to the dock!"

"I was looking for Geoffrey Crookshank," Molly said to Grandage, "to ask him about a charter trip."

"He's not been here since first thing this morning. Stopped in to buy a new gaff, he did."

"A gaff?"

Grandage stepped over to a wall draped with nets and stacked with rolls of line and other fishing equipment. He picked up a short spear. "Some gaffs have handles and hooks on the end, but Geoff, he bought one like this. The traditional sort for a traditional bloke, eh?"

A virtual lightbulb winked on over Molly's head. "You use that to get the fish on board the boat, right?"

"And move 'em around once you've got them there, aye." Grandage hung the gaff back on the wall. "You're not wanting a fishing charter, then. More of a tour of the coastline?"

Molly barely heard him. She visualized Geoffrey, gaff in hand, stepping silently onto Willie's boat. Willie would have come up out of the cabin, spun and might have had time for no more than a grunt of surprise before... Quickly she spun toward the door. "I'll come back, thank you."

The last thing she heard before she shut the door was the voice of the second loremaster beginning his own yarn. "There he was, old Charles Crowe, his hold full of a king's ransom in gold, and the gypsies swearing to reclaim it and get their revenge, as well. His ship came into Blackpool on the wings of a storm...."

CHAPTER TEN

LEADING THE NEWSPAPER office behind, Michael strode down Dockside Avenue and discovered Rohan sitting on the steps of the Mariner's Museum. "Sorry, I kept finding more people to talk to."

"Any luck?" Rohan pulled himself to his feet and stretched.

Michael could almost hear his friend's muscles creaking. He, too, would be grateful for a session of hang gliding or the like. But not yet. "You be the judge," Michael answered, and filled Rohan in on his conversations with Callum, Betsy and Fred.

Rohan whistled at the first, rolled his eyes at the second and shook his head at the third. Finally, he concluded, "Willie did find the coins in the tunnels, eh? I've never seen him out with the tunnel rats. But then, a football team and the seven dwarves could be walking around in that maze and one never cross paths with the other."

"There is that. How's Naomi getting on?"

"Stunned. Scared, too. There's more at stake here than Dylan's name, mate."

"Oh, yes. That's why I want a word with Alfie about the gold."

Michael held the heavy doors of the museum's vestibule open for Rohan, then followed him into the dim, slightly musty interior. Normally, he'd have paused at the displays of local artifacts, including fossils, rock samples and items associated with pirates—logbooks, spyglasses, compasses, pistols, cutlasses and daggers. But not today…

Wait a minute. Michael took a closer look at one glass-topped case. The spot where a curved dagger had once rested was empty, its shape outlined on the faded backing cloth. "Now where has that gone?" he asked, not that Rohan had an answer.

Michael took the first flight of the marble steps two at a time, then reminded himself to appear to be more of a casual passerby than a bloodhound following a scent.

They found Alfie Lochridge in the reading room. When he saw the two men strolling along inspecting the portraits on the wall—including one of Charles Crowe, his dark eyes aloof—Alfie stroked back his long gray hair as though to proclaim, *I'm ready for my close-up, Mr. De-Mille,* and adjusted his pince-nez. "Well, if it isn't Michael Graham. And—what's your name, young fellow?"

"Rohan Wallace," said Rohan.

"Part Scots, are you? Fancy that." Alfie smiled at Michael. "I hear we've had another murder here in Blackpool. Willie Myners, was it now?"

"I'm afraid so," said Michael. "Did you know the man at all?"

"Only in passing. Though he did catch me on the front steps just yesterday, as I was returning from having a look at the *Black Sea Pearl*—trust Trevor Hopewell to arrive with a fanfare, eh? Willie had the neck to ask me for an appraisal of what he called 'valuable artifacts'." Alfie's fingers made quotation marks.

"Did he show you the artifacts?" Rohan asked.

"Good heavens, no. He patted his pocket and leered at me, is all. Can you imagine? What could that toe-rag have that could possibly be of value?"

Alfie was apparently the raisin on the Blackpool grapevine, his stem disconnected from the stalk. "What about three Wallachian gold coins and a silver thaler?" suggested Michael.

Alfie stared. The pince-nez fell off his nose and swung back and forth at the end of its cord. "You're joking."

"No, I'm not joking. But Wallachian coins have turned up here before, right?"

"Yes, two lads unearthed several back in the 1840s. But those disappeared into the Crowe's Nest, never to be seen again. I had to call in a favor or two from the British Museum to borrow a similar coin from their numismatics collection to illustrate the story during the first Seafaring Days. And what a struggle that was, initiating the festival!" Alfie jammed his pince-nez onto the bridge of his nose. Behind them, his ash-brown eyes glinted. "If Alice Coffey and her crew had their way, the town would be famous as the residence of Little Bo-Peep and her woolly lambs, not the haunt of shady characters from Harold Skull-Splitter the Viking to Blackbeard the Pirate. Speaking of shady characters, Willie found himself a bit of the Crowe treasure, did he?"

"So it seems. If you didn't take the bait, might he have tried Trevor Hopewell?"

"That's logical. Hopewell's mad for historical artifacts, the more valuable the better."

"I guess his reputation precedes him," said Rohan.

"Very much, yes," Alfie said. "Plus I spoke with him late yesterday afternoon when he came to collect the dagger."

"The one from the display case downstairs," said Michael.

"The Arabian with the curved blade and the scrolled hand-guard, right. He made us a very nice offer. I'm not quite sure of the dagger's origins. I suspect it was made no earlier than 1900 or so, even though Aleister claims it's a souvenir of Charles Crowe's voyages. But *caveat emptor,* right?"

"Another possible murder weapon?" whispered Rohan from the side of his mouth.

Michael nodded.

Alfie was still talking. "Hopewell offered on that Wallachian coin the first time he visited here, but, alas, it wasn't the museum's to sell."

It was Michael's turn to stare. "The coin from London? Three years ago?"

Rohan added, "Hopewell said he'd never been here before."

"And he told us he'd never seen Wallachian coins of..." Michael drew a blank. "What's his name, Vlad the Impaler or some early ruler."

"Are you calling me a liar? Come along, I'll prove it to you." Alfie stamped across the floor, each step resounding like a gunshot, and stopped by a lectern topped with a visitor's book and chained-up pen. From the shelf below, he pulled out another book dated three years earlier. He thrust it toward Rohan. "See for yourself."

Rohan turned the pages. "Um, if Seafaring Days was held over the August bank holiday weekend then, like it is now, then we're looking at a date of..."

Michael leaned over his shoulder. Some visitors' names and remarks were neatly written, some were scrawled. "There! 'Trevor Hopewell—excellent collections.'" It was written in a flowing hand better suited for a quill pen than ballpoint.

That explained why Hopewell was so quick off the mark when Fred had said something about the coins this morning. *But that doesn't explain why he lied.*

Smirking, Alfie replaced the book and straightened his bow tie, its bloodred fabric imprinted with tiny skulls and crossbones. "That was a careless lie, wasn't it? He could have said he'd seen such coins in London. But to these fanatical collectors, acquiring pieces is a sport. There's always one more item to attain."

Murder, thought Michael, is no sport. "This time round, then, Hopewell bought the dagger. I doubt that means he's no longer interested in the coins, though."

"You've got that right. He was asking me about Charles Crowe's activities as a ship builder and master, what routes his ships followed, what sort of contacts he had in Eastern Europe, Africa, the Near East and the Orient. Did any of his ships come to grief on the way back to England, and so forth. I finally referred him to the Customs House for maps of sunken ships in the area."

"Molly and I met up with him outside the Customs House this morning, though he didn't go inside. His first mate—Martin Dunhill—reminded him about a phone call and something to do with corporate law."

"Ah," Alfie said with a nod. "Perhaps Hopewell's looking to dive on some of the wrecks just off the coast. The legal ramifications experienced by independent salvors are complex enough to keep a battery of lawyers in business. I've written the prime minister with a list of changes to our own laws of treasure trove—no need to let the sticky fingers of the Crown have first choice, is there?"

Sensing Alfie preparing to get on his soapbox, Michael said, "Sorry, Alfie, must run."

"Come back when you've time for another chat." Again Alfie smoothed his hair off his collar. "I'll be happy to set you straight."

"Good to meet you," Rohan said, and managed to avoid

laughing until he and Michael made it to the bottom of the stairs. "Full of himself, isn't he?"

"There's a reason no other museums will take him. He knows his history, though." The men walked toward the marina, still dominated by Trevor Hopewell's tricked-out yacht.

"The *Black Sea Pearl*," said Rohan. "Isn't that the ship in the first *Pirates of the Caribbean?*"

"That was just the *Black Pearl*," Michael replied. "I wonder if the fact that Hopewell added 'Sea' to the name of his own pirate ship means anything. Romania borders on the Black Sea, and he does seem keen on Charles Crowe's activities there."

"Are you thinking 'collector' is merely a polite way of saying 'treasure hunter'?"

"In Hopewell's case, yes. Let's have a word or two with him, eh?" Considering that there might be a reason the man had a Jolly Roger flying from his mast—never mind that the masts were intended for decorative purposes only—Michael led the way through the crowd gathered near the crime scene, up the *Pearl*'s gangplank and onto the deck. A sailor coiling a rope spotted them and nipped below. Within moments, Martin Dunhill appeared. His smile of welcome was pinched around the edges, sending creases deep into his jowls. "Ah, it's Michael again. And Rohan, was it?"

Michael asked, "Is Trevor aboard just now?"

"No, he's off to Whitby this afternoon. Some wrinkly historian offered a tour of the sites mentioned in *Dracula*."

He didn't add, "appropriately enough," and Michael didn't suggest it. "Well then, Trevor may have mentioned to you that I'm a video game designer and my newest game is based on pirate legends…"

Martin's smile was congealing fast. *Get to the point.*

That's just it, Michael thought wryly, a point—one at the end of a knife or dagger. "I'd like a few photos of Trevor's knife collection, especially the Arabian dagger he bought from Alfie Lochridge. I'd been intending to take a photo or two of it there in the museum, but was just too late." He held up his iPhone, glad Dunhill hadn't seen him taking the same photos with his camera during his tour of the ship the day before.

"Very good, then. Come below." Not bothering to conceal his annoyance, Martin guided them down the narrow steps. He stood by while Michael took photos of the weapons in the display case. The Arabian dagger was there, nestled next to the Highlander's dirk, with its own neat computer-printed label. The items formed such a fine collection Michael wouldn't have been surprised to see Monty Python's holy hand grenade of Antioch, suitably polished and labeled, among them.

Finally, he tucked his phone away again. "Thank you. Very helpful."

"Are you thinking one of them's the murder weapon?" asked Martin.

Michael stopped, his hand still on his phone in his cargo pants. Beside him, Rohan's shoulders twitched in an infinitesimal shrug. Right now, offense was the best defense. Straightening to his full height, Michael asked Martin, "So you've heard of the murder?"

"Who hasn't? There's not a Blackpooler who's not full of it—no play on words intended," Martin added, which just proved he *had* intended the play on words.

"I've heard that the victim, Willie Myners, was here yesterday afternoon to see Trevor."

"He was, but I intercept loads of confidence tricksters bragging they've got something special to offer the boss."

"Willie's gold coins were rather special, I should think."

Martin snorted. "That's the rumor."

"Had you and Willie met before?" Rohan asked.

"Being responsible for security, I meet a variety of villains. I knew Willie for what he was, an old lag, a criminal, not the sort you expect to have a genuine gold coin. Or more. Some are claiming he had sacks of the things." Martin's eyes narrowed. "But rumor usually over-states the situation." With a gesture, Martin urged Michael and Rohan toward the hatchway. "When did the murder happen, exactly?"

"Supposedly about half past ten this morning," Michael answered.

"Is that so? And here's me walking through the vendor's stalls, meeting up with you, your lovely wife and Trevor at the Customs House. Missed the whole thing, didn't I? Pity." Martin emitted a dusty chuckle.

Pity has nothing to do with it. Michael said, "Thank you for your time," and he and Rohan emerged onto the deck and walked off the ship. On the pier, they looked back.

"He's a cool one," said Rohan. "What about those knives? If Hopewell or Dunhill murdered Willie for his coins, they cleaned up the evidence."

"And they didn't get the coins for their pains. For Willie's pains, rather." Michael gazed down the pier toward Willie's boat. With all the people standing about gawping, he could hardly see the new van and the remaining police car. The tall chap with the beak of a nose stood at the edge of the pier... Ah, that was it. He had a dive team searching the water around and beneath Willie's boat.

"We'll not get closer to those knives or any others on board the *Pearl*," Michael told Rohan. "The police could do, but they'd need a warrant."

"And they'd need actual evidence, not just supposition and hearsay, to get it. Maybe we should let the police do the legwork, Michael."

"They're *doing* the legwork. We're just trying to make sure they don't miss anything, is all.… Is that Robbie Glennison?"

A thin young man, his eyes bulging, his complexion so white it was almost gray, hovered on the edge of the crowd, hands in pockets, shoulders curled, head hanging. He jerked away when Maurice Paddington bustled up and pushed by, but Paddington didn't seem to notice him. The inspector marched on by Fotherby and Krebs and up to Ross. Words were exchanged, Paddington making tight little gestures, Ross unmoving and replying in monosyllables. Every one of the navy of cameras pointed and clicked.

"What's Paddington going on about now?" asked Rohan.

"Just as a guess," Michael replied, "he's telling the Ripon team to not spend any more time here than is strictly necessary. Blackpool is his patch and he doesn't take kindly to outsiders."

Nodding imperturbably, Ross stepped back, allowing the divers to clamber up a ladder and onto the pier. Michael peered at them, not just interested in the details of their gear, but to see if any of them was holding an evidence bag.

"Doesn't look like they found anything," Rohan said.

"Now *that's* a pity…"

Krebs went to attention. "You! Glennison!"

Good, Michael thought. Callum must've called the police about his missing knife, and Paddington and crew were taking it seriously.

Robbie turned and ran, limbs flailing, soft soles thudding on the pier.

"Here, you!" shouted Fotherby, and gave chase.

Robbie was heading right for Michael and Rohan. The two men exchanged a glance and a nod, and braced for impact.

CHAPTER ELEVEN

MOLLY STEPPED OUT OF the Bait and Tackle Shop in time to see Michael and Rohan seize a running Robbie Glennison. The young man went limp in their grasp and crumpled to the water-stained planks of the pier.

Molly reached them just as Fotherby did, mere seconds ahead of Luann Krebs. Within moments Molly, Michael and Rohan found themselves in a tightening circle of humanity, the familiar faces of the townspeople—the Norton girls, Daisy, Margaret and Randall Coffey—outnumbered by those of visitors.

Fotherby dragged Robbie to his feet, but then, out of breath, could only stare accusingly at him. Robbie's watery eyes focused on his battered, unlaced sneakers. "I didn't do nothing," he panted. "I didn't kill nobody."

Claiming his other arm, Krebs pulled him away from Fotherby and leaned in close. "No one's accused you of anything, Robbie. Yet. Why'd you run?"

"Fotherby," said Robbie. "He knocked me about Friday, at the Smokehouse. I didn't want nothing to do with him."

Fotherby discovered his voice. "You deserved a bit of knocking about, lad. If you ask me, keelhauling wouldn't go amiss."

Funny how no one had asked him. Molly extended a hand to Michael and he clasped it tightly in his own.

Paddington elbowed his way through the crowd and

regarded Robbie with such a triumphant smile his round head resembled a jack-o'-lantern. "What's this? Running away?"

"I didn't kill nobody," repeated Robbie, wilting even further, so that Fotherby and Krebs both had to hold him up.

Before Paddington could approach the subject of hot tempers and cold steel, a woman's voice spoke from the back of the crowd. "He was with me at the time of the murder."

The spectators parted like the Red Sea before Moses. Microphones made gantries over the gap. Cameras clicked. Temperance Collins made her entrance. In the sunlight her hair shone a brassy shade unknown to nature. Her fortysomething body was sausaged into twentysomething clothing and she balanced herself like an acrobat on nosebleed-high heels.

"Robbie was with me at the time of the murder," Temperance repeated, still speaking loudly even though she was now only inches from Paddington's moustache. "I saw him going through the bins behind the Blackpool Artist's Gallery about half past ten, and we had us a few words, didn't we, Robbie?"

Robbie nodded eagerly. "Nothing wrong with a bit of bin-diving, Inspector."

Paddington flinched, either at Robbie's breath or the thought of rooting around in someone's trash.

"I set him to work cleaning my floors. The antique Baltic pine's lovely, but needs waxing after every opening. Still, we girls have to have our stiletto heels, don't we?"

Krebs gagged. Fotherby's eyes weren't focused on Temperance's face. Paddington's eyes were focused nowhere but.

"Miss, um, Mrs. um, Collins…" Paddington stammered.

Temperance ignored him and turned to the cameras. "That's www.Blackpoolartistsgallery.co.uk. Unique art and artifacts. Representation for the artistic soul who can't be bothered with business. Investment opportunities galore for those who can." Her eyelashes, thick as caterpillars, shivered in a wink.

Paddington exploded. "Madam! You cannot just walk into a murder investigation and, and— If Robbie was with you this morning, then the pair of you are coming to the station. Fotherby, Krebs…" He elbowed his way through the crowd and across Dockside Avenue, his features now looking less like a jack-o'-lantern than pumpkin pie.

Fotherby hovered at Temperance's side as she sashayed in the same direction, with Krebs doing a Darth Vader stranglehold on Robbie behind them both.

"Mon, is she tellin' the truth?" asked Rohan. "Or is she only wantin' publicity?"

"Dylan said Temperance wouldn't exhibit any of Naomi's 'artistic soul,' or represent her," Molly pointed out.

"Leaving Willie to represent her," Michael said. "This is according to Betsy Sewell, who's selling some very nice maps drawn by Naomi."

"Really?" Molly's mind scrambled, trying to work out some way Temperance's snub could be turned into motivation for Willie's murder, but came up empty.

"And I thought we were making progress," Michael went on, "when Callum told me Robbie had taken one of his filleting knives."

"One of the ones used for red herring, I guess," Molly said, but no one smiled.

The van from Ripon inched down the pier and onto Dockside Avenue, followed closely by the police car.

Cameras and phones clicked. Then the Scene of Crimes team, too, was gone, the show was over, and the onlookers ebbed like the tide.

Molly, Michael and Rohan were left behind like flotsam on the beach.

Rohan squinted into the sky. "The sun's over the yardarm. I'm goin' for a pint and a pie at the Dockside. Michael? Molly?"

"Thank you, no," Michael told him. "Molly and I need to compare notes, decide where to go from here. If anywhere, that is."

"We have to go somewhere," said Molly. "If Robbie's alibi is good, then Dylan's still on the hook."

"What about having a tunnel crawl?" Rohan asked. "Maybe we can find out where Willie came up with those coins."

"But just blundering around the tunnels won't help," Molly said quickly.

Michael's hand tightened on hers. He knew how she felt about the tunnels. "Molly's right, mate. We need some hint of where to go. Though it wouldn't hurt to have a gander."

"No, it wouldn't. Give me a call when you're ready to go underground."

"That I will," Michael told him.

Molly waved as he walked away. "It is time for happy hour, or tea or something, but now I'm not hungry. More frustrated than anything, I guess." She led Michael to a bench near the Mariner's Museum that overlooked the harbor, and sat down close beside him.

The sun eased toward the hills to the southwest, and shadow stretched over the town, tucked as it was beneath the cliffs. But light still shimmered on the North Sea to the east. The lights along the crescent of Dockside Avenue began to wink on. So did those draped from the *Pearl's* masts. Musicians filed into the bandstand and began tuning up, while gulls emitted mocking squawks.

Molly's tense muscles started to relax. This evening she'd intended to wear an outfit that looked like a Mardi Gras version of a pirate, from billowing satin blouse to gilt-buckled shoes, but she didn't want to return to Thorne-Shower Mansion to change into it.

"The murder's the fly in the ointment," she said aloud.

"The murder. Yes." Michael took a deep breath of the sea air.

Molly produced her phone and its list of names. "If only it was as easy as Santa Claus checking his list, going to find out who's naughty or nice."

That was a lame joke, and it drew only a lame smile from Michael. "Willie wanted Alfie at the museum to evaluate some 'valuable artifacts,' but Alfie sent him away with a flea in his ear. Nothing new there. But I did prove that Trevor Hopewell lied. Twice. He was in Blackpool three years ago, and while he was here he saw the British Museum coin and even made Alfie an offer on it."

"Whoa!"

"He also bought that Arabian dagger from the museum. It's on the *Pearl* now, along with the Highlander's dagger. Rohan and I talked Martin Dunhill into showing us the display."

"Could one of those be the murder weapon? Hard as it is for me to consider Trevor getting his hands dirty."

"Ah, Trevor, the golden boy," mocked Michael. Changing the subject, he told her, "Fred showed me his next front page, all about Charles Crowe and the gypsy gold."

"Oh, that'll help!" Molly said, partly laughing, partly groaning. "There's not a person in town who doesn't know Willie had gold coins of some kind. Rebecca, for example, thinks they're stamped with Dracula's image. Daisy Coffey could put Fred Purnell and Tim Jenkins out of work."

"Right."

Molly sifted through her conversation with Rebecca. "Here's something. Aleister was late to church, even though Lydia, Aubrey and Addison Headerly were there in plenty of time."

"Perhaps his car broke down."

"He's got a new one, an Alfa Romeo."

"There you are, love. An unreliable new car."

Molly smiled indulgently. "It was in the shop—that was where *he* heard about the coins. I bet Aleister was blindsided by the sudden appearance. Maybe he did kill Willie to keep him quiet about the treasure."

"It would have been easier to have bought the coins and let Willie leave town."

"Aleister doesn't necessarily take the easy way out, as we've seen before. His efforts last spring to suppress his family history regarding those stolen paintings blew it all up even bigger—and he's doing it again."

"Well, yes. Mind you, he might be playing double or even triple agent with his family history, all to confuse the issue."

"I wouldn't put it past him." Molly added a few notes to her list. "Or Trevor could have stabbed Willie, then cleaned up and made it to the Customs House where we saw him. As for Martin Dunhill, Rebecca noticed him hanging around the festival at the time of the murder. And…"

"And?" Michael prodded.

"Michelle was also wandering around the pier and the

marina this morning. She may have been trying to make up her mind to confront Willie about Naomi."

"Ah."

"Geoffrey lied, too. He stopped by the Bait and Tackle Shop early today and bought a gaff. Jamey Grandage showed me a similar one. It's basically a spear."

"Ah," Michael said again. "A gaff wouldn't create quite the same sort of wound as a knife blade, but it would take a postmortem exam to tell the difference."

From the corner of her eye, Molly saw a familiar figure and thrust her phone into her purse. "Look! There's Dylan! He's free!"

"For the moment," warned Michael, even as he leaped to his feet and led the way to the corner of Compass Rose and Dockside, where Dylan and Naomi stood talking to Fred.

Or where Fred stood talking to them, rather, while they kept taking steps backward, trying to get away. At last Fred gave up, greeted the Grahams with a cheery, "Grand evening, isn't it?" and headed toward the ice cream van parked nearby.

Dylan turned to Molly. "Thank you for getting onto the lawyer. Even Paddington's little cell is not a place I'd like to spend time in, to say nothing of one of Her Majesty's prisons."

"No problem," she returned. "I hope we can help clear your name, too."

"So do I." Naomi's red lips were smiling, but her eyes were desolate. After an awkward silence, Dylan pointed past the museum toward the whitewashed flanks of his own shop, a spectral glimmer in the shadows below Glower Lighthouse. "Fancy a cuppa? Naomi's made short-bread."

"Had to keep myself busy," she explained.

They needed the Grahams like they needed two more wheels on a bicycle, Molly thought. "Thank you, but we, ah, thought we'd go listen to the music, see what people are wearing for costumes, you know…"

"Do the festival," Michael concluded.

"All right then," said Dylan. He looked at Naomi. "Get on home, love, I'll catch you up."

Naomi's gaze moved from Dylan's face to the dim shape of the bicycle shop and its dark windows. She folded her arms across her navy blue pullover. "Well, it's been several days since I've heard the footsteps behind the walls, whether you think I'm hearing them or not, Dylan."

"Just echoes from the pub at the lighthouse," Dylan told her.

"Yeah." She headed at a swift walk toward the shop, then stopped and spun back around. "Listen, I don't know what to say, how to help—there's too much…" Barely holding back a sob, she whirled and ran to the shop. Her shadowy figure disappeared inside and the windows flared with light.

Dylan turned to Michael. "I don't know what to say, either, mate."

Resting a brotherly hand on his shoulder, Michael asked, quietly but urgently, "Dylan, I'm sorry, but is there any possibility Naomi killed Willie? It wouldn't have been difficult for her to lay hands on a knife of some sort and sneak up on him."

"You're asking whether she killed the man and is standing by, letting me take the blame. Is that it?" He shook his head so firmly his crest of hair shuddered. "No. She can't be putting me in the frame. I can't believe that of her. I can't believe that she murdered him. She thought he was her way out of here."

Molly caught Michael's eye. Naomi could still get out of Blackpool if Dylan went to jail. In fact, she'd come out ahead, because she wouldn't be burdened with Willie as the price of her escape. But the woman was obviously crushed by what had happened; Molly had no trouble giving Naomi the benefit of the doubt.

"Get some rest, Dylan," Michael urged his friend. "I'll phone tomorrow, let you know how we're getting on. Rohan wants to have a look at the tunnels to see if we can trace Willie's path."

"Does he? Well, if you find anything, give me a shout. I'll be here trying to make up for the business I've missed this weekend. Good job tomorrow's a bank holiday. Thank you for everything, Michael, Molly. Sorry to be such a bother."

"I just hope we're helping," Molly said.

"Don't worry, Dylan," said Michael, although Molly could tell from the edge in his voice that he had plenty of worries. At least he could share them with her.

Side by side, they strolled through the twilight back toward the festival. The Dockside was heaving with customers. Voices, the clink of glasses and Coldplay's latest hit mingled with the waltz coming from the harbor side bandstand.

"Does Dylan know Willie was acting as Naomi's agent?" Molly asked.

"Maybe she's not telling him, afraid that would be rubbing salt in the wound."

"Hmm…I wonder if there's anything else she's not telling him."

"Rohan thinks she's in shock."

"A murder would be shocking enough, let alone the victim being your lover. Not that I can call the relationship that." Molly tucked her hand behind Michael's arm and squeezed. "It's sad, though. Not one person in town has anything good to say for Willie."

"Except for Michelle Crookshank, assuming she's not covering up for herself or her father." Michael's free hand indicated Geoffrey Crookshank walking along behind several tourists, burdened with fishing gear and a picnic basket, his new gaff under his arm. Its point stuck out before him like a knight's lance—a lethal one. "When it comes to murder weapons, the police are spoiled for choice."

"Agreed." Stopping at the end of the pier, they gazed up at the *Black Sea Pearl,* draped with fairy lights. "The police, including the detective from Ripon."

"Perhaps he means to come back here tomorrow."

"Tim Jenkins says his name is Ross, that he interviewed him once." Molly straightened from her comfortable lean against Michael's side. "The Ripon team went over the boat where Willie was murdered, but did they do the same with his flat?"

"The victim's home would be a normal part of an investigation."

"You have to wonder what the police could find that Daisy doesn't already know."

"And is talking about?" asked Michael. "The murder's almost driven the possible robbery out of our minds—and likely out of Paddington's, as well. Given the state of the place, I'm inclined to believe it was a robbery. The question is, did the person who turned over Willie's flat yesterday afternoon kill him this morning?"

Molly visualized Willie's desk. "There was a strip of dark blue cloth caught on the bracket of Willie's desk lamp, remember? Did you notice the pullover Naomi was wearing? It's dark blue. Was she wearing that when you found her on the boat this morning?"

"No, she wasn't. What of it? It's the same as finding sheets of her notebook paper on the desk—it's no mystery she was in Willie's flat. Perhaps it was her Dylan heard running away."

"Yeah, she might have been there looking for the coins for herself."

"Did she know about them? Willie only said his 'ship had come in.' Even if she did, that wouldn't mean she killed Willie."

"No," Molly agreed. "No, it wouldn't."

The sprightly music made her toe tap. When Michael's sober expression evaporated, she threw herself into his arms and they whirled away in a waltz.

Faces spun past. There was Randall Coffey dancing with Emily Crowder, both of them wearing vaguely piratical garments. Liam McKenna had added a plastic cutlass to his belt and an artificial parrot to his shoulder, while Holly in her gypsy costume could have been auditioning for the opera *Carmen*. Lydia Crowe had opted for a Cleopatra outfit.

Other people were dressed as Vikings, seafaring Celtic monks, Romans and red-coated marines of Nelson's era. Several wore generic vampire or mummy costumes, or, like Molly and Michael, were dressed in everyday garments. No matter what their clothing, everyone seemed to be having a good time. When the music stopped, Michael pulled out his iPhone and started taking photos. Molly smiled—she'd learned long since that anything could spark an idea for a game character or situation. Although she'd just as soon he wasn't inspired by Temperance Collins, who was posing in a harem slave outfit two sizes too small for her.

"Look there," said Michael.

Aleister Crowe wove his way through the crowd,

nodding and smiling to the peasants. His Admiral Nelson-at-Trafalgar costume was correct right down to the last swag of gold braid, except Aleister very obviously had both arms. He was wearing a patch over one eye, and Molly noted it was transparent gauze. Far be it from Aleister to miss anything.

From the opposite direction came Trevor Hopewell, resplendent in the ruff, cloak, doublet and hose of an Elizabethan sea dog, expertly made and garnished with gold-threaded embroidery. "Sir Francis Drake," Molly said to Michael. "What do you want to bet?"

"Naval commander, privateer, slave trader, explorer—Drake suits Hopewell's fantasies right down to the ground," Michael replied.

So many people took photos that Hopewell literally glittered in the flashes. Aleister stepped forward, signature smile creasing his face. He swept off his hat and bowed deeply. Hopewell returned the bow, his hand on his dagger.

Michael focused on the long sheath and the long, tapering fingers wrapping around its top and clicked another photo.

The music started again. Martin Dunhill, still in white and blue, offered his hand to Charlotte Abercrombie, who gathered up her hoop skirts for a dance. Addison Headerly appeared at Lydia's side, holding his plumed helmet under his arm—he was probably posing as Julius Caesar or Mark Antony, Cleopatra's lovers. But Lydia turned to Hopewell, and Addison's face fell like Antony's must have at the battle of Actium as he watched his fleet sink.

Here came Paddington in a Victorian policeman's uniform—more navy blue cloth, noted Molly. She wondered if he was familiar with the old Keystone Kop movies. He stopped beside Randall Coffey, asking, "Have you seen

Daisy? She left me a message, wanted a word, but she never turned up at the station."

Randall looked around. "Margaret says she left the shop some time ago."

Fred Purnell jockeyed for position. Tim Jenkins and his cohorts fanned out for maximum coverage. Fotherby strutted around the periphery of the crowd, breaking up groups of onlookers, while Krebs stood beneath a street-light, arms folded, watching him.

Then a woman's scream cut through the music, and a man's voice shouted, "Help, police!"

CHAPTER TWELVE

MICHAEL THRUST HIS phone back into his pocket as the crowd surged toward the pier. He whirled in that direction, then, when Molly whirled with him, grabbed her arm and stopped her. "Wait. Let's see what's happened."

Molly pressed herself into the protective circle of his arm. "Not another murder. Please, not another murder."

Despite their best efforts, the crowd carried them forward. Paddington used his torch as a truncheon to clear a path for himself and for Fotherby and Krebs. Lights outlined the weathered eaves of Grandage's Bait and Tackle like spotlights at a Hollywood premiere. But this was no film, Michael told himself. This was no game.

James and Barbara Norton stood clasped together next to a stack of barrels draped with drying fishing nets. In the ripple of light and shadow beyond lay a body curled on its side. A pool of crimson glistened in the darkness and the same crimson smeared the wide gray planks of the pier. The crowd grew so quiet Michael could hear the gurgle and lap of water against the concrete seawall below.

The beam from Paddington's torch threw the body into sharp relief. Athletic training shoes. Polyester trousers. A white shopkeeper's apron stained deep red. A hand splayed on the pier, a smear of red trailing from the forefinger. Gray pincurls around a slack gray face.

"Daisy Coffey," said James. His face was as white as

the cap, belt and spats of his Royal Navy uniform. "We were walking along the pier, enjoying the sunset, and I stepped back here to look over the grommets on the nets—we sell grommets at the hardware shop…"

"There she was. She's been there a good time. She's cold." Barbara's tiara glittered as she trembled.

Out of the corner of his eye Michael saw Trevor Hopewell standing to one side, unnoticed by the crowd. Even as Michael and Molly looked at him, he slipped off toward the *Pearl,* Martin Dunhill a shadow at his side.

Paddington started barking orders. Fotherby pushed people away from the scene.

Molly and Michael didn't have to be urged to leave. "That answers my question," he said as they plodded away. "D.I. Ross will be back in Blackpool tonight."

"Maybe this time—well, we don't know whether he found the knife used on Willie, whether this one is different…" Her voice trailing away, Molly eyed Tim Jenkins, who was chattering into his microphone, and Fred Purnell, who was darting to and fro with his notebook and camera.

Michael didn't need a camera—the scene behind the Bait and Tackle Shop was seared in his memory.

Molly asked, "Did you see that smear of—of blood right next to her index finger? A curved line ending in a straight one? It looked like she'd written the number two on the plank."

"I thought so as well, love, but that's likely our imagination. Our minds tend to create patterns."

"Better than giving in to chaos," Molly replied.

Aleister, his admiral's hat tucked beneath his arm, escorted the gaunt shape of Alice Coffey toward the crime scene, Margaret and Randall Coffey not far behind her. Geoffrey and Michelle Crookshank sat close together next to the ice cream van. Rebecca Hislop stood outside her stall, her hands clasped, her eyes wide. Liam and Holly McKenna lingered beside the bandstand, talking to Temperance Collins. Really, Molly thought, the McKennas played the part of gypsies to the hilt, appropriately enough... Something Iris had said tickled the back of her mind, but she couldn't quite grasp it.

"Any one of these people could have stabbed her," said Michael.

"Not Rebecca."

"Now the question isn't whether the person who ransacked the flat killed Willie..."

"The question is whether that same person killed again. This time to eliminate a witness, what do you want to bet? A very talkative witness."

Feeling sick, Michael drew Molly even closer against his side. Slowly, they walked past the weatherbeaten sheet metal of Coffey's Garage, to the boarded-up train station where the Land Rover was parked.

Shadows filled the landscape beyond the lights of the town, but the sky to the west still glowed a deep peacock-blue even as stars pricked the sky to the east. The lights of their own home soon shone like a lighthouse before them, and Iris greeted them at the door. "There you are! The town's buzzing like a hive of bees, is it?"

"Have you already heard?" Michael asked.

"Daisy didn't have the only wagging tongue in town," replied Iris.

"But she's the one who lived next to Willie Myners." Molly walked into the house and Michael shut the door against the night. "What's that I smell?"

"A curry," Iris said. "I thought you'd need a good meal after your day. I've just brought the dishes over from my kitchen."

"Thank you," Molly said. "You're a friend indeed."

They sat down with Iris and ate spicy chicken tikka masala over basmati rice with yogurt-and-cucumber raita. But, delicious as the food was, it was the cool pint of beer that Michael appreciated most. The slightly astringent taste seemed to clear the cobwebs from his mind.

Across from him, Molly drank deeply of her iced tea, something Iris would never have prepared if she hadn't grown familiar with it in the United States. "Sit, sit," the housekeeper commanded when Molly started gathering the empty dishes. Efficiently, she cleared them away herself.

The front door opened, admitting Irwin and his stony expression. "Some to-do in town," was all he said as he pulled out the fourth chair at the table.

Iris returned from the kitchen, carrying four servings of thick, milky rice pudding, then passed around cups of tea. "All right then. Tell us about it."

Molly, with the occasional comment from Michael, led Iris and Irwin through their day, from the original murder scene to its terrible repetition, and from various shops and assorted conversations. At last she concluded, "Gold, there's a motive for murder. Willie's coins, and everyone thinking there were bags full of them."

"Thanks partially to Daisy, God rest her soul," said Iris.

"But Paddington assumes Dylan killed Willie out of jealousy," Molly reminded them. "Or maybe Geoffrey killed him for revenge. We've got to think outside the box. Or the treasure chest."

"I'll do my best." Michael scooted back from the table.

Molly, too, rose from her chair. "Let's get the dishes washed, Iris. Then I'm going to make some notes, hopefully work out a schedule of who was where when. I'm guessing Daisy was killed about seven, while we were dancing and everyone was milling around the square. Just about the whole town was there except Dylan and Naomi. And Robbie."

"There's Trevor Hopewell—Daisy said she'd seen the yacht and him, and we know he lied."

"Do you think he did it?" Molly asked.

"I don't know what to think, love." Michael started for the door, then turned back. "Do you need help in the kitchen?"

"Get on with you," Irwin urged. "You, as well, Molly. I'll help Iris."

"Cheers." Molly headed to her office just off the ball-room and Michael went upstairs. Within moments he was deep in the branching paths of the World Wide Web.

Now that he searched for specific information about Trevor Hopewell, he discovered that the man had quite a media footprint. But then, the media loved a treasure hunter, especially one who'd more than once skirted the law to obtain the artifacts he desired. Fitting out his yacht as a pirate ship revealed more about Hopewell than he intended.

Michael downloaded the photos he'd taken earlier that evening. There was Headerly with his plastic breastplate, and Lydia in her sequin-bedecked collar and headdress, and… What was that?

Michael enlarged his last photo of Hopewell, then cut out one portion of it and enlarged it. Even in the increasingly pixilated image, he could see that Hopewell's hand at the top of the ornate sheath wasn't holding a hilt at all, but what looked like a stick.

There was no knife in the sheath.

Michael skimmed through the photos he'd taken of the

weapons collection on the *Pearl,* both the ones he'd made this afternoon and those from his tour the day before. The reason he didn't remember seeing an Elizabethan dagger in the display case was because there hadn't been one. There hadn't even been a space for it. Assuming Hopewell had ever had a dagger. But having gone to the trouble of obtaining a sheath of the proper era to complete his costume, why wouldn't he have the blade to fit in it— especially when money was no barrier.

Michael went back to this evening's shots of Hopewell. There, in the very first picture, taken just as he entered the scene, his face was turned toward Martin Dunhill.

Dunhill. With a few keystrokes, Michael changed the direction of his search.

His breath slowly escaped his pursed lips. Numerous members of the Dunhill family had criminal records, Martin alone having gone to prison for robbery as well as for assault.

A soft knock on the door frame heralded Molly's entrance. "Have you found anything?"

"Indeed." Michael showed her the photos and the search results. "So here's Hopewell with a personal assistant who's known to the police."

"Oh, boy," she said. "And there was Martin Dunhill telling Willie he didn't want any drugs on the *Pearl.* Did the two men meet in prison? Trevor hiring Dunhill to work security on the yacht is like hiring the fox to guard the henhouse. Maybe we should warn him."

"I should think even a pretty boy like Trevor Hopewell would have done a background check on his employees. Maybe Dunhill's gone straight. Or maybe Hopewell knows exactly what he's got, and Dunhill's in on his schemes. Just because Hopewell's got a film-star face and bags of money doesn't mean he's not a killer."

"No, it doesn't." Molly grimaced. "But the missing dagger could point to Dunhill as much as Trevor. Maybe more—look at Trevor's expression." Her fingernail tapped the screen. "His mouth is open, like you caught him in midsentence. His chin is stuck out and his eyebrows are tight. He's angry. Maybe Trevor was dressing Dunhill down for, say, losing a sixteenth-century dagger?"

Michael looked again. She was right. Dunhill's expression, far from being respectful, as befit his status as second banana, was resentful.

"Just one problem. Dunhill was at the festival at the time of Willie's murder."

"Yes," Molly conceded. "We saw him there ourselves. And I'd just as soon we had only one murderer, thank you."

Michael knew better than to gloat over winning the point. Putting on his most congenial expression, he asked, "Did you make your schedule?"

"Oh. Yeah. I played around with it, made columns with names and so forth, but there are still too many blank spots. However, when I was going through my e-mail I remembered something. Do you remember Iris saying yesterday that even though the McKennas are from Cumbria, they should get their Yorkshire history straight? Well, it turns out they're from Appleby."

"Appleby?"

"I worked with Appleby Council to get a grant for facilities for their big horse fair every year. Horses, gypsies, fortune-tellers. That Appleby."

Michael felt his eyebrows rise to his hairline. "You mean Liam and Holly might really be gypsies? That there's something to that story of a Romany blood oath to reclaim Charles Crowe's gold?"

"Maybe Daisy overheard Liam telling Willie he had no choice but to show them where he found the coins."

"If that's what they wanted, though, why kill him?"

"Maybe all he found was the four coins, not the Crowe mother lode, so they—or someone else—killed him in frustration." Molly slumped. "Yeah. Frustration. That's about it."

"Enough is enough for one evening, love. We'll have a word with Paddington tomorrow, see if this angle has occurred to him." Michael tried to think of other possibilities, but his brain lost traction and he surprised himself with a yawn. He shut down his computer.

Molly's yawn almost unhinged her jaw—he could count every pearly tooth. "I'm off to bed," she said.

"Are you all that sleepy, then?" he asked with a smile.

She leaned against his chest and turned her lips up to his. "I don't know. Let's go see."

A CLIPPER SHIP, SAILS taut with a following wind, breaking the waves of a sea filled with golden icebergs—Michael's dream shattered and he jolted awake. Molly's voice in the darkness, slurred with sleep, groaned, "What was that?"

"What was what?" But even as he spoke, he heard the blare of the house security alarm that had thrust him back into consciousness.

His phone on the nightstand erupted with the 007 theme music just as Molly's on the other struck up "Thriller," making a discordant duet. Michael didn't have to glance at the screen to know who it was.

"Mr. Graham, this is Holdover Security," said the polite, professional voice. "We just recorded a break-in at your house and want to make sure you and your family are all right."

"We'll let you know." Swiftly Michael used his phone to connect with the security system controls and switched off the alarm. He launched himself out of the bed and into his slippers, Molly doing the same on the other side. They raced down the stairs into the front hall.

Lights were blazing around the house, triggered by motion sensors. From the parking area came Irwin's bellow. "Here! You! Stop just there!"

Michael threw open the front door. Beside him, Molly called, "What's going on?"

Irwin Jaeger waved a cricket bat into the darkness, shouting, "And good riddance to you!" A chill breeze made his striped pajamas flutter on his wiry limbs and raised gooseflesh on Michael's arms.

Iris ran from her cottage into the glare, her short, white hair forming a halo around her face. "What's all this?"

Irwin lowered the bat, straightened his glasses, and joined the Grahams and Iris in the front hall. "First the alarm went, and a moment later Holdover phoned. I heard footsteps, someone running down the drive, so I thought I'd help him along a bit. He climbed the front gate, I reckon."

"You should have called for help," Iris told him.

"Who should I call, then? P.C. Fotherby?" Irwin's hair stood on end like so many iron filings stretching toward a magnet. "If I'd laid my hands on the villain…"

The man would be mincemeat, Michael concluded silently. Raising his phone, he informed Holdover that the situation was under control. Then he inspected the neo-Gothic arched window beside the door. One of its diamond-shaped panes was smashed, the glass littering the tile of the floor and crunching beneath his slippers. A rock the size of a brick lay in the midst of the destruction.

"That stone's from the herbaceous border by the driveway," Iris noted.

"I'll stop by Norton's tomorrow and buy a new pane of glass," said Irwin.

"So who was trying to break into our house at—" Molly glanced at the clock ticking away imperturbably at the foot of the staircase "—four o'clock in the morning? I'll tell you one thing. It wasn't Michelle Crookshank."

"At least this time we were here and they didn't get in," said Michael, remembering the mayhem they'd discovered after the theatre murder last spring.

"The villain was after the silver tea service, I daresay," said Iris. "You get back to bed. I'll sweep up the mess."

"Thank you, both of you," Molly said. She trudged up the stairs, Michael at her heels. At the landing, she turned to him. "They weren't after the silver tea service."

"No." Michael wrapped her waist with his arm and felt the flutter of her heart. All the alarms in the world couldn't restore a feeling of safety, not after such violation. "I guess there's not much point to calling the police now. We'll face it in the morning."

MICHAEL SAT DOWN AT the table in the breakfast nook and sniffed the air. "Iris is cooking again?"

"Oh, yes," Molly replied. "She thinks an army marches on its stomach."

"We're no army."

"I've noticed." Molly seemed rather colorless this morning, as though she'd had a session with a vampire during the night.

He leaned over to kiss that cheek reassuringly, and welcomed her smile. Then he turned to business. "I viewed the feed from CCTV cameras mounted round the house. All that's visible is a dark shape chucking a rock through the window, then legging it down the drive."

"Great. Things are really getting out of hand." She indicated the morning's *Blackpool Journal,* propped against the teapot—the everyday Portmeirion china one. "Fred's done himself proud this time. 'Crowe Treasure To Be Revealed At Last'."

"Fred removed the question mark for this edition, I see."

Molly scanned the front page. "It's a shame Fred's article is sharing space with one about Daisy's murder. Yes, D.I. Ross was here with the Scene of Crimes team. No, he doesn't have anything to say… I guess we can't accuse Fred of murdering Willie and Daisy just to increase circulation."

"That's thinking too far outside the box, love."

Iris carried in two plates brimming with eggs, bacon, tomato, mushrooms and beans. "Here you are. A proper fry-up will get you up and going."

Molly raised her fork as though girding herself for battle.

Michael dug in. "You were born and bred here in Blackpool, Iris. What do you think of the legend of Charles Crowe and the gypsy gold?"

"The story's been going round for a donkey's years," Iris answered, "since long before my time. But as for the facts of the story itself, like any tale it's grown in the telling, with each teller thinking, 'This will make it better, this will improve it.' I've always believed there was very little behind it all, but after the last couple of days, I'm not so sure."

An electronic chirp sounded in the distance. Still chewing, Molly leaped up and raced into the other room. When she came back, she told Michael, "Last night I e-mailed one of my contacts at the BBC."

"The BBC?" asked Iris.

Michael explained, "Yesterday morning, at Havers Customs House, Dunhill called Hopewell away for a phone interview with—what did he say? The BBC's legal department?"

"When Fred asked about it, Trevor said something about corporate law. But he lied about that, too. He's being sued for illegally taking items from a shipwreck at Tobermory Bay, on the Island of Mull. It's all very hush-hush, since the case hasn't yet come up in court."

Michael nodded. "I'm not surprised."

"Hopewell's another of those chaps who thinks his wealth excuses him from obeying the law," Iris said. "I'd not put it past him to have sent a thug up here last night. I'll freshen the pot." Iris carried the teapot back into the kitchen.

Sitting back down, Molly stabbed her fork into a mushroom, sending it flying onto the table, where it left a grease mark on the polished wood. "Okay, maybe you were right about Trevor."

"Not necessarily. Hard to imagine Mr. Perfect murdering—"

"You can stop with the insults, already. I'm not attracted to Trevor. He's nice to look at, is all."

Michael put down his knife and fork and raised his brows at Molly. "Excuse me?"

"You're even nicer to look at, okay?"

He smiled. "Okay, sorry for getting off topic. It might not have been the murderer breaking the window, it might have been someone after the gold coins. Daisy Coffey could have been putting it about that we still have the coins."

"Poor Daisy." Molly plucked a piece of toast from the rack and broke it in two with a snap. "She was murdered because she knew things she wasn't supposed to know. And here we are, trying to find out things *we* aren't supposed to know. I don't think anyone tried to break in at all, Michael."

"You mean the rock through the window was a warning." He considered his own piece of toast, spread with bloodred jam. "This would be a fine time for a shopping trip to London, Molly. You could visit Harrod's, buy yourself some new shoes."

"You think you can distract me with shoes?" She was slathering her own piece of toast with butter, knife flashing. "Why don't you, oh, go snowboard down Mount Everest or something?"

"I'm not backing off," he told her.

"Neither am I," she retorted.

For a long moment they glared at each other, then, as one, their expressions relaxed into rueful smiles. "Here's me," Michael said, "annoyed with you for trying to get me to back off, and all the time I'm wishing *you'd* back off."

"So I guess all we can do now is keep on keeping on," Molly replied.

Michael's smile tightened into a grimace. "Right."

CHAPTER THIRTEEN

MOUNDS OF WHITE AND gray cloud floated like galleons in the blue of the sky. The water in the harbor was so calm that every boat left a wake like a knife-edge, and the ocean beyond rose and fell in a lazy swell. The damp, still air seemed dense, and Molly's hair was a heavy curtain on the back of her neck.

She and Michael grabbed the last two parking places behind the old train station—he'd driven his own car to town so he could go back to the house for his tunnel gear, if necessary—and they walked up Dockside Avenue. Below the seawall lay the abbreviated beach, a strip of wet sand and pebbles striped by ridges of rock and dotted by blotches of seaweed. Human figures poked into every crevice and waved metal detectors over the ground. But Molly doubted that Willie had found his coins beach-combing.

Rohan met up with the Grahams outside the Blackpool Café, a paper cup in his huge, calloused hand. "Good morning," he said with a grin. "You two are slow off the mark today."

His grin faded as Michael told him about the early morning alarm, concluding, "It was just harassment, I expect."

"You sure you don't want to take a long vacation until all this blows over?"

"Or until Dylan ends up in prison?" Molly asked. "I'm

afraid we're committed, Rohan. Or maybe we should be committed."

Expelling a long sigh, Rohan said, "Adam Abercrombie and Grace Norton are tellin' me there's traffic jams in the tunnels. Everyone and his dog is searchin' for the spot where Willie found the gold coins, and mon, I think we should be down there, too."

"Great." Molly wrapped her arms around her waist so tightly they were gouged by the tiny rhinestones decorating her T-shirt.

"Speaking of the tunnels," Rohan went on, "last week Connor Abercrombie saw Willie Myners leaving the one that comes out in the old toy shop just behind Olivia Tarlton's book shop. I'm goin' to see Olivia now, about refinishing her grandmother's dining-room table. I'll take a look at the toy shop while I'm there."

"That might give us something to go on," Michael said.

"Grace and her sister, Hannah, also noticed Willie hangin' about the Customs House cellar. That's the best-known tunnel entrance in town—you've been there yourself, Molly."

Shivering, Molly remembered the ancient wooden door in a dark corner, the stones around it oozing moisture and the tunnel mouth exhaling a dank breath. "Give me a cliff top in a gale, no problem, but I have trouble digging the Christmas decorations out of the closet."

Michael could do cliff tops and caverns both. At the moment, though, he was looking at something beyond Molly's back. "What's Jenkins on about now?"

Rohan and Molly glanced around to see the reporter using duct tape to mark out a spot on the sidewalk, one with a particularly photogenic view of the *Black Sea Pearl* and the harbor. His crew, which had now increased to four, was jostling other news teams beside Grandage's, where police tape still festooned the barrels and the fishing net.

"As if the murders weren't enough to stir everything up," said Molly, "Fred's article about the lost treasure has unleashed utter madness."

Rohan nodded agreement. "So when are we joining in, Michael?"

Michael reached for his phone, but Molly was quicker, raising her wrist to check her watch. "It's a quarter to ten."

Michael inspected the screen of his phone. "All right, let's do it. Half past eleven at the toy shop, Rohan?"

"Sounds good. See you then." Rohan strolled closer to the media action.

Michael put his phone to use, calling Iris and asking her to get his thermos ready and his equipment laid out, while Molly led the way to the police station. Just as she reached for the doorknob, the door flew open and Fred Purnell spurted out. "Oops, sorry there, Michael, Molly." His color was high and his eyes bright. Two cameras hung on his chest like oversized medals and a notepad peeked from the breast pocket of his shirt.

From the interior of the building came Paddington's voice. "I'd bear that in mind, if I were you!"

"I'm not you," Fred retorted over his shoulder. "And a good job I'm not, else no one in town would have a clue about current events! Next time, just phone me and I'll stop in. No good having P.C. Krebs bring me in and scare the children."

"See that there's no next time," shouted Paddington.

"Is he threatening you with jail again?" Molly asked Fred, as he edged into the street and she and Michael maneuvered into the doorway.

"Of course he is. I gave him my speech about freedom of the press, to no more effect than usual, but I'm not going to faint in amazement at that." Gaining the sidewalk, Fred turned toward Dockside Avenue. "Paddington's had word from Ripon about the postmortem on Willie and a preliminary report on poor old Daisy. Me, I'm trying to organize an ever-so-accidental meeting between Tim and Aleister Crowe. Crowe's on board the *Pearl* just now… Sorry, must dash." And dash he did, trotting down the street and away.

"The man's a glutton for punishment," Molly remarked to Michael.

"So are we." Removing his aviator sunglasses, Michael waved her ahead of him into the building.

Luann Krebs sat at a desk just behind the counter, facing a computer. With a sharp glance over her shoulder, she closed the window on the screen in front of her, but not before Molly glimpsed the heading, "Controlled Drugs Act."

"Can I help you?" Krebs asked.

"We want to see D.C.I. Paddington," Michael replied.

"What is it now?" called Paddington from the back, and with a shrug Krebs returned to her computer.

Molly and Michael found the inspector ensconced behind his battered metal desk and its tidy stacks of folders and forms with this morning's copy of the *Journal*. A paper cup of muddy instant coffee steamed into the air. His face was flushed a shade somewhere between strawberry and pomegranate.

"Good morning," said Michael.

"What is it now?" Paddington asked again, not even taking his eyes from the file in his hands.

"Someone broke one of our windows in the wee hours of the morning, that's what," said Molly.

"The CCTV cameras showed a man running away," Michael added.

He looked at them then. "You've called attention to yourselves with this gypsy gold business, haven't you now?" Paddington reached for another folder and extracted a form. "Vandalism," he said slowly as he wrote. "Thorne-Shower Mansion."

Michael helped himself to a chair and pulled another one forward for Molly. "I'd say the *murderer* has called attention to himself. First Willie, then Daisy."

When Paddington didn't respond, Molly asked outright, "How *are* the investigations going?"

"Ross thinks Daisy Coffey was killed with the same knife that did in Willie Myners. A flat blade about seven inches long. Which he hasn't found, never mind his fancy team dragging the water below Grandage's."

"What were you saying last night," Michael cut in, "about Daisy leaving you a message?"

"You heard that, did you? Yes, she said she wanted a word, that she had an idea how Willie's murder was done. I thought at the time she was just making herself important, but…"

"She did live right next door," said Molly. "She did report the break-in—according to Fotherby, although he got there awfully fast."

Paddington frowned. "It doesn't matter, does it, whether she knew how the murder was done or not? She told everyone she did, the killer heard, and he lured her to a dark, quiet place and murdered her."

"What about the number," Michael prompted, "that Daisy drew in her own blood?"

"What?"

"Wasn't that a number two right next to her forefinger?" asked Molly.

"No, it was a smear caused by her twitching about, poor thing."

Molly wasn't so sure about that, and, judging by the furrow between Michael's eyes, neither was he. After a moment of silence, she went on, "Please tell us you're not still thinking Dylan's the murderer. Why would he kill Daisy?"

"She reported him breaking in to Willie's flat, that's why. If he killed Willie for revenge, then it goes without saying he's capable of murdering Daisy for the same reason."

"He didn't kill Willie," Michael stated. "He didn't break in to Willie's flat. Someone was there when he got there."

"So he says, but there's no evidence supporting that claim. Your posh lawyer may have him out on bail, but we'll lay him by the heels yet. Unless he's covering for his wife. That's always a possibility." Paddington leaned back in his chair, his weight making its frame squeal piteously, and sipped from his cup.

"Have you cleared Robbie Glennison, then?"

"Yes. He was with Temperance Collins at the time of Willie's murder—Thomas Clough saw him cleaning the floors in her gallery, just as she said. And Robbie was safe as houses here at the station when Daisy was killed last night. First thing this morning, Fotherby took him to the train station in Darlington, made sure he got on the London train. That's one step toward righting things here in Blackpool."

"But only one," Molly said. "You say there's no evidence Dylan's telling the truth about Willie's flat...."

"Fotherby secured the crime scene, didn't he?"

"Sure he did. How about the dark blue bit of cloth hanging from the lamp? Or was Fotherby more concerned about the gold coins? You do have those now, don't you?"

"Yes, they're in my safe."

Michael said, "Have you ever asked yourself why Fotherby didn't turn them in until *after* Willie was murdered?"

Paddington's eyes narrowed. "Yes, Graham, I have. Internal police affairs don't concern you."

Did that mean Paddington was suspicious of Fotherby? Molly asked herself. *Good.* "Speaking of Fotherby, what did he do with Robbie Glennison's filleting knife?"

"It's gone in to Ripon."

"Could it be the murder weapon?" Michael asked.

Molly knew he was headed in the same direction she was. If Willie's nuisance factor had started to outweigh whatever Fotherby might be getting from him, the constable could have gotten the bright idea of using the knife to kill Willie and letting Robbie take the rap. Discovering Robbie was working at the gallery yesterday morning might have come as a nasty shock.

Whether that shock translated into Fotherby's killing Daisy, Molly asked herself, was another matter, especially since they had no more proof of his guilt than Paddington had of Dylan's.

"No," said Paddington, "I doubt the filleting knife is the weapon that killed Willie. I think Ross is a by-the-book chap, and more power to him. The sooner we get these murders solved, the sooner he can stop commuting in from Ripon and we'll have us peace and quiet here in Blackpool—as much as we can with the tourists bringing in con artists like the McKennas, and pickpockets and other criminals."

Not necessarily, Molly thought. The crowds would only go away when they got tired of searching for gold. But one issue at a time. "The tourists bring in business, too. As for the McKennas, are you just assuming they're con artists or have you checked them out?"

Paddington smiled condescendingly. "I know my business, Mrs. Graham. Yes, I checked them out. They've got a misdemeanor or so in Cumbria, a couple of fines."

"Are they really gypsies?"

"What?" Paddington stared.

"The legend of Charles Crowe," Michael explained. "What if the McKennas are gypsies who are pursuing the treasure? They lived downstairs from both Willie and Daisy."

"The legend of…" Paddington laughed. "Gold causes murders, there's no doubt of that. But gypsies? You really are going on a bit, aren't you?"

From the front room came the ring of a phone and Krebs's voice answering. From outside the window came the sound of footsteps and voices. Between his teeth, Michael asked, "What of other possible suspects, like the Crookshanks?"

Paddington snorted. "The lass couldn't have killed a mouse, not in her condition."

Having no imagination, Molly thought, could be quite a handicap. "And Geoffrey? He bought a new gaff at Grandage's the morning of Willie's murder."

"Did he, now?" Paddington reached for another paper and jotted that down. "That's a long shot, though. A gaff doesn't fit the medical examiner's description."

"No, but—"

"Geoffrey's not going anywhere, not with Michelle to look after." Paddington threw down the pen and reached for his pipe. "Anything else?"

"There's the *Black Sea Pearl*," Molly suggested. "Trevor Hopewell has had quite a few shady dealings in regards to valuable artifacts, and Martin Dunhill has a criminal record."

Michael smiled at her implicating Trevor, but not smugly, thank goodness.

"Yes, I know. But in order to search the ship, I'd be obliged to produce a warrant, and no warrant's forthcoming without cause." Paddington shut the file in front of him with such force, paper flew into the air. "Now. Should I give you the lecture about leaving the investigation to the professionals, or did you learn your lesson the last time? You can't depend on your friendship with Dylan Stewart to keep you safe."

"He didn't kill anyone," Molly insisted.

"It wasn't him chucking a stone through our front window," added Michael.

"Then you're caught between a rock and a hard place, aren't you?" Striking a match, Paddington smiled with satisfaction. Huffing, Molly rose from her chair.

Michael was already opening the door of the office. "Thank you, Inspector."

Behind the smoke, Paddington's eyes gleamed. "You're welcome. Mind how you go, eh? Two murders, Seafaring Days, tales of treasure—I've got quite enough to deal with here. I don't need the pair of you walking into trouble."

"We'll do our best to oblige you," Michael said as Molly fled first into the corridor, then out of the building.

They paused on the steps, looking up and down Walnut Grove Street, catching their breath. As maddening as the inspector was, he was right. She and Michael *were* caught between a rock and a hard place—how to prove Dylan's innocence while not getting hurt themselves.

Daisy hadn't been trying to prove Dylan's innocence, but she'd gotten hurt anyway.

At the sound of "Move Along," Michael pulled out his phone. "Dylan, how's… What? Yes, yes, of course, we'll be right there."

Molly almost asked, "What is it now?" but she didn't want to sound like Paddington.

"Dylan says Naomi has something to show us." Michael's large, warm, reassuring hand in the small of her back urged her down the street and toward the bicycle shop.

Within moments, Molly and Michael were walking up the stairs and into the living room of the Stewarts' small flat. The room was shabby but tidy, Molly noted, decorated with posters of such masterworks as *The Scream* and *The Kiss*. Naomi huddled on the couch, a cup and saucer rattling between her trembling hands.

Molly sat down beside her and placed a steadying hand on her forearm. "What's happened, Naomi?"

"Someone tried the doors and windows of the shop in the wee hours this morning. And I swear a man followed us when we ran up to Coffey's for milk and bacon." Naomi's eyes darted around the room, the smudged makeup above them as dark as the circles below.

"There are loads of folk in town," Dylan told her. "Maybe some drunk was trying the doors. How're you sure there was a bloke?"

"I could feel his eyes on the back of my neck," Naomi insisted. "Every time I looked 'round, someone ran into a shop or an alley."

"But why?" asked Dylan.

"Gold," Michael stated.

Molly said the same thing in more words. "Everyone

on the planet knows that Willie found gold and thinks more is free for the taking, finders keepers."

"Yeah. It's all about money," Naomi said. "I made that plain enough myself, didn't I, Dylan?" She crashed the cup and saucer down on a nearby table, and picked up a spiral notebook. "I don't know if there's anything here that will help, but you're welcome to it. Take it to the police. Do whatever needs doing. Daisy Coffey was murdered because she was connected to Willie and I don't want to be next."

Molly remembered seeing Naomi drawing in the churchyard. She also remembered the loose sheets of paper lying on the desk in Willie's flat. As Michael sat down and picked up the book, Molly leaned in closer. Yes, Naomi's notebook held the same kind of paper—thick, quality leaves with a high rag content.

Slowly, he turned the pages, revealing sketches of tombstones, the church, the Crowe mausoleum, the light-house and the black-and-white front of Betsy Sewell's Curio Shop. Two pages showed early drafts of the map of Blackpool, this time with expertly rendered caricatures of some of its citizens. Paddington looked like a teddy bear with a moustache, Fotherby like a badger, Betsy herself like a cat crossed with a sphinx. And there was Alice Coffey, a dried-up bat in a witch's hat.

"You've got some skill with a pencil," Molly said.

"The map you did for Betsy is quite nice," added Michael.

"Map?" Dylan asked from behind the couch.

"I did a map of the town," Naomi explained. "Temperance, she wanted none of it. Willie thought I did good work. He took it to Betsy and she bought it, made copies to sell."

Dylan nodded. "Oh. Well. That's good. If you'd told me about it, I'd have found some way to help."

"Right," Naomi said, but her voice held more contriteness than sarcasm.

If all this ever blew over, Molly started, and quickly corrected her thought to *when* it all blew over, she'd bypass Temperance and use her connections to set Naomi up with a dealer in Newcastle or even London. The caricatures were very nicely done, and so was the map. Molly's eyebrows puckered. The map reminded her of something….

Michael turned another page. There, arranged diagonally across the paper, lay Willie's coins. Naomi had used a fine pencil for the details, the stamped lion, the letters of *Transalpina*. A charcoal pencil added shadows, so that the drawings looked almost like photographs. "These are great, Naomi."

"Thanks."

And Dylan repeated, a little more heartily than was really necessary, "Really great."

"I could use some drawings in my new pirate game," Michael told her. "A treasure map, with X marks the spot or a message in antique handwriting."

Molly nodded. "Good idea. How about a witch, or a gypsy or even Holly McKenna's Mademoiselle Fate. Maybe you could do a Tomb Raider character based on yourself."

A flash from Michael's blue eyes said, don't overdo it. He reached the back cover of the notebook, closed it and returned it to Naomi. "Thank you, but…"

"There's more." From the knitted bag hanging on the arm of the couch, she brought out several pages of drawing paper, folded and blotched with dirt. "Would it help if you had a map of where Willie discovered the coins?"

"Yes," Michael stated.

Dylan leaned over the back of the couch while Naomi unfolded the papers, revealing several crudely drawn maps. "Willie made these," Naomi said. "Used my paper without asking, but that's the way he was. Thought he was entitled—that if he didn't get what he wanted, then he was being cheated." Her purple fingernail, the polish chipped, pointed at the smudged pencil lines winding in and out like the ancient streets in London's City. "These are the tunnels, right? And these dots and squares are entry and exit points."

Michael tilted his head first this way, then that. "I'm not sure I recognize any... Wait. There. That triangle might be the entrance from the old toy shop—it's the only one I know of with a peaked lintel. But there's a square just there, close by. Hmm. If that's a tunnel leading from the book shop, it's a new one on me. I wonder if Willie ever did any work for Olivia?"

"Is that why someone was watching our shop?" Dylan asked. "Wanting to get into the tunnels through my cellar?"

"Or maybe," Naomi said, her voice quavering slightly, "they assumed I knew where Willie found the coins and that I'd show them—with the right kind of persuasion."

Dylan's hands settled on her shoulders, perhaps less as support than to keep her from jumping up and running away.

"But I never went into the tunnels with him. He went exploring on his own, save the time he had Robbie Glennison do a bit of digging. And wasn't that a big mistake, he said. Robbie kept insisting on a share of the gold. *He* killed Willie, I reckon."

"I reckon not," said Michael. "He's been cleared and left town. And he was in jail when Daisy was murdered."

Dylan sagged. "Paddington's still after me, then. I was alone when Daisy was killed, repairing a mountain bike downstairs."

"And I was here, watching the telly." Naomi sighed from the depths of her soul. "Take the maps, Michael. You and Rohan, you find where Willie struck lucky, and then no one will be after me, eh? Like they were after Daisy. She was a snoop and a gossip, but there was no call murdering her. And Paddington badgering poor Dylan here. It's a scandal."

Well, yes, it was, Molly thought.

"If you uncover more gold, we could share it out among us," Naomi added, a faint glow in her eyes.

"The treasure might be priceless, but I'm not sure it's worth this cost."

"We'll be all right, lass." Dylan tightened his grasp of his wife's shoulders and she slumped back against him, closing her eyes wearily. "We'll find some way of getting your work in the right places. There's no sense in worrying about the bleeding gold when we've not got it."

"That's the cleverest thing I've heard in days," Michael remarked. Folding the maps, he tucked them into his pocket. Then he landed a reassuring punch on Dylan's massive bicep. "I'll be in touch."

"Take care," Molly told them both. As soon as she and Michael were back on the street, she said, "Great, Paddington threw Robbie out of town before anyone knew to ask him where Willie had him dig. He'll be impossible to trace now."

"These maps give us something to go on." Michael pulled out his phone and touched Rohan's icon. "Seems Willie opened up new parts of the tunnel system. That was either brave or foolish, depending on where those parts are. Rohan? I need you to have a look at Olivia

Tarlton's back room—there may be an entrance there. I'll be along as soon as I collect my gear."

Michael snapped his phone back into his pocket, settled his sunglasses on his nose and turned to Molly with a grin. "Off we go, then!"

"Off *you* go," she replied. "I'll meet up with you at the toy shop, okay? Eleven-thirty?"

"Okay," he said, and with a kiss on the tip of her nose, headed for the car park.

CHAPTER FOURTEEN

MOLLY WAVED UNTIL Michael vanished into the throng filling Dockside Avenue, then let her hand fall to her side. She shouldn't worry about him exploring the tunnels. It was her own claustrophobia getting to her, that was all. Much better to stiffen her upper lip and keep busy than to cling to him.

The vendors were looking harried, not expecting to still have so much business even though it was a holiday Monday. With the crowds of crime-watchers and gold-seekers, Blackpoolers were proving there was more than one way to uncover treasure. Like fishing charters, Molly thought, spotting Geoffrey Crookshank leaving Rebecca's stall with a bouquet of flowers wrapped in cellophane. She moved to intercept. "Good morning."

"Morning." Geoffrey's eyes were even redder than they'd been yesterday, and the bags beneath them darker. If he hadn't been up all night, then he'd been having nightmares.

"How's business?" Molly asked. "My husband and I saw you with some customers last night. He was admiring your new gaff."

The battered eyes didn't blink. "Yeah, I bought me a new gaff, the old one's rusted away. I got to make Michelle and me a living. Especially now, with the little one to look after. Just came from the hospital—my grandson was born this mornin'. Six pound five ounces, he is. Bright little chap with dark hair. Came into this world just as the sun was rising. Sorry, can't stop any longer." Geoffrey's wizened form disappeared into the mob scene.

"Good luck," Molly called after the new grandfather, but he didn't seem to hear.

Paddington had one thing right: Michelle wasn't going anywhere, and neither was her father. The postmortem report on Willie didn't completely exonerate Geoffrey, and Daisy might not have been killed with the same weapon. Still, Molly told herself, there was no need for her to twist herself into a pretzel to come up with some off-the-wall solution involving Geoffrey and his gaff. A straight line is often the best throughline, as Michael said about his games.

Except in the tunnels, of course.

A man and woman pedaled by on two of Dylan's rental bicycles. Several young men wearing backpacks the size of steamer trunks walked past, each holding what had to be one of Naomi's maps. Where *had* she seen one of those? Molly asked herself.

In front of the *Black Sea Pearl* stood Fred Purnell, Tim Jenkins and a couple of camera people. In front of them stood Aleister Crowe, in his dark suit looking like his namesake bird. People were gathering, and the railing of the *Pearl* was lined with gawkers, including Martin Dunhill. A flicker of shadow and light in one of the portholes might be Trevor. Molly slipped closer.

"Think you're playing at?" Aleister demanded, his voice quiet but menacing.

Fred stood his ground. "I'm reporting the news."

"Rubbish! You're legitimizing rumor and innuendo about my family. 'Crowe treasure' indeed! Gypsies and gold coins and other lies." Aleister leaned casually on his cane, but his shoulders were poised, like those of a raptor about to swoop down on its prey. "Newspapers go out of business for spreading rumors about the wrong people. You would be wise to print a retraction, Mr. Purnell. Now."

"Well, dear me," said Fred, looking around vaguely, "I don't seem to have a printing press on me at the moment."

Aleister rolled his eyes. His voice dropped even further, into a cold purr. "Take care, or my solicitor will be filing a suit for libel. As for you and your cameras, Mr. Jenkins…"

"Mr. Crowe," said Tim, "as members of the press, we're within our rights to ask questions."

Aleister emitted a short, humorless laugh. "I beg to differ."

"Be my guest. It's a free country. In the meantime, have you a statement to make about Willie Myners's murder? What about Daisy Coffey's?"

"No," said Aleister. "I have nothing to add."

"Can I quote you on that?" Tim asked.

For a long, breathless moment, Aleister stared at Tim and at Fred as well, his face impassive, frozen as an iceberg. Then he turned and strode away, swinging his cane.

Fred and Tim exchanged satisfied grins. Molly was surprised they didn't high-five each other. But no, Fred strolled off toward Willie's boat, Tim's team trailing behind him like ducklings behind their mother.

Aleister bore down on her. "Mrs. Graham. Where is your spouse? Is it wise to leave you alone? Don't you feel exposed, what with a killer on the loose?"

Molly stared into Aleister's cold eyes. Yes, she had probably spoken with a killer in the last couple of days. She assumed she was not speaking with one now, but then, with Aleister, it was never safe to make assumptions. He knew way too much about who was doing what and when. Maybe he even knew that there *was* a treasure, and where it was hidden.

"For someone who wants to quell those rumors," she said, "you're sure trying to call attention to them. Have you ever thought of just ignoring them?"

"Rumors about gold won't simply fade away. Give my regards to your husband." Aleister strolled away, not into a dark alley but toward the ITV team.

Turning her back on him, Molly directed her steps toward the old toy shop—and found herself within hailing distance of Holly and Liam McKenna, who were handing out flyers.

Even without his black tricorn hat, Liam would've fit right in as one of Blackbeard's crew. His beard bristled, his earrings flashed and his bald skull gleamed. Beside him Holly tossed her head, making her long ebony hair shimmy like a belly dancer. When a couple of male passersby stopped to admire her, she pounced. "How about a tour, lads? The true stories of Blackpool, the ones the Council and the civic leaders don't want you to hear."

Liam chimed in. "Witchcraft, secret passageways, wreckers luring ships onto the rocks, rich men cheating their way into a fortune—it's all here, folks! There you are, next tour's at noon." He handed a flyer to a plump middle-aged woman, then spotted Molly. "Hullo, luv. On your own?"

"For the moment," Molly replied. "How's business?"

"Brilliant," said Liam, with a smile that revealed uneven yellow teeth. "Can I interest you in a seance? You're sure to have some extinct relation reaching out to you from beyond the grave."

"What about extinct Blackpoolers like Charles Crowe?

Where do you and Holly get the stories you tell on your tours?"

"Where don't we get 'em? They're in the air, luv. In the ground, in the water. Old James Norton, he's got the goods going back generations. And Daisy Coffey had a tongue on her could kill a horse. There's nothing in this town she or one of her pack didn't know. A drop of the barley, or a stiff G and T, and Bob's your uncle—all the scandal you'd ever want to hear. Or pass on, for money. I reckon that's what got Daisy killed—her tongue."

Molly nodded. At least she and Michael didn't have Daisy's reputation as a busybody. Not yet, anyway. "Were you aware of the Crowe legend before you came here to Blackpool? That's just the sort of story you hear from the Romany."

Liam cocked his head to the side. "Just 'cause there's gypsies in the story doesn't mean it's a gypsy story. Everyone's got tales of curses and treasures, not just them."

Liam said "them" instead of "us," but that didn't prove a thing. "You live in the Oceanview, don't you? Just downstairs from the two murder victims? There's new material for you."

"But it's the same old story. Poor sod, Willie. There he was, rabbiting on about getting what's coming to him, and by gawd, so he did! Charles Crowe's curse laid him low!"

"Getting what…" Molly repeated.

"Said his ship was coming in loaded with gold. Holly and I didn't give a toss—he was always sounding off about something. But when we got home Saturday night, here's Daisy bleating about you and Stewart and Fotherby making off with a bag of gold. Clever, ain't you, luv?" Liam's bright black eyes narrowed calculatingly.

Molly imagined his tattooed arm lobbing a stone

through Thorne-Shower's front window. "It was only four coins. Fotherby took them and locked them up at the police station."

"Ah, that's a shame." Liam's shoulders rose and fell— easy come, easy go.

Holly wafted by, her dark eyes considering Molly, dismissing her, then pouncing on a set of backpackers. "How about a tour, lads? Behind the scenes in haunted Blackpool!"

Molly decided to try one of Michael's straight lines. "Did you know Willie was dealing drugs?"

"Couldn't miss it, could we? Even without the folk 'visiting' at all hours, carrying their little bags of pills, there's the smell. We burn incense, but Willie, he was burning something else."

"Did you hear Willie arguing with a woman not long before he was killed?"

"He was always quarreling with someone. Michelle Crookshank, Naomi Stewart, Douglas Fotherby—"

"Fotherby?"

"Reckon we've got a cop on the take, eh? Why else hang about the Oceanview and ignore Willie's dealing? But then, Luann Krebs is no stranger, either, keeping her finger in the pie." Smiling, Liam patted the side of his nose with his forefinger. "No business of mine, though. My work's on another plane of existence. Speaking of which, I'd better be getting to it. You like ghost stories, sonny?" Liam extended a flyer toward a little boy. The child's father snatched him away.

"Thanks," Molly told Liam, but he was already out of earshot.

Like a shark, Molly supposed, he had to keep moving. He and Holly were con artists, but they were highly entertaining ones, even if Liam was too cagey to reveal anything outright. That bit about P.C. Krebs, for example, didn't give her anything new. The Grahams had already seen her outside the Oceanview. Catching Willie in the act would have helped make her reputation, but it was too late now.

Her phone sounded from her purse and she whisked it to her ear. "Michael?"

"Never mind the toy shop, love. Rohan's found an entrance in Olivia's bookstore."

"I'm on my way."

Mulling over clues and suspects, trying not to spin her wheels with worry, Molly headed up Pelican Lane. The Turn the Page Book Shop occupied part of an old building that had once been Olivia Tarlton's grandmother's house. The upper story was cantilevered out over the skinny strip of sidewalk, as were those of several nearby buildings, making Pelican Lane into a canyon. But the overhanging eaves were ideal for suspending large baskets of flowers and vines. Olivia's spilled over with geraniums, and the ones hanging from the B and B next door were heavy with nasturtiums.

The ground-floor windows of the book shop displayed stacks of bestsellers, history books, classic novels, and, front and center, an array of Iris's historical romances. Olivia herself waited in the doorway, her hair held back from her face by a red scarf like a seaman's neckerchief. "There you are," she said to Molly. "Michael's just arrived."

MICHAEL COULD TELL BY a certain stiffness in Molly's expression that she didn't want him to go into the tunnels. But it wasn't as though tunnel-ratting was any more dangerous than rock climbing or scuba diving, not if you kept your wits about you. She said nothing about her qualms, though, simply filled him in on her encounters with Aleister and Liam while Olivia led them to the scene of the action. Michael could only shake his head in irritation at both men.

They found Rohan's denim-clad bottom framed by a low, square opening in the wainscoting of Olivia's back parlor. A dusty panel lay propped to one side, below an expanse of wallpaper in a faded cabbage rose pattern. A print of Queen Mary and King George V still hung on the wall. Their Majesties' faces looked sternly down as Rohan eased out of the aperture. Dusting his hands, he said, "You'll have to stoop, Michael. The ceiling's low, but this tunnel heads right for the one behind the toy shop. I phoned the Abercrombies and the Nortons, and Connor and Grace are on their way."

"No worries." Michael reached into his rucksack for his hard hat, settled it on his head, then shrugged the rucksack itself onto his back. The clammy, wet-dog odor emanating from the tunnel was perfume to him, but Molly wrinkled her nose.

Connor and Grace pushed into the room. At fourteen, tomboy Grace's short hair and slender body could have been that of either a boy or a girl. So could the grin on her elfin face as she donned a hard hat, switched on her torch, and brandished a garden spade. "I'm ready!"

Seventeen-year-old Connor's hazel eyes and dark hair reminded Michael of his mother Charlotte's, save that Connor was a foot taller and six inches thinner. He was wearing his own battered rucksack and hard hat, and carried a small pickax.

"I can't believe Willie found a secret door behind the wainscoting," Olivia said, "though, now that I think about it, Granny always claimed the room was haunted, that she'd hear voices in the distance and feel a cold draft."

"Wait for me!" Lydia Crowe catapulted through the doorway. Her workmanlike coveralls, boots and the hard hat flattening her pinned-up blond hair made her look like a completely different person from the giggling girl who'd dragged him into a dance Saturday afternoon, Michael thought. "You weren't going to go without me, were you? Just because of all that rubbish about old Charles Crowe stealing gold from Dracula? Who cares after all these years?"

"Aleister does," said Molly.

Lydia's lower lip protruded. "Tell me! I've been hearing nothing else from Aleister. He had us into the Tea Shop after church yesterday for another lecture on preserving the family heritage. It's not my fault I'm a Crowe."

"Um…" Michael glanced at Molly. Her eyebrows rose and fell in a shrug. Rohan looked from Connor to Grace and back to Michael. "Not at all," Michael told Lydia. "Let's get on, then."

Imprinting Molly's smile and blown kiss on his mind, he ducked into the opening.

MOLLY STOOD WITH OLIVIA until each of the tunnel rats had made their way into the darkness. The light from the various torches winked out and the sound of footsteps diminished and died.

"Well then," Olivia said. "Is Iris working on another historical novel?"

"She's just starting one set during Bonnie Prince Charlie's rebellion in 1745," replied Molly, even though the story that was running through her own mind was that of Theseus wending his way through the Cretan labyrinth until he came at last to the Minotaur.

If Michael and the tunnel rats found the gold, would that reveal the killer? Was the murderer biding his time until someone located the treasure for him? Lydia had a point, though. In the long run it didn't matter whether the gold had been Charles Crowe's or where he got it from, it only mattered that it existed. That it was believed to exist.

"See you later," Molly told Olivia.

Plotting her next move, she walked past the enticing piles of books and stepped out of the shop—and almost collided with Addison Headerly, who was peering through the window. In everyday clothing, his freckles emphasized by the sunlight of the last few days, he seemed no older than Connor. "Oh, sorry," he said, taking a step backward and almost falling over the curb into the street.

"Don't apologize. I ran into you. I don't believe we've formally met—I'm Molly Graham."

"I know. Your husband does those brilliant games.… Um, Addison Headerly. Pleased to meet you."

Gravely, they exchanged handshakes. "Were you looking for Lydia? She's gone off with Michael and the other tunnel rats."

"Well, I, um—I asked her to lunch, but she said she was busy. I guess she was, this time, but…" His words came in a rush. "No Headerly's good enough for a Crowe. Aleister's made that clear. It all goes back to an ancestor working on one of Charles Crowe's ships. I don't know what went wrong, but there's been bad feeling ever since."

"It's not your fault you're a Headerly," Molly told him, almost repeating Lydia's words. "But people have long memories in Blackpool."

Her sympathetic smile was perfectly genuine. She could question his taste, but she couldn't question his devotion. She *could* ask him about something Lydia had just brought up, though. "We saw Lydia, Aubrey and Aleister at the Tea Shop yesterday afternoon, but you weren't with them."

"I wasn't invited. I probably shouldn't have wasted the effort going to church—well, going with the Crowes, that is. Especially when Aleister himself couldn't be bothered to show up on time."

That's right, Rebecca had heard the same thing from Sandy Mason. "Why was he late?"

"I'm not sure. He was in a fine state when he arrived, though, I can tell you that."

Was he? Molly made a note of that.

With one more yearning glance into the shop, Addison turned away. "I'd best be getting on— Oh, my God!"

Leaping forward, he seized Molly in a bear hug and dragged her into the street.

CHAPTER FIFTEEN

MOLLY PUSHED AT Addison's chest, threw his arms aside and broke free. Spitting out the wool fuzz from his sweater, she demanded, "What do you think you're doing?"

A tattoo of footsteps and several people converged at the spot, among them her caretaker, Irwin Jaeger, who must have been down the street, and Olivia Tarlton from inside her shop. "Molly!"

"Ma'am!"

"Are you all right?"

"What happened?"

Their voices were like a chorus around her.

Addison's pointing forefinger trembled.

Molly followed its direction, to see a wire basket lying half-crushed on the sidewalk, spilling peat moss and orange nasturtiums over the curb into the street. With her head squashed against Addison's chest, she hadn't heard it hit. But thank goodness he'd seen it falling. If it had landed on her, she'd be lying in the street herself right now, and the color staining the cobblestones wouldn't be orange. "Oh," she said, her voice squeaking and her knees turning suddenly to jelly.

Olivia looked up at the cord dangling from a window of the B and B. "It must have broken."

Irwin set down the bulky plastic bag he was holding, emblazoned "Norton's Hardware." His large, capable hands inspected the end of the cord extending from the handle of the basket. "Cut through. Wait here." He dived into the B and B. Voices echoed. A moment later, the upstairs window flew open and Irwin looked out. "No one's here. Whoever cut the cord legged it down the back stairs and away. The owner was hoovering the carpets, didn't hear a thing."

"Oh," Molly said again, and to Addison, "Thank you."

"It was cut on purpose? But why would—oh. You're, um— Glad I could help." He turned and hurried off toward Dockside Avenue like someone escaping contagion.

No, Molly told herself, *why* wasn't that hard a question.

Irwin emerged from the door of the B and B, followed by a plump woman wearing an apron and wielding a broom and dustpan. "Sorry, dear. The people renting the room left this morning and I hadn't cleaned it yet—I can't believe anyone would play a joke like that. The very idea, a perfectly good basket, and you might have been hurt." She set to work clearing up the mess.

A joke, thought Molly. *Hardly!* She remembered Aleister's words that morning: "Exposed. Isn't that how you feel, with a killer on the loose?" Had that been a threat, soon to be put into action, or was he simply playing his usual role of sinister mastermind?

The show over, the other passersby wandered away. Fred Purnell and Tim Jenkins were nowhere in sight, fortunately. Freedom of the press was a more palatable concept when the press was not making free with your own predicament.

"Come inside, and I'll make tea," offered Olivia.

Molly imagined sweet, milky tea washing away the acid in her mouth. She thought of chocolate, or whisky or some other restorative. She visualized Michael working his way through the tunnels, when she was the one who needed the hard hat. He'd be more upset than she was when he heard about the basket attack. "Thank you, but I'd better keep on moving."

With a dubious nod, Olivia returned to her customers.

Molly offered Irwin what she hoped was a jaunty grin. "We've been warned off, but we're in too far to quit now. A good thing Addison has quick reflexes."

"Good job the killer's timing was not quite on," Irwin said grimly.

"Trust you to call a spade a spade. This just proves that we're onto something, doesn't it?"

Irwin's steel-wool eyebrows almost shook hands over the rim of his bifocals. "Right."

Molly flexed her knees—good, they'd solidified, even though the back of her neck still felt like crepe paper— and strolled on up Pelican Lane. Collecting his bag, Irwin fell into step beside her. She changed the topic. "You got the new pane of glass, I see."

"Yes, ma'am. And I had a coffee with James Norton— the older one, the father. He's right excited about Seafaring Days and the murders and the coins and all."

"I bet he is," Molly said.

"Usually he's going on about the war and U-boats along the coast and such, teasing me because of my German family, but not today. Today he wanted to talk about the Crowes."

"Who doesn't?"

"He knew Aleister's grandfather, Ophelia's brother. Philip kept dismissing stories of the hidden gold just as Aleister does, even as he got involved in some rather questionable business himself."

"Yeah," Molly said. "Tell me about it."

"James was saying that when his own grandfather was a boy in the 1860s, he was friends with older folk who'd known Charles. Charles was a self-made man, clever and daring. Once he made himself some money in the shipping trade, he started helping out folks round Blackpool—for a price. Pretty soon he owned most of the town, and he'd uncovered most of the town's secrets. James compared him to a Mafia boss. Either you paid him off and kept your mouth shut or you vanished, and your family counted themselves lucky if your body washed up on the beach."

"And here we are, several generations later, still dealing with his secrets." Molly stopped in front of the Style Shop, which faced the Calm Seas churchyard. "I'm going to stop in here."

Irwin opened the door for her. "Get yourself another pretty frock, ma'am. That'll ease your mind."

Molly laughed out loud. "Irwin, if Iris heard you giving me that advice, she'd wallop you with a soup ladle."

His moustache couldn't quite hide his smile. "It made you laugh, though. I'll get on to the house, start repairing the window. Have a care now, and don't go off on your own. I don't want to tell Michael you've been hurt."

"Neither do I. Thanks." Molly stepped into the shop.

Angela Ogbourne's Style Shop occupied a recent building that had no history. On the other hand, the structure was sound enough that it wasn't one of Rohan's habitual job sites.

Angela was folding chiffon tops that reminded Molly of scoops of rainbow sherbet while several customers browsed. With her artfully mussed dark hair, skintight jeans and sandals decorated with faux jewels, she could have fit in on any London street. "Hullo, Molly."

"Good— I guess it's afternoon now, isn't it?"

"Half past twelve or thereabouts," said Angela.

"You didn't happen to get in any Stella McCartney jackets, did you?"

"Molly, I can't afford Stella McCartney. No one else in Blackpool can, either—well, except for maybe Lydia Crowe, but she doesn't have your taste."

"I saw her at the Tea Shop yesterday after church. Pretty fabric in her blouse. A silk blend, I'd bet. But I'm not so sure about the skirt."

"You've got that right. I saw her going into the church while I was opening up. The short skirt, the sexy shoes, like she was out for a night of clubbing."

Molly turned her back on the clothing, accessories and shoes, and gazed through Angela's plate-glass window at a vista of the churchyard and its ranks of tombstones. "Did you see Aleister going into the church yesterday morning, too?"

"You can't miss Aleister, not in one of those navy blue suits. Savile Row, has to be. Still, when he dresses down in a tennis sweater or his polo togs, he's quite dashing."

Smiling, Molly reminded Angela of the question. "Aleister? The church?"

"Oh, my, yes. First Aubrey and Lydia arrived, and met up with that young chap Lydia's been leading on. They went inside. Then Aleister appeared and stopped like a bird dog spotting a pheasant. He positively swooped across the churchyard. A minute later, Luann Krebs came rushing over. Aleister must have phoned her." Angela placed the last top on the table.

"And then?" Molly prompted.

"Turns out there were two chaps dossed down in sleeping bags in front of the Crowe mausoleum. It was sad, seeing them running among the tombstones, carrying all their things out the gate and away. I reckon they're still running. Aleister can tear more strips off you with a whisper than most people can with a shout."

"Absolutely."

Angela's meticulously lined lips crumpled. "Those two must have had nerves of steel. Naomi Stewart says she's heard bony fingers scratching at the inside of the mausoleum door—Charles Crowe himself, probably, come up from the crypt wanting to make more money."

"I wouldn't be surprised," Molly said, even as she ruled out Aleister as Willie's killer, and by extension, Daisy's. Assuming there was only one killer in Blackpool, not two.

"Speaking of money," Angela went on, "what's all this that Daisy Coffey, rest her soul, was putting about? That chap Willie had a bag of… Why yes, madam?"

A middle-aged woman held up a print dress, in a pattern that looked like an explosion in a flower shop. Her beringed fingers waggled through a rip in the seam. "Will you discount the price?"

"Certainly, madam. Five percent. Then I'll ring Sandy Mason at the Launderette and tell her to expect you. She'll mend the seam and press the dress, as well."

"She'll charge you for the service, not me," said the woman.

"Of course." Angela's smile stiffened but she motioned the woman to the counter.

With a smile and a wave, Molly retreated back to the street. Sandy had patched Michael's cricket and rugby outfits, and hemmed up one of Molly's jackets. She made a good living in Blackpool, where traditional concepts of make-and-mend lingered as long as ghost stories.

Molly gazed through the covered lych-gate into the churchyard, but she didn't really see it. She visualized

Michael and the others walking, crouching, even crawling through the tunnels. She imagined Willie Myners lying mortally wounded on his boat, and Daisy Coffey dead behind the Bait and Tackle Shop—what a way to go.

She tried several different scenarios, with several different murderers—Trevor Hopewell, Fotherby. Maybe Martin Dunhill had found a device like Hermione's time tuner from *Harry Potter*. Maybe one McKenna had killed Willie while the other murdered Daisy Coffey. But she came up short on every one.

Liam and Holly McKenna's office occupied a small room above Margaret Coffey's grocery shop, the space they rented from her in return for reading her fortune. She wondered what Margaret knew about her tenants.

Carefully walking next to the curb, taking no short cuts up dark alleys and looking over her shoulder as often as she looked right and left, Molly made her way to Dockside Avenue.

The large window in the front of Coffey's Grocers displayed yet another of the McKennas' posters, along with the usual stacks of soft drinks and boxes of potatoes and apples. Through the window, Molly saw Margaret totting up a basket of snacks, drinks and sunscreen for several tourists.

Molly strolled into the shop with its scents of ripe fruit and dusty spices, chose a cheese and chutney sandwich from the half-empty rack and dithered over a cooler of drinks until a lull left Margaret alone at the till.

Molly set her sandwich and a can of Diet Coke down on the counter. "I'm so sorry about Daisy."

Margaret's face beneath its helmet of brown hair was the color and texture of dough that had risen and then fallen again, and revealed as much emotion. She scanned

Molly's items. "That'll be three pound sixty-five pence, please."

Molly pulled a five-pound note from her pocket and handed it over.

Margaret tucked the bill into the register and said, "Daisy. I told her again and again that tongue of hers would cause trouble, especially with a lag like Willie Myners living next door. But she thought she was viewing a real-life crime program. Still, I shan't be saying 'I told you so' when I talk with her again. She was my sister-in-law. She deserves some consideration."

"When you talk with her again?" Molly asked.

Margaret counted out the change. "Holly McKenna says soon as Seafaring Days is finished, she'll try and contact Daisy for me. She's only passed over, mind you, she's not gone."

"Well, ah, yes, er, no…" Molly got her own tongue under control. "I know a lot of people claim to have occult skill. Holly really does?"

"Quite. She's very perceptive. You see so many charlatans about these days, but not Holly and Liam. They did a reading for me just before I opened Sunday morning that was pitch-perfect. Trouble from the sea, they said. Strangers in town. Money coming my way."

None of that was at all hard to predict, Molly thought. If the McKennas had predicted Daisy's death, now, or Willie's… A man stepped up behind her, ready to check out. Molly had time to ask Margaret only one more question. "You must have opened early Sunday morning, for the festival."

"No, I opened bang-on eleven, as always. Holly and Liam arrived at half past ten, and I opened at eleven." Margaret slammed the cash drawer. "Would you like a bag for those?"

"No, thank you." Molly gathered up her sandwich and drink and stepped aside, imagining Liam and Holly bent over Margaret's hand—or crystal ball, maybe—just as someone plunged a knife into Willie Myners. That crossed them off her list.

Outside, Molly was lucky enough to find an empty bench in the shade of the town hall. There had been times here in Blackpool that she thought she'd never be warm again—the chill of the sea, fog and the winter winds cut to the bone. But now even the puffy summer clouds had evaporated, leaving the sky clear, and sunlight filtered through a moist haze. The water in the harbor could have been glass. The skull-and-crossbones flag atop the *Black Sea Pearl* hung limp as a black shroud.

Even in the shade a trickle of sweat ran down Molly's back. She looked across at the Blackpool Café, thinking that a seat on one of the balconies would be the most comfortable place in town right now.

Apparently, she wasn't the only one with the idea. Aleister Crowe was sitting at a corner table with Tim Jenkins, the remains of a lunch spread between them. Aleister's fingers were steepled, as though he were a finance officer interviewing a loan candidate. No telling what sort of story Jenkins was bargaining for, but Aleister would no doubt come out ahead.

Her phone trilled. Choking down the bread, cheese and chutney that was in her mouth, Molly checked the screen. The call wasn't from Michael, damn it, but was an unknown number, probably a business contact. "Molly Graham."

"I suggest you take that flower basket seriously. The next time, neither you nor your husband will walk away."

The male voice was cold, the vowels rounded, the

consonants partly swallowed, in a posh accent so strong it was a caricature of Trevor's or... Molly darted a glance at Aleister. He was still talking to Jenkins.

She scrutinized all the passing faces, recognizing only a few. Who had seen her at the book shop?

Who was the killer who was now after her?

"Hello?" Molly said again, but there was no reply. She tried returning the call, but it rang unanswered. When a one-size-fits-all voice-mail message came on, she restored the phone to her purse and clasped her hands to keep them from trembling when, despite the warmth, an icicle slipped down her spine.

The taste in her mouth was no longer that of cheese and chutney, but the acrid tang of fear.

MICHAEL'S BACK CREAKED. If anything, Rohan had exaggerated the height of the tunnel running from the book shop. The petite Grace had to crouch. Michael had to bend double.

He followed the beam of his torch through a passageway as narrow as a snake's throat, its low ceiling a rough, pointed arch. Drops of water plunked on his hard hat, echoing the splats of booted feet feeling their way through the brown slurry of the floor. The wet-dog smell hadn't really weakened, but he'd gotten used to it.

"Have a care!" said Connor, and Michael ducked before he knocked his head against a stone block protruding from the oozing ceiling.

As with other parts of the labyrinth beneath Blackpool, this tunnel was lined with stone. It was mostly mortared rubble, patterned with pale roots like the fingertips of ghosts. Occasionally, the shape of a well-cut limestone ashlar would loom from the darkness, blocks perhaps left over from Charles Crowe's multiple building projects.

The tunnels themselves predated Crowe. Michael half expected to see Stone Age drawings of extinct animals on the walls.

He squeezed himself through an opening so constricted he had to turn sideways, stepping over a low pile of tumbled stone, and emerged in a wider, relatively taller tunnel. Warily, he stretched, his back twanging. This ceiling was also too low for him to stand erect, but still he felt as though he had just walked into York Cathedral with its soaring arches.

"I know where we are," said Rohan. "This is the tunnel running behind Compass Rose Street. There's a branch that eventually comes out in the dell below Ravenhearst."

"I've only gone up that branch the once," Michael told him. "The ground's boggy there, and the ceilings have shifted and cracked. They could collapse at any moment."

"And it's Ravenhearst," said Grace, without needing to add any further cautions.

Michael took a few steps farther on, then pulled Willie's penciled maps from his pocket. In the light of his torch he compared them to each other. And suddenly they made sense.

"I see what Willie was doing. These lines are meant to be the tunnels going right into the hillside, these are the ones paralleling the major streets and these are the ones running into some of the buildings, like the warehouses along the docks—those are Crowe's work, as well. There's no saying what he was getting up to there."

"Excuse me," Lydia piped up. "Crowe here."

"You said yourself, you can't help being a Crowe."

"Yes, but you don't have to imply—"

"Give it a rest," Connor told her, and she did.

Rohan swung his light around to inspect the aperture they'd just crawled through. "Look at the stones knocked from the wall, and the fresh chisel marks. There's an empty beer can and another piece of that drawin' paper—nothing on it, though. Willie's work, for sure. Is this where he found the coins?"

"If so, he left no traces of them," said Michael. "See this wiggly line? That's this tunnel, behind the bookshop. If a wiggly line means a tunnel he opened up on his own—there's a fool, rushing in where an angel wouldn't risk his shoe leather—then this line's a new tunnel, as well."

Rohan leaned closer to the smudged paper ringed with light, his dark eyes gleaming. "But there's only one tunnel leadin' from the lighthouse, with no branches."

"My granddad saw Willie at the lighthouse just last week," said Grace. "He claimed he was doing some work on the masonry, but Granddad thought he was up to no good. Said he looked dirty."

"Let's take the low road to the lighthouse, then." Michael folded the maps and thrust them back into his pocket. Like most puzzles, this one seemed easy once he'd figured it out. Although he'd been a long enough time doing it. When had Naomi said something about hearing footsteps behind the walls of the bicycle shop, just below the lighthouse?

Single file, the tunnel rats made their way along the underground equivalent of a promenade, water rushing and echoing in the distance. Michael thought of flooded tunnels and collapsing roofs, then pushed the images away. Exploring the tunnels was exciting, not frightening.

They walked past the Customs House entrance and around a group of tourists standing about like sheep with torches. Michael made a mental note to come back and police the area—visitors were leaving bits of rubbish, and more than one had even carved his name into the lumpy limestone walls.

Several branchings and various wanderers later, Michael led the way into a narrower, lower path. The cellar of the lighthouse lay ahead, carved out of rock centuries ago like an ancient chambered tomb. A breath of chill, fetid air wafted past his face, and he shivered, reminding himself he didn't believe in ghosts, or curses or even... Well, no. He did believe in gypsy gold, now.

"There." The light of his torch sliced through the gloom to expose a stone shoulder, a hidden buttress supporting the bedrock that was Dockside Head. "That's the place Willie marked on his map."

"That's the Oxter," said Rohan, with a chuckle at the old Scots word for *armpit*. "Most tourists never get any farther, mon. They come this far, lose their nerve, and go back to the lighthouse pub for a pint."

Stepping around the shoulder, Michael focused his light into the dank alcove just behind. "This has never been more than a dead end and a rubbish pit—and a loo. The smell alone's enough to keep people away."

Lydia made a noise of disgust.

"But now the rubbish is piled to one side, see? And the far wall's as smooth as my plastered parlor. There's nowhere else in the tunnels you've got such an even coating of mud." Michael stepped into the alcove. So did the others, the vapor of their breaths wafting like specters through the multiple beams of light.

Light that revealed, behind a coating of mud displaying handprints and the marks of a trowel, a regular pattern of square on square... Bricks. A doorway blocked with bricks.

"Yes!" Michael said, but restrained himself from

pumping his fist in the air. "Back off a bit—here, this one's loose. And this one, as well." Carefully, he pried at a brick and pulled it away, then another and another, opening up a small, rectangular space. Beyond it gaped nothingness. He aimed his torch through the hole and peered inside.

"What is it? What do you see?" chorused Lydia and Connor, while Grace asked, "Is it another tunnel?"

"No, it's not a tunnel." The damp, moldy smell leaking through the aperture combined with the smell of the alcove clogged Michael's throat. Still he managed to choke out, "It's a room. And it's occupied."

CHAPTER SIXTEEN

THE OTHERS JOSTLED FORWARD, eager to look through the hole. "Stop!" Michael ordered. "You'll have the wall down! The bricks were once mortared together—see the traces along the edges—but Willie only stacked them back in the opening."

Rohan waggled a brick here, pressed a brick there. "There's only a few been removed, just enough to squeeze inside. The others are still solid."

"That bloke in there's none too solid," said Connor, the whites of his eyes glittering in the torchlight.

Quelling his thrill of horror, Michael scanned the room again then, moving only one muscle at a time, climbed inside. Rohan followed. Between them, they almost filled the floor space.

The skeleton lay curled in the far corner, as though its original owner had simply fallen asleep. The skull lay on its side, the empty eye sockets staring into eternity, the jaw hanging askew. The dark brown ribs rose from the muck in parallel rows, and the arm bones were angled in two vees in the front. The legs were likewise bent... Well, no. *Leg*—there was only one. The other ended at the knee. A brown ridge extending from it was a waterlogged, partially decayed wooden leg.

Shreds of cloth still clung to the limbs and the chest, now as dark brown and sodden as steeped tea leaves.

Beams of light danced over the oozing walls as Grace,

Lydia and Connor clustered in the opening. Rohan knelt down to get a closer look at the body. Michael averted his eyes—poor chap, surely he hadn't been walled up in here—and saw something an arm's length away from the fan of finger bones.

Or, rather, saw the absence of something. Four round shapes were imprinted in the mud, just the right size to be three Wallachian coins and a Dutch thaler. In fact, by bending over and focusing his torch, Michael could see where the fine ridges rimming the coins had corrugated the shallow depressions in the dirt. Except for the places where fingers had very recently gouged the indents away.

"This is where Willie got the coins," he said.

"He didn't notice this, mon." Rohan lifted away what had once been the breast of a coat. Gold glinted beneath. "It's another coin, a big one."

The disc gleamed all the brighter for resting against brown tatters and browner bone. Michael peered at it. "No, it's a medallion. Palm trees, sailing ships—those clouds must be puffs of smoke. Looks to be a battle scene." Squinting, he read the letters engraved below the picture. "'Shared Losses All Round.' This should help identify the body, don't you think?"

With a scramble and scrape, Grace headed for the lighthouse entrance—or exit, depending. "I'll phone Paddington."

He should phone or text Molly, Michael told himself. But his phone wouldn't work underground any more than Grace's… That wasn't quite true. Michael produced his iPhone and with cold, muddy fingers started taking photos. In the shadows caused by the camera flashes and the wavering torches, the bones seemed to shift uneasily. *Just illusion, Michael, relax.* he told himself.

Muttering, "The guy's glad to be found," Rohan stepped back to the wall and examined it. "The bricks are laid in a Flemish bond pattern, typical of the eighteenth, early nineteenth, centuries. Over the years the mud ran down and roots grew over them till they blended in with the rest of the wall."

"How'd Willie find the place, then?" asked Connor.

"He actually looked instead of just passing by," said Michael.

"Or he may have come along at just the right time to spot a crack, or a slip or water leaking from between the bricks or somethin'," Rohan said.

Connor replied, "He was lucky."

"For a few days. Then his luck ran out." Michael stood up.

"Only four coins," Lydia said. "That's hardly a treasure."

"It was to Willie. He could have set himself up nicely selling those coins. A collector like Trevor Hopewell would have bought that medallion as well, but you can't blame Willie for not getting any closer to the skeleton."

Lydia said, "Still, this doesn't prove that the rumors are true. All of them, that is."

"Tell that to the reporters and the trippers," Connor said, as voices echoed down the tunnel.

Rohan climbed back into the tunnel and stood guard in the opening, shooing away everyone who wandered up—after lecturing them about going into the tunnels without proper equipment. Before long, footsteps reverberated, and Paddington's voice bellowed, "Make room, make room!"

The inspector himself hung back, letting Dr. Harvey Parker, who was also acting as the local coroner today, climb into the small chamber. "This is a day and no mistake," he remarked. "First a birth, then another death."

"Not a recent death, not like Willie and Daisy," Michael told him, "but not unrelated, either."

Parker knelt by the skeleton. "Well, well, well. This acid soil usually eats away bones, but these were placed just right. It's a man—you can tell by the narrowness of the pelvic arch. His leg was amputated well before his death. See how the end of the bone has grown over? But then, there's a primitive wooden prosthetic there, preserved by the damp."

"The battle on the medallion," Michael said. "Perhaps he was wounded in it."

"That's not what he died from." Gently, Parker turned the skull in its muddy nest. "He was killed by a shot to the head. See the entry wound?"

A jagged hole in the back arch of the man's skull testified that he'd been taken from behind.

Parker trained his torchlight into the hole. "I do believe the bullet is still there—no other reason for a squashed bit of lead inside a chap's skull, eh? Probably killed him instantly."

"He wasn't walled up in here, then?"

"If he'd been trying to get out, you'd expect to find him lying next to the bricks. I think it was more a matter of his body being hidden here."

"Another murder?" groaned Paddington from the doorway.

"I think this one is old enough to be outside your jurisdiction," Parker told him. "Still, we'd best call Ripon."

"Might as well put that chap Ross on my payroll!" Paddington stamped away.

"You get on—I'll keep watch here," Rohan told Michael. His eyes strayed back down the tunnel, beyond the oxter.

"Thanks, mate." Michael gave Rohan his flask of tea, and along with Parker followed Connor, Lydia and Grace out of the tunnel. He stepped into the cellar of the lighthouse with a sense of relief and made his way up the uneven stairs and out into the light of day with an even bigger one. He closed his eyes against the sun, blurred by humidity as it was, and let the warm, damp air dispel the chill clinging to his body. This must be what Molly's claustrophobia felt like. Eagerly he inhaled the odors of the sea, traces of diesel from the marina, cooking food from the lighthouse pub.

"Michael." It was Molly's voice. Her arms embraced his rib cage, regardless of his mud-stained garments. "They're saying you stumbled on another body."

Opening his eyes, he feasted them on her face and form, then rested his chin on her hair. Her perfume, the scent of a garden in June, wafted into his nostrils and the tight muscles of his face relaxed. "It's a very old body, just a skeleton, in a little room off the tunnel. That's where Willie found the coins. There were only the four."

He looked around to see the customers of the lighthouse pub watching him; the flagstoned veranda with its tables provided ringside seats. Luann Krebs was rolling out her crime scene tape, a job she was getting very good at by now. A sound like chirping crickets was Fred Purnell's and Tim Jenkins's cameras clicking in harmony. Michael was starting to think of them as the gruesome twosome.

"No more coins?" asked Fred.

"Can I quote you on that?" Jenkins prodded.

"Go right ahead," Michael told them, "if it will keep

folk from blundering about in the tunnels causing rock-falls and leaving rubbish."

Fred turned to Molly. "What's this I hear about someone dropping a basket on your head?"

"What?" Michael's entire body tensed as she relayed to him what had happened.

"Thank goodness for Addison's peripheral vision," Molly concluded, but from her glance to Jenkins and Fred, Michael knew she hadn't told him everything. "Tim, did I see you with Aleister at the Café?"

"Had us a nice leisurely lunch. He's trying to convince me there's some plot by the townsfolk to make his family look bad and is even offering an exclusive interview about it, for a price. But then, he was paying for the food, so I listened to him until I'd had my pudding."

"Oooh," Fred said. "Aleister as master of mayhem. I like that… Ah! Dr. Parker! Over here!"

Parker was trying to slip away down the steps to Dockside Avenue. At Fred's cry, he doubled his speed, leaping down the stairway and across the car park, spry as a mountain goat.

Tim pursued him, chiming, "How about a statement, Doc?" A few members of Tim's crew followed, while the crowd of locals and tourists stood postulating scenarios involving gold, curses and murders.

As if he *did* have a sixth sense, Liam McKenna, black eyes sparkling, materialized to hand out more flyers. "What's hidden in these tunnels? What do the powers-that-be here in Blackpool not want you to know—that the curse has claimed another life? A miasma of evil permeates the secret passageways, flowing out into the streets."

From her place in front of the lighthouse door, Krebs gave him her worst scowl and took up a stance, fists knotted at her sides, like a tae kwan do champion facing a challenger.

Liam waved, fingers waggling, and continued working the crowd.

Taking advantage of the distraction, Michael and Molly hurried down the steps and didn't stop until they stood in the lee of the bicycle shop. From inside came Dylan's voice extolling the virtues of multiple gears and braking systems, but for once Michael didn't want to talk to him. "I take it Jenkins was with Aleister when a psychopath was chucking baskets at you?" he asked Molly.

"Yes. And he was with Aleister when someone called—a man—and said I should take that flower basket seriously, and next time, neither you nor I would walk away. I didn't recognize the voice—the accent reminded me of Aleister's, to a degree, but Aleister and Tim were right in front of me."

"Was the accent like Trevor's?"

"Sort of. I did find out that Liam and Holly were with Margaret when Willie was killed, and that Aleister was in the churchyard, ditto. I'm still assuming we've only got one killer, not a pack of them going around offing Willie and Daisy, and trying to scare me…" Molly wiped a sheen of sweat from her forehead and lifted the hair off the back of her neck.

The gesture would have fanned Michael's senses, if they hadn't been so thoroughly chilled by other matters. Like death, and the fear of it. "The villain's after us now."

Molly forced a smile. "You're getting a reputation for being nosey."

"Me? No one's dropping baskets on me!"

"Not yet. Don't hold your breath." Molly tensed against Michael's chest. "We can't let it stop us. In for a penny, in for a pound. Besides," she added, "I really, really want to know whodunnit. Especially now that they're doing it to me."

"What happens to you happens to me, love." Michael could only hope that, like cats, he and Molly had nine lives.

"Cheers!" shouted Dylan from around the corner, apparently sending a customer on his way.

"And there's still Dylan's name to clear," Michael breathed into Molly's hair.

She replied, "That is the point of the exercise, isn't it?"

"Yes, it is, though we've gotten a ways beyond Dylan. Look here." Michael pulled out his phone and showed Molly the photos of the bones and the medallion. "Half a tick, I can't go walking into the library like this, but I want to identify that medal."

"Won't the library be closed for the bank holiday?"

"I'm betting with all these tourists and treasure hunters, Mrs. Hirschfield wouldn't dream of not opening. She's probably never seen so many people in the library."

Molly laughed and pushed him on into the bicycle shop. He gave Dylan the short version of recent events as well as his rucksack and helmet, and borrowed a greasy rag to clean the mud from his boots.

When he went back outside, Molly was waiting. "You sure you want to waste the effort researching something that's old news? Or are you just getting ideas for your game?"

"You never know what's important," he retorted.

"Fine. I'll walk you to the library." She took his arm.

They talked about the man Daisy heard Willie arguing with, and how many other people she'd spoken to, and whether the third time in Blackpool would be the charm for D.I. Ross. By the time they arrived at the library, Michael was considering a mind-meld, just to save so much talking.

Molly rose on her tiptoes to kiss his cheek. "I'm going to the hospital to see if I can talk to Michelle. There may be something she hasn't told us, and with a new baby, maybe she'll have her priorities straight."

"Phone or text if you need me, eh?"

"And you, if you need me." Molly strode off down the street, leaving Michael to look at her retreating form and think, *I'll always need you, love.*

Trying not to imagine heavy flower baskets crushing Molly's beautiful head, Michael hurried through the vestibule and into the old Victorian mansion that housed the library.

Michael had been right about the library being open— and the number of people inside. Two people were reading recent *Blackpool Journals,* the pages threaded through long staves. Another inserted microfiches into the reader. A young woman worked at a laptop computer. An older gentleman in the window bay was actually reading a book.

Mrs. Hirschfield presided from behind the circulation desk. Michael made a beeline toward her. "Hullo, Mrs. H."

"Michael, nice to see you again. I hear you've been busy lately."

"Never a dull day in Blackpool," he replied.

He'd come to her because she knew all there was to know not just about Blackpool's history, but about general history, as well. Finding a photo on his phone that showed the medallion without too much background, Michael extended it toward her. "I'm looking to identify this."

Mrs. Hirschfield's clawlike hand—she made Alice

Coffey look plump—grabbed his wrist and angled the phone so she could see it. "That's a Tenerife Medallion!"

"Tenerife? In the Canary Islands?"

"One and the same. The medallions were struck to commemorate the Battle of Santa Cruz de Tenerife in 1797. That's the one where Admiral Nelson lost his right arm. Don't think he was an admiral at the time, mind you. Or that losing his arm slowed him down any." She tilted her head like a bird inspecting a worm. "Where'd you find that?"

"In the tunnels. Long story."

"One involving Willie Myners's gold coins, I expect. Or Charles Crowe's gypsy gold?"

"Could there be any connection between Charles Crowe's gold and this medallion?" Michael asked.

"Well, Charles Crowe was serving with Nelson at the age of fourteen—they grew up fast in those days—not so many made it to my age, ha!" Mrs. Hirschfield bustled out from behind the counter and led Michael to a bookshelf, where she selected a book.

Beyond the shelf gleamed the glass case holding Charles Crowe's model of Blackpool, with miniature versions of Havers Customs House, the old town hall, the Mariner's Museum and St. Mary's Church. There were even models of Crowe's warehouses with their simple clapboard-and-stone walls and roofs, along with tall-masted ships at anchor in the harbor. A small Glower Lighthouse stood on Dockside Head.

Crowe had renovated, not built, the lighthouse. It was so old its origins were lost in the mists—or, more appropriately, the sea frets—of history. A room just beneath and beyond it would have been a logical place for Charles to hide his ill-gotten gold. But there had been only four coins in the room. In the tomb.

Michael took several steps forward, fascinated by the model's wealth of detail. The tiny columns were fluted, the windows framed, the roofs covered by micro-slates. Even the parapet of the lighthouse was ringed by a tooth-pick-size railing, and lilliputian panes of glass encased the light itself.

There was something about that model… Michael raised his phone and took several photos. When he had a chance to catch his breath, he'd enlarge and manipulate them, try to figure out just what intrigued him so much.

"Hey, Michael!" Mrs. Hirschfield spoke in a hoarse whisper.

Michael forced his attention away from the glass case and walked back to the table. Mrs. Hirschfield handed him a book with a photograph of the same medallion. "This it?"

"Yes, that's it." The picture was in black-and-white, but the trees, the ships, the smoke, the inscription, "Shared Losses All Round," were unmistakable. "Could Crowe have served in the battle?"

"No, he was twenty-eight in 1797, had been a civilian ship owner for five years—well, there's an outside chance…" She flipped to another page. "Nelson was at Tenerife to intercept the Spanish treasure ships coming in from the Americas. With his taste for treasure, maybe Crowe was there, as well. He had his fingers in a lot of pies, not just ones in Eastern Europe."

"Or maybe the medallion has nothing to do with him at all." *And neither does the body,* Michael added to himself.

An elderly woman, probably younger than Mrs. Hirschfield, entered the library and walked up to the desk. The librarian thrust the book into Michael's hands. "Here you are. You've got a good head for puzzles, you'll solve this one, too. Tell Molly hello—oh, and thank her for writing up the grant to fund the library reading program."

"I will," said Michael, and made a note to ask Molly to tackle the issue of getting the library more computers.

Mrs. Hirshfield strolled toward the woman, leaving Michael with the book and his thoughts.

He set the book down as his eye strayed to the shelf and landed on one particular spine. Black words on a red-and-yellow dust jacket read, *History of Wallachia: The Sign of the Dragon.*

The name Dracula, Michael knew, was a form of *dragon.* He pulled the book out and paged quickly through it.

There was the story of Vladislav III, who had minted the gold coins. His sixteenth century had been turbulent. So had the seventeenth, eighteenth and nineteenth centuries, with Wallachia sometimes allied with the Ottoman Empire based in modern-day Turkey, sometimes struggling for independence from it. The Treaty of Adrianople in 1828 had allowed Wallachia to trade outside the Ottoman Empire, signaling substantial economic growth. That was the era of Charles Crowe, a man focused mostly on economic growth of the personal sort. Michael turned to the index.

Crowe, Charles, page 237. *Aha.* Crowe had very briefly represented a British trade delegation to Wallachia. A man like him would have seen a time of unrest as a time of opportunity. He had probably played dangerous, clever and lucrative games—someone had paid him in gold to do something he didn't do, or he'd transported gold between factions but took it for himself. As for the gypsies…

In the index, Michael read several references to

powerful Romany clans, but nothing that tied them to Britain, let alone to its envoy, Crowe.

Crowe might have earned his gold quite honorably, but if so, why hadn't he allowed his family access to it? Why were the modern-day Crowes still protecting it? Where did gypsies or Romany or any aggrieved Wallachian family come into the picture? And, for that matter, was the treasure the whole story, or was there more going on here than the glitter of gold?

Now that he had something to go on, Michael's next step was to take his questions to the Internet.… His pocket vibrated. He took out his phone and read a text message from Molly. I may have found Willie's burglar. Meet me at the Café.

What? Jamming his phone back into his pocket, he hurried out the door. With any luck, Molly's suspect would be a sandwich and a pint. Instead of growling at the thought, his stomach sank.

Molly, alone with a possible criminal. He didn't like that at all.

CHAPTER SEVENTEEN

MOLLY CROSSED MARINER STREET, her mind busy with crime—too much of that—and punishment—not so much, yet—and stepped through the front doors of St. Theresa's.

The temperature inside wasn't much cooler than outside. The warm air congealed in runnels of sweat down her temples and back. She thought of the huge bathtub at Thorne-Shower Mansion, of her selection of soaps and candles. But she was on another scent right now.

She found Michelle Crookshank propped up on several pillows watching a cartoon, a red-faced and blanket-swaddled baby lying in the plastic cradle at the foot of the bed. "Hello," Molly said. And, with as much enthusiasm as she could muster, "What a beautiful baby! Congratulations!"

Michelle looked around, her eyes beyond weary, almost shell-shocked. Her pale lips didn't quite manage a smile. "Thanks."

There was only one bouquet of flowers in the room—probably Geoffrey's—wilting on the windowsill. "Sorry to break in on you right now, but, well, yesterday morning…"

"When Willie died." Michelle fell back against the pillows. "Yesterday morning. What about it?"

Do the girl a favor and get to the point. "You told

us you were home making sandwiches for your father's clients. But you were seen walking around the marina."

"Yeah. I lied. Thought I'd save myself the trouble of being a witness."

"Are you a witness? Did you speak to Willie at all?"

"No. He was with Naomi—that's what Jamey Grandage said, leastways. Willie was with Naomi, and there I was out to here with his baby. I reckon he was planning to leave with her, not me. No need to saddle himself with a kid, eh? Then someone pinched his coins. Too bad. So sad." Her voice caught.

"Did you see him at all on Sunday morning?"

"Did I kill him, you mean? Take my kid's father away?" Michelle looked toward the cradle. "Poor little mite. He'll be better off without his dad."

"He has a fine grandfather," said Molly.

"Yeah." Michelle's exhaustion rolled off her in waves.

"Did you notice anyone on Willie's boat? Or even in the area?"

"That yacht's in the area, ain't it? All the men in their twee striped shirts, swabbing the decks, polishing the brass, carrying on crates of fruit and veg and wine. And there's Willie's boat, drifting away into the harbor."

"You saw the boat drifting away?" She must have walked by right after the murder.

"Yeah, me and one bloke on the dock."

"A bloke on…" Molly stood up straighter. "Who was it?"

"I dunno. He was crouched in the shadow behind Grandage's, half-hid by some barrels and that fishing net."

Behind Grandage's…

"All I could see was a dark blue coat," said Michelle.

A dark blue coat. How many people in Blackpool had dark blue coats? "Did he have blond hair?" Molly asked.

"Might have had. Might not. Couldn't properly see, could I, through the net." Michelle looked again at the television screen. The baby stirred and emitted a tiny sound, like a kitten.

"Thank you." Molly backed away, skirting the curtain that partitioned off Michelle's bit of the ward. She should send flowers. Or a basket of tiny garments. Or plain hard cash. Something Michelle could use, though right now Michelle could use some rest.

Molly walked out into the sultry afternoon, visualizing that strip of dark blue cloth caught in the bracket of Willie's desk lamp. Paddington had assured them that Fotherby had secured the crime scene. Did that mean he'd collected the strip of cloth? Or did that mean he hadn't done anything more than take the gold coins?

It was past time for D.I. Ross and his team from Ripon to test that bit of cloth against—what? A yachtsman's jacket? A police constable's uniform? A posh Savile Row suit? Aleister could have ransacked Willie's flat. Just because he hadn't killed Willie or sent a basket crashing down so close to Molly that if it hadn't been for Addison Headerly—

She stopped dead. Addison had been wearing a dark blue frock coat that day at the Festival, the same day as Willie's break-in. Maybe he'd arranged Molly's falling-basket save with a confederate, to deflect suspicion. But why? No one had been suspicious of him to begin with.

Had the police been chasing wild geese for two days?

Well, Molly told herself, sometimes it took a wild goose to catch a wild goose. She made such a sharp turn on Coffey's Way that she caused a three-tourist pile-up behind her. "Sorry," she called over her shoulder, and sped on up the steep alley, the cobblestones breaking into steps every few paces.

The Clean and Fresh Launderette was a popular spot. Today several youths lounged in the plastic chairs, chatting and listening to their iPods, while the washing machines sudsed and the dryers whirled. In an alcove at the back sat Sandy Mason behind her sewing machine, her dark brown eyes peering out over the top of glasses.

"Hello, Sandy. The air seems fresher in here than it does outside." Molly glanced past Sandy to a row of garments bagged in plastic.

"It's the new detergent packets," Sandy said. "I don't have anything of yours just now, Mrs. Graham."

"I'm looking for a navy blue coat or jacket."

"There's the only one I've got. It's not Mr. Graham's, though. He had that black leather the one time but I repaired the cigar burn."

The burn in his leather jacket served Michael right for smoking a cigar. Molly stepped around the table and lifted a plastic-swathed dark blue coat from the rack. All right! It was a Regency-era frock coat! Her gamble had paid off. "Did this have a rip in the sleeve or hem?"

"That it did, a strip torn clean away from the side seam. I pieced in another bit of fabric and it didn't turn out too bad. Probably not up to Lydia's standards, though."

"Lydia Crowe? She brought this in?"

"She brings me things all the time. Last week had me raising the hem of a brand-new frock all to glory." Sandy raised a needle and thrust a thread through the microscopic eye. "Lydia was with the young man who brought it in."

Molly checked the paper tag. "Edison Hatherly?"

"Thought that's what he said—he was mooning over her, mind. Wasn't paying me any attention at all. Do you know him?"

"Yep. I sure do." Reading the tag, Molly pulled out her phone and tapped out the number penciled on it. It had better not be Lydia's phone number.

It wasn't. "Addison," said the young man's voice.

"Hi. This is Molly Graham. I—um, my husband and I would like to talk to you. Can you meet us at the Café at, say, three-fifteen? Quarter past three," she added, in case he couldn't tell American time.

"Could do, but there's no need to thank me, I was merely there when the basket fell—"

"See you there!" With an internal *woo-hoo!*, Molly hung the coat back up. She should be thanking him, not raking him over the coals. But a sleuth had to do what a sleuth had to do.

"Thank you. You've been a big help!" Molly called to Sandy's puzzled face, and dashed out of the Launderette as quickly as she could while texting Michael.

Passing Fotherby preening himself on the corner, she spotted her better half—make that her other half—standing outside the Café.

Between them, up the middle of the street, walked Liam McKenna shepherding a group of tourists. His spiel had already evolved from the one he'd been giving outside the lighthouse. "Sea captain helping Charles Crowe to hide the gypsy gold. But the curse struck him down where he stood, froze his heart and made his tongue cleave to the roof of his mouth!"

Never mind the skeleton's one leg and the bullet inside his head, Molly thought.

Just behind Liam's group came a second one, this one guided by Holly in her "Gypsies, Tramps and Thieves" persona, whether genuine or not. Funny how all but two of her group were men—including the younger of the Crowe brothers, Aubrey.

Martin Dunhill was walking along at the end of the procession. Molly darted across the street toward Michael, noting that his eyes, too, followed Holly.

Wait. She glanced back around. That wasn't Dunhill at all, but a similarly heavy-jowled, dark-haired man dressed in a seaman's blue jacket. He was walking along with two other men clad in Hopewell's traditional striped tops, all three wearing red neckerchiefs. They were on shore leave, she supposed.

She stepped over the curb and slipped her arm around Michael's.

"Willie's burglar?" he asked. His suspicious scan of the area included Fotherby, both McKennas and Hopewell's crew members.

"Michelle admitted she was walking around the marina on Sunday morning. She saw Willie's boat drifting away. And she saw a man in a dark blue coat watching from behind Grandage's, from the exact spot where Daisy was murdered Sunday night."

"A dark blue coat? Like the strip of blue cloth caught by the bracket of Willie's lamp?"

"Yep. It's a long shot, I know, but…" She traced her train of thought to Addison's frock coat.

"Well done, Molly. There's an empty table on the balcony, quick." He and Molly claimed the table, ordered fish and chips and two beers—a pint of ale and a half-pint of lager—and had five minutes to discuss maritime history and Wallachian politics and how they affected the history and legends of Blackpool, before Molly spotted Addison.

The young man sat down and shyly accepted Michael's thanks for saving Molly's life.

The waitress served the beer and took Addison's order for a Coke. Molly drank deeply from her foam-flecked glass, filling her mouth with the paradoxically cool taste of sun-warmed barley and hops. Across the table, Michael's brilliant blue eyes sent a signal. *Get on with it.*

"Addison," she began. "How did you catch your frock coat on Willie Myners's desk lamp?"

He stared at her, the color draining so abruptly from his complexion that each freckle stood out like a bomb crater. "How did you know?"

"Long story. We're not going to turn you over to the police, just tell us why you broke in. What were you looking for?"

The waitress delivered the food and Addison's Coke. He took a swig and a deep breath. "When we were on the *Black Sea Pearl,* I heard Willie talking to Hopewell's first mate. Dunhill?"

"Dunhill," Molly confirmed.

Michael shook malt vinegar onto his planks of fish and thick-cut chips.

"Willie said he had a gold coin from the Crowe treasure," Addison went on. "Dunhill didn't believe him. But I thought, maybe he did have a coin, and maybe I could buy it from him—Aleister's always trying to quash rumors about that treasure. He's obsessed with the family reputation. Learned that at Ophelia's knee, I expect. I figured if I got the coin for Aleister, he'd put in a good word for me with Lydia and Ophelia."

"What happened at Myners's flat?" Michael asked between bites.

"I knocked. I heard someone inside, but no one answered the door. I tried the knob, but the door was already open. I went in. Someone ran down the back stairs. I caught a glimpse of him in the kitchen yard. Heavyset chap, dark hair—that first mate from the *Black Sea Pearl,* I think."

Molly and Michael nodded in unison. *Dunhill.*

Addison gazed into his glass. "I'm ashamed to admit I considered stealing the coin, if I could've found it."

Love was a harsh master, Molly concluded.

"But the flat had been ransacked. For all I knew, the coin was already gone. I started to look but I hardly had time to root around on the desk before someone knocked on the door so hard I feared he'd break it down."

Dylan. So Addison was the intruder Dylan had heard and then seen running away. But he claimed he wasn't the person who'd turned the place over, and Molly didn't doubt him. She wouldn't put it past Dunhill, though, to be searching for the coins.

"I caught my coat on the lamp bracket, but I was so frightened I just pulled it loose and ran down the back stairs. The chap at the door could've been the police. I'd seen P.C. Fotherby in the next street as I walked up and reckoned Daisy Coffey had phoned for him. She lived just next door."

Michael said, "It wasn't Fotherby who tossed the flat? He wasn't the chap you saw running through the yard?"

"Not unless he teleported himself from the street to the flat," Addison said.

First Dunhill, then Addison, then Dylan then the Grahams themselves. The scene at Willie's flat had resembled one from a Three Stooges routine. Daisy could have sold popcorn.

Daisy hadn't called the police, though. She'd seen Fotherby outside, too, and figured the situation was in hand.

Which it was, but in a way that favored Fotherby, not the law. He must have also heard the less-than-discreet conversation between Willie and Dunhill on the *Black Sea Pearl*. He'd given Dylan and the Grahams every chance to locate the coin for him, and had come up trumps when they'd found four.

"You promise you won't hand me over to the police?" Addison looked from Michael's sober face to Molly's.

He didn't need to know that without the original strip of cloth, the police wouldn't be able to prove a thing. "No, we won't. You can tell them yourself," Molly said, and snagged a bit of potato from Michael's plate.

Addison gulped his Coke and burped. "Sorry. I've made a mess of it all, haven't I? It's all about money."

"It usually is," said Michael.

"Aleister's even asked his solicitor about claiming Willie's gold."

"Is this the same solicitor who's going to sue Fred Purnell for spreading rumors that the gold exists?" Molly asked. "Trust Aleister to cover all his bases."

"No one's going to get rich off Willie's gold save the lawyers," Addison stated.

All Molly and Michael could do was raise their glasses and touch his in silent agreement. She upended her half-pint, draining the last of the golden lager into her mouth. From the corner of her eye she saw two police cars crawling through the pedestrians thronging Dockside Avenue. "Hmm. The team from Ripon is here. Again. Michael, Ross is going to want to talk to you, since you found the body."

"What body? Where?" Addison asked, probably the last person in Blackpool not to have heard about the new—albeit very old—murder case.

The Grahams quickly filled him in, then paid for the

food and accepted Addison's thanks for the Coke and for not marching him off in handcuffs. Then they ran.

By the time they reached Dockside Head, the squad cars were sitting in the car park below the lighthouse and a couple of constables were unrolling a second ribbon of crime-scene tape. Before the police could move the watching people back to a perimeter line much farther from the scene, the Grahams slipped by and up the steps.

The red-haired detective was now standing in the lighthouse door, his hands folded behind his back while Luann Krebs made her report. So bloated with importance that her barely convex chest almost touched the front of his suit, Krebs wound down with "And Michael Graham..." just as Michael's long legs carried him into the scene.

He introduced himself to the detective, adding, "And this is my wife, Molly."

"Detective Inspector Jason Ross," said the detective, his beak of a nose turning from one Graham to the other, taking their measure. With his red hair and freckles he reminded Molly of Addison after a self-confidence transplant, except he didn't speak in Addison's university-trained accent but in a soft Scots brogue. "You're the Grahams, are you now? I heard about your assisting the police in solving the theatre murder."

"Assisting the police" was often a euphemism for "under suspicion and being questioned," but Ross meant it straight. It was discomforting to learn that both her and Michael's names were permanently enshrined in the annals of the North Yorkshire Police Authority.

The constables, finished with the tape, climbed the steps. "Show my team the scene, please," Ross told Krebs.

Peeling herself away, she led the men into the lighthouse.

"D.I. Ross," Molly went on, "did your forensics team ever get any evidence from the break-in at Willie Myners's flat?"

"No. I was informed that P.C. Fotherby was seeing to it, but we never received a report."

"Well then," Michael said, but was interrupted by a stir in the kibitzing crowd, somewhere between the microphones and the cameras.

It had to be Paddington coming to protect his turf. Sure enough, the all-too-familiar bearlike figure emerged from the throng and labored up the steps to the lighthouse. "Always in the thick of it, aren't you?" he asked, his baleful gaze landing like a wet towel on both Michael and Molly.

"More so than you know." Bracing herself and without naming her sources, Molly told him the whole story— Willie Myners's flat, Fotherby watching the place and taking the coins but not delivering any evidence to Ripon, the rumors going around town of his complicity in Willie's drug trade. Michael interjected the occasional fact-check.

Paddington's face darkened to its patented red-fruit shade. "You're saying that P.C. Fotherby is bent? On the take?"

Ross's face had changed neither expression nor color. "I wouldn't have thought there'd be enough profit selling drugs in such a small town to make bribery worthwhile."

A woman's voice said, "But you still don't know everything yet."

They looked around to see Luann Krebs emerging from the lighthouse, her eyes shining with zeal.

"If this is about those damnable coins," said Paddington. "Fotherby might have taken his own sweet time handing them in, but he said he'd been distracted by the festival, which is true enough, so I had a word in his ear about efficiency. But this…" His voice ran down into a sputter.

A glint in Ross's pale blue eyes registered the approaching figure of a raw-boned man in a constable's uniform. "That's the man himself, is it?"

"Yes," said Michael.

Ross gestured as subtly as a shepherd to his sheep dog. One of the constables still standing in the parking lot stepped into Fotherby's path and engaged him in conversation.

Smooth, Molly thought.

Paddington's eyes narrowed. "Krebs?"

P.C. Krebs stood to attention. "Sir. As I'm sure you're aware, there've long been reports of drugs trade all up and down the coast and into the interior, overseen by a group of villains in Newcastle."

"There is that," said Ross. "I've just seen a new report. The dealers are creaming off the drugs—pharmaceuticals, for the most part, with a bit of marijuana on the side—from legitimate shipments brought in from India and China. You're suggesting this Willie was your local agent?"

Before Krebs could answer, Michael interrupted. "Shipments? Like those made on vehicles belonging to Hopewell Transport?"

"Ah," Ross said.

Paddington looked back at Krebs. "Is Hopewell involved?"

"I've not yet pursued the case from the top down, just from the bottom up, so to speak," she replied. "The interaction between Willie Myners and P.C. Fotherby made me suspect Fotherby was bent. I followed him several times to Myners's flat…including Saturday afternoon. I have pictures of money and illegal substances changing hands between Fotherby and Myners."

Paddington stared, his throat emitting a sound like that of a teakettle on the boil.

"I was just about to hand in my report when Myners was murdered. But it's all on my computer, in a file titled 'Controlled Drugs Act'."

Molly nodded. So did Michael beside her. That's what Krebs had been up to, then. Finally, something that made sense.

"Well then," said Ross. "Inspector Paddington, is it possible that Fotherby killed Myners?"

"He had motive, whether he had the opportunity, I don't know," Molly said.

"D.I. Ross was talking to me," Paddington informed them, his face now the color of ripe cherries. "Fotherby was with me at the station Sunday morning, seeing to his paperwork, at the time of Willie's murder, and he was walking to the festival with me Sunday evening when Daisy was murdered."

Ross signaled again. The constable who had intercepted Fotherby moved aside and Fotherby climbed the steps to the lighthouse door. Paddington greeted him with a tight, "Douglas. May I have a word?"

Michael and Molly faded away, out of the line of fire. Michael stared up at the whitewashed cylinder of the lighthouse. Molly gazed into the distance. The blue of the sky was muted, as though covered by gauze, and darkened to Prussian blue where it met the sea. An early-evening sea breeze stirred the sultry air and rippled the water in the harbor.

Ross, too, had taken a step back while Paddington leaned into Fotherby's face, screaming his tirade, bits of spittle flying off his lips. Fotherby's heavy features lengthened and his mouth fell open. Gobbling, he replied, "Now, Guv'nor, you can't be thinking— I was waiting at Myners's flat to read him the riot act, tell him to shape up or ship out—ha-ha, ship out."

Paddington was not amused, the color of his face that of a red flag waved before a bull.

Fotherby's attempt at a smile evaporated. "Yeah, yeah, I was watching for Willie on Saturday—I can talk to the man, can't I, without breaking any laws?—I saw that chap from the *Pearl* go up the steps…"

Molly and Michael moved closer again.

"Martin Dunhill," said Fotherby. "He sneaked into the flat, didn't he?"

"Well, did he?" Paddington demanded.

Yes, Molly answered silently. That's who Addison saw. That was corroborating evidence.

Ross inspected the spit-shined leather of his shoes, but his ears twitched like a cat's.

"Yeah, it was Dunhill," Fotherby said. "Just caught a glimpse of him, with the neckerchief and all, but that's who it was. Then I saw that lad's been chasing young Lydia go in after him, and then Dylan—the murderer, right?"

Paddington didn't rise to the bait.

"And the Grahams, there." His voice rising to a sound like that of fingernails down a blackboard, Fotherby turned toward them.

Before he could speak, Molly told him, "Don't you dare blame us."

Paddington took so firm a grasp of Fotherby's collar that the constable's voice was choked off. "It's time you were seeing our cells from the inside. Come along." And, to Krebs, "Good job, lass. Good job."

Despite the condescending "lass," Krebs's thin face lit with a grin, one that grew even wider as Paddington dragged the now slumping Fotherby away.

CHAPTER EIGHTEEN

MICHAEL HAD BARELY exchanged a smile of satisfaction and relief with Molly before Rohan appeared in the lighthouse door. Squinting up at the sun, which was sinking toward the high ground to the west, he said, "Mon, I thought I'd missed the entire day and gone into the night. I wouldn't have made it without the tea, Michael, thanks."

"Meanwhile," Molly said, and filled him in from the medallion to Fotherby's fall.

"All right! One more copper off the streets—oh, sorry there, didn't catch the name. Rohan Wallace." Rohan extended his hand toward Ross, then, seeing how mud-encrusted it was, let it drop to his side.

He was so much grimier than Michael remembered. He wondered if Rohan had taken the opportunity to do some exploring on his own, despite the danger.

Ross introduced himself to Rohan, then pulled out a small digital recorder and proceeded to pump Michael and Molly for information. He walked them through the entire sequence of events at Willie's flat, Krebs interjecting a question or two of her own. By the time Ross had saved all the particulars, several men bearing boxes and bags were walking out of the lighthouse. Krebs danced attendance on them down the steps to their cars. Funny, Michael thought, how her body language had gone from pompous to self-confident.

"We'll be taking the bones and other evidence to the police station now, sorting out what needs to go on to Ripon. I'll suggest to D.C.I. Paddington that he interview this Addison Headerly." Ross traded his recorder for several business cards, handing them to Michael, Molly and Rohan. "Give me a shout if anything else happens, eh? Oh, and if you can recommend a B and B or hotel, I'd be obliged. I'm thinking I'll stop here for the night, have myself a good look round. Settling the events at Myners's flat is all to the good, but that was only the preliminary to two murders."

Molly said, "We have guest rooms at Thorne-Shower Mansion, Inspector, though it's a bit out of Blackpool proper."

"Yes, please join us." Michael visualized enlightening conversations about police procedure and more over drinks.

"We'll let our housekeeper know to expect you. Anyone can direct you to the house." Molly waved in the general direction of home.

"Thank you kindly." Ross's smile made a perfect rectangle below his nose, like a base beneath a column. With an affable but still professional nod, he followed his team and Krebs toward the police station, drawing quite a few of the onlookers with him. The cries of "Inspector, Inspector!" died away in the distance.

Rohan said, "The guy in the secret room is one murder Paddington and Ross won't be able to solve."

"I wouldn't be so sure," Molly told him. "I bet that murderer had the same motive as the man who murdered Willie—to get the gold coins."

"You said last night we needed to think outside the box," Michael replied.

"Well, yes. There's blackmail, as you mentioned earlier,

though ultimately that's about money, too. People do kill for love, or hate or to keep a secret hidden."

"A secret dealin' with a family reputation?" suggested Rohan.

"The bones in the tunnel may not have anything to do with the Crowes," Molly acknowledged, "but, darn it, that medallion indicates the same time period, and there were definitely Wallachian coins involved with that murder, too."

"Unless," said Rohan under his breath, "there's more to the story than the gold."

"Aleister Crowe can't have killed Willie," Michael reminded Molly. "You proved that yourself. There's only one possible name now."

"Yeah, that of a coin collector, treasure hunter and drugs dealer named Trevor Hopewell."

"Posh prat like Hopewell probably thought we'd assume he wasn't up to doing his own dirty work," muttered Michael.

"But it was Dunhill that snuck into Willie's flat," Rohan cut in.

"Sure," said Molly. "Dunhill could have been looking for the coins to sell to Trevor himself, take out the middleman. Or Dunhill could have told Trevor about the coins, and Trevor ordered Dunhill to shake Willie down for them."

"Hopewell also lied about visitin' Blackpool three years ago."

"And about having seen a Wallachian coin before," Molly said. "So what else has he been lying about?"

Michael replied, "Not about wanting to see the maps of sunken ships, not at all."

"That's it!" Molly exclaimed. "That's where I saw one

of Naomi's maps of Blackpool! On Hopewell's desk, along with charts of the coast."

"And he does have a big collection of weapons..." Michael's thought slipped down a dark alley and he tried to follow.

"Knives," Rohan said. "Like the murder weapon."

"The murder weapon *twice over*," said Molly. "If it's not Hopewell's Elizabethan knife, then what is it? If it is, then where is it? The police dive team searched the water around Willie's boat, and they dragged the area beneath the pier where Daisy was found..." Her brown eyes lit with the luster of amber. "Oh, boy. That would be genius."

"You're thinking that after killing Daisy, Hopewell chucked the knife into an area that had already been searched."

"Beneath Willie's boat," said Rohan. "It's been there less than twenty-four hours—should still be visible."

"Worth a shot." Michael galloped down the steps, across the car park and into the bicycle shop. It was easier to keep his diving gear there with Rohan's and Dylan's than to haul it all down from Thorne-Shower Mansion every time he wanted it.

Dylan was stooped over a bicycle tire. "Dylan!" shouted Michael. "We need the scuba kit!"

Rohan ran through the door after him and dumped his rucksack and Michael's flask behind the counter, next to the paraphernalia Michael had left there earlier. Molly made a third, her chest rising and falling very attractively beneath her T-shirt.

Dylan looked up, still holding a patch in one hand and a tube of glue in the other. "Right you are, but what—"

"We think the murder weapon's in the water beneath Willie's boat," Molly explained.

Dropping the patch and the glue, Dylan hurried to a storage locker. Within moments Rohan and Michael were back out on the street burdened with neoprene dry suits, swim fins, air tanks—and Dylan, who seized his own equipment and headed out, leaving Naomi in charge of the shop.

"Good luck," she called from the door, adding a quiet, "Please, please end this."

The three men and Molly pushed through the people thronging Dockside Avenue and the town square. Many of the vendors had given up and broken down their stalls, but others were still doing brisk business, among them Peggy Hartwick and her pastries and Thomas Clough and his meat pies. Rebecca Hislop, though, had folded her tents and stolen away. Flowers, Michael supposed, only held up so long, especially in this weather.

Although the sea breeze was easing the heat. At the *Black Sea Pearl*'s masthead, the Jolly Roger gave a desultory flutter. The water in the harbor rippled and splashed against the pilings of the pier.

Molly held the oars while Dylan, Rohan and Michael piled their things into Dylan's little boat. But when she said, "Oh, hello," Michael looked up.

Geoffrey Crookshank's seamed and stubbled face peered over the edge of the pier. "What's all this?"

"We're diving for the murder weapon," Michael answered.

"Let me help you then, lads. I'll steady the boat while you dive. Willie was a rotter, but he was my grandson's father, and I'd like to see his killer behind bars." Geoffrey's large red hands took the oars from Molly's small white ones. She handed them over with a smile of thanks, no doubt aware that despite her frequent workouts, she lacked upper body strength.

"Thank you." Michael made room in the boat and Geoffrey clambered down a ladder—as the tide ebbed, boats rode farther below the decking of the pier.

Unfortunately, taking Geoffrey on board meant no room for Molly. With a brave smile, she threw off the mooring ropes, stepped back and gazed around. And stopped, her brows rising.

Even as the boat's outboard engine turned over and began thrumming, Michael followed the direction of her eyes. A masculine shape stood at the railing of the *Black Sea Pearl,* topped by a glistening white yachtsman's cap. Trevor Hopewell.

The man Michelle saw behind Grandage's hadn't been wearing a hat, or so Molly reported. But that proved nothing. It was the man's dark blue coat that was important—not the blue strip of fabric caught in Willie's desk lamp, although that had been a useful diversion.

Hopewell had a navy blue jacket. So did Martin Dunhill. So did others of Hopewell's crew, like the ones Michael had seen walking along with Holly McKenna. But it was Hopewell who had means, motive and opportunity. And if he wanted to stand there watching while Michael, Rohan and Dylan—the man he was happy to send to jail in his place—proved his guilt, then fine.

Michael waved to Molly. She looked back at him just in time to respond with a wave of her own, annotated by a grin. Dylan, having guided the boat to a spot near Willie's shabby cabin cruiser, cut the engine.

Leaving Geoffrey at the oars, fine-tuning their position, Michael, Dylan and Rohan pulled on their neoprene suits. Zippers and seals, fins, regulators, masks—within minutes the three men were rolling off the gunwales into the water.

The water closed over Michael's head and its chill sent

a shock wave through his body. He blinked at the sudden plunge from daylight to dusk. Slowly, methodically, he took a breath of stale air from his mouthpiece and swam toward the bottom of the harbor. The lumpy expanse of mud was broken not only by jutting ribs of bedrock, but also by the regular shapes of man-made debris—wood planks, an anchor, a cement block, a broken chain.

Michael blinked up at the underside of Dylan's boat, the oars like wings. The sleek chevrons of Willie's cabin cruiser and the *Pearl*—large as a basking whale—hung nearby. Each of the other boats in the marina became less distinct the farther away it was, and the pier itself diminished like an exercise in perspective as he went deeper until all was consumed by the blue-green-brown shadow of the sea.

A prickle ran down his back, not water leaking into his suit, but his senses alerting him to shapes moving in those shadows.... There was nothing beyond fish and other sea creatures, Michael told himself. Not even the mermaids he was depicting in his new game. He forced his attention to the search.

Dylan and Rohan were quartering the area near the pier, fading in and out like ghosts. Every now and then one of them would pull the odd tree branch or whiskey bottle from the mud with a small explosion of silt. Flexing his legs, Michael, too, coasted along, trying to distinguish the shapes.

That long stone trough looked like a sarcophagus, right down to the rounded end. And there—a human form? He thrust himself closer, and saw that it wasn't even as interesting as an old bowsprit, just a plastic mannequin from a clothing store.

Despite his gloves, his hands were growing cold. His ears reverberated hollowly with the sound of deep water and his own breath. *Come along, come along, we've got to find it. It's got to be here!*

Again, Michael looked up, taking his bearings. There was Willie's boat. There was the pier, its pilings wearing flowing skirts of seaweed that camouflaged the high- and low-tide marks.

He examined the mud beneath him. Two beer cans. A sudden spatter of little fish. A long, dull gleam…

There it was! Michael fumbled at the evocative shape, his hands stiff, then grasped it and held it up to the others.

An Elizabethan dirk or dagger, its wire-wrapped handle emitting a furtive gleam of gold.

Rohan made a triumphant gesture. Dylan pointed heavenward, either in gratitude or to say, *Let's get out of here.* In a clump, they swam back to the boat, levered themselves up the ladder and tumbled onto the deck.

Before Michael could even remove his mouthpiece, Geoffrey was pointing toward the pier. "There's something caught on that piling, at the high water mark. Can you see it?"

Working his lips and mouth, inhaling the free air, Michael peered in the direction Geoffrey pointed. A reddish blotch like a misshapen starfish clung to the gray wood. "I'll check it out. In the meantime, here, have a care."

He handed the knife—the murder weapon—to Geoffrey. Geoffrey held it between thumb and forefinger, his arm extended, the way he'd hold a live grenade.

Michael's hands were too cold to manipulate his phone. He searched the decking of the pier, meaning to content himself with an enthusiastic wave and a thumbs-up at Molly.

She was no longer standing where she'd been when they set out. Where had she gone? And why?

"You looking for the missus?" asked Geoffrey. "She was having a blether with Montcalm."

"Oh, thanks." Of course Owen Montcalm would come to see what was happening in his marina. Good for Molly, keeping him distracted.

Starting the engine, Dylan maneuvered the boat up to the pier and partially beneath it. Michael balanced out over the gunwale and yanked a piece of cloth from where it had caught on the thornlike splinters of the piling. A good thing the tide was ebbing or Geoffrey would never have seen it. The dive team from Ripon probably hadn't noticed it because it was in the shadow of the pier and the tide had been high.

"That's one of the *Pearl's* neckerchiefs," said Rohan.

This time it was Dylan who extended forefinger and thumb. "It's barely touched the water. It's more damp than wet. Likely Hopewell dropped it when he leaped from Willie's boat to the pier—thought it went into the water when it actually blew onto the piling. Those brown stains…you suppose they're…"

Willie's blood. No one had to say the words.

Dylan found two clean plastic bags in a locker. Michael had Geoffrey slide the dagger into one, and Rohan slipped the neckerchief into the other. As Dylan guided the boat back to its usual docking place, Michael considered the weapon. Its wooden handle beneath its mesh of gold wire was somewhat swollen and buckled. If there was any blood caught in that mesh, or any fingerprints on it, only sophisticated forensics techniques could recover them. But the Ripon team had such techniques at its disposal.

Dylan killed the engine and left Geoffrey to see to the mooring ropes. Michael sealed the bags, then joined Rohan and Dylan as they tidied up their equipment and stowed it in the locker—no need to drag it all back to the bicycle shop, not just now.

"Thank you, Michael," Dylan said. "And Molly, too. This whole thing, Naomi vanishing, the murder, the coins, it's—"

"Not over yet," Michael finished for him. "Not until we've had an arrest. Let's get these bags to the police station." He turned toward the pier and froze.

Geoffrey was now talking with Owen Montcalm, but Molly was nowhere to be seen.

CHAPTER NINETEEN

MOLLY LOWERED HER HAND from waving good luck to Michael and the others. Her grin contracted into a sigh of frustration. There had to be something she could do.

Chatting with Owen Montcalm wasn't that something, she added to herself when the weather-beaten old man in his oil-stained coveralls strolled toward her. "Hullo there. What's himself up to?"

Even as she answered with something neutral, the hair on the back of her neck quivered. She spun around, toward the *Black Sea Pearl*.

Trevor Hopewell was still standing at the stern railing, peering across the harbor through a pair of binoculars, the lenses catching the muted light as the sun sank behind the hills to the west and shadow flowed over the town. Was he watching the divers? Did he suspect what they were looking for?

If he didn't now, his guilty conscience would very quickly work overtime once he saw the three men diving beside Willie's boat.

She had to distract him. And how better to do that than make sure he really didn't have the dagger that went with his Francis Drake costume? It was possible that Michael, Dylan and Rohan were searching for the wrong weapon. There was some risk that she could be walking into the lion's den, but if Michael did find Hopewell's knife on the ocean floor, he'd have the police on the boat in a shot.

Muttering some sort of excuse to Montcalm, she took a few hasty steps toward the yacht, then stopped and moderated her pace. Casual, she told herself. She was moving along because there was nothing to see in the harbor, that was all.

Molly loitered up the gangplank just as Martin Dunhill emerged from a hatchway. He smirked rather than smiled, his dark, beady eyes sweeping her up and down like an exploring hand. His jowls displayed less of a five-o'clock shadow than a ten-o'clock eclipse. If he went several days without shaving, he could easily play Wolfman to Aleister Crowe's elegant Dracula. Even his uniform was disheveled, his collar open.

His eyes returned to her face. "Good afternoon, Molly. To what do we owe the pleasure of this visit?"

Her own smile was refrigerated. "I'd like to speak to Trevor, please. I was hoping to take some photos of the costume he was wearing last night. I have a friend in public relations who's always looking for interesting photos of important people."

That was laying it on a bit thick, but the taking-photos ploy had worked for Michael. She pulled her iPhone from her pocket and held it up, "I'd also like a picture of the pocket watch on Trevor's desk. Is it a family heirloom? That's the sort of human-interest story my friend loves to blog about."

Whether Martin was convinced or not, he turned on his heel, clambered up a nearby stairway-cum-ladder and called to Trevor, "You've got a visitor, boss. Molly Graham. Wants to take photos."

Instantly, Trevor was wafting down the ladder, every tooth gleaming. "Molly. How good to see you. What's this about a photo-op?"

She repeated her spiel, this time with a much warmer smile and the merest flutter of her lashes.

"How clever of you to recognize Drake!" Trevor replied. "I'd be glad to show the outfit off for you. I had it made by the costumer who did the clothing for the Elizabethan *Blackadder* television series, for one, and a Helen Mirren film for another." Leaving Martin to do whatever he did on deck—skulk, Molly thought—Trevor escorted her below and out of sight of the recovery expedition at Willie's boat.

She paused beside the display case in the corridor. "The dagger you were carrying with your costume. Is it in the case here?"

"Ah, well, you see..." Trevor's chin wobbled. "The dagger has gone missing, more's the pity."

"It has? When did you last have it?"

"My valet tells me it was with the costume Saturday evening. It must have disappeared during the day on Sunday, whilst I was visiting Whitby. My valet had gone with the rest of my crew to enjoy the Seafaring Days festivities—with my permission, of course. My crew's very much taken with your lovely town."

"I bet they are."

"Your Inspector Paddington warned me of the local criminal elements when I first arrived. I can only suppose some villain made his way on board despite Martin's vigilance. I had a word with him about that."

Yes, we saw, in Michael's photo. But Trevor had lied before, Molly reminded herself. His pose as a charming upper-class twit was an act. He was a hardened drug dealer and murderer. And yet, if the expression of mingled chagrin, irritation and frustration creasing his chiseled features was only an act, he deserved an Oscar.

"Fortunately the dagger's not genuine, but an authentic

reproduction, if that's not a contradiction in terms," he went on with a deprecating smile. "It has a seven-inch Damascus blade with a haft made from oak taken from Drake's own ship, the *Golden Hind,* and wrapped with gold wire and tiny gold beads. I have a publicity still of it, if you'd like to have a copy. I'd be delighted for you to take some casual pictures of the entire costume. You said you'd like to take photos of the watch, as well? It was my grandfather's. It's somewhat battered to be a collector's item but of sentimental value even so. Please, come through."

Molly followed his extended arm into his office and stepped up to his desk. She raised her phone and took a couple of snaps of the watch.

Yes, there was Naomi's map, now folded away to one side of a nautical chart of the Yorkshire coast. Pointing toward it, she once again deployed her eyelashes. "I see you have the map drawn by one of our friends. Lovely, isn't it? Did you get it during your tour of the town?"

"No, no, it was sent to me before I came here. Helped to convince me to come, in a way. Although…" Again that deprecating smile, which now spread into a sheepish grin. "I must confess, Molly, I shaded the truth a bit: I've visited Blackpool before, to see the Wallachian coin displayed at the Mariner's Museum three years past. This is the sort of thing one keeps quiet to dissuade other collectors, mind you."

To say nothing of other treasure hunters, Molly thought, but she kept her own smile in place. Why was he suddenly being honest? Was he taunting her with his cleverness— you'll never catch me, ha-ha? Or did he genuinely have nothing to hide? If so, she and Michael had made some terrible miscalculation.

She tried a direct question. "So you were aware that more Wallachian coins have turned up here?"

"Can't pull the wool over your eyes, can I? Your reputation as a detective is well-deserved."

Yes, Fred had said something at the Customs House about her and Michael being detectives. *Thank you very much, Fred.*

Trevor tapped on the glass dome encasing the watch, making it sway back and forth like a reproving nod. "Willie Myners, of late but I gather less-than-lamented memory, contacted me via e-mail last week, then, at my request, he sent the map via Royal Mail."

"Did you talk to him about the coins?" Molly took a step to the side, so that she had an unobstructed path to the door, just in case Hopewell was bragging before he pounced. But his relaxed stance tended the other way, toward a door in the back of the room.

"No. In my caution I neglected to fill Martin in on the complete picture. He recognized Willie from his days in prison."

"You knew Martin had been in prison?"

Trevor's blue eyes widened. "Why, yes—not as a criminal, of course, but as a guard. He has a sterling record, one of the reasons I hired him to work security for me."

It was Martin Dunhill, then, who was the liar. He must have forged his references and hidden his record. He might well be using Trevor's transportation network to obtain and move drugs, Trevor being none the wiser. And yet, Trevor still had to be the murderer.

Didn't he? They'd seen Dunhill. He'd spoken to Trevor.

"Well, then." Hopewell walked on toward the rear door. "I'll adopt my Drake persona for you, if you don't mind waiting a bit. There's a fair number of fiddly little laces and the like. Feel free to ring for tea. My chef bakes a lovely currant scone."

"Thank you." Molly had no intention of ringing for tea or anything else. As soon as Hopewell shut his door, she was heading for the other one. Just as she slipped her phone into her pocket, though, she thought of the sinister warning she'd heard earlier...

She whipped her phone out again and found the number of that call. She remembered every word of the ever-so-posh voice: *I suggest you take that flower basket seriously. The next time, neither you nor your husband will walk away.*

Dialing the number again, she held her breath. But she heard nothing in the office or in the private quarters beyond, no pop tunes, no ring tones, no answer. If Trevor had used the numbers she and Michael had given him to threaten them, then his phone was not within earshot.

Michael could use his technological expertise to trace the call. So could Ross's people. But right now... Molly pocketed the phone again and sprinted out of the office, along the corridor, up the ladder and across the deck to the gangplank.

Michael stood at its foot, talking to Martin Dunhill. Or at him, rather. Martin stood with his arms crossed, not so much barring Michael's way as showing how little it mattered whether he passed or not.

Hearing Molly's steps down the gangplank, he turned and smirked again. "There she is, Michael. Untouched, it appears, although appearances can be deceiving."

"Don't I know it," Michael retorted. He took Molly's arm and guided her away from the yacht, shielding her with his own body from Martin's eyes. Several paces down the pier, he bent toward her ear and hissed, "What was all that in aid of? What if Hopewell had gone for you?"

"So you're allowed to go into danger and I'm not?"

"Neither exploring the tunnels nor diving is the equivalent of paying a visit to a murderer!"

"He was watching you and the others! If he'd seen you pulling up the dagger—which he did lose— Did you find it?"

"Yes, that we did. Dylan's gone home, but Rohan's on our cabin cruiser. He phoned Ross and is keeping an eye on the dagger. And on one of Hopewell's neckerchiefs, as well. A bloodstained neckerchief. We spied it caught beneath the pier."

They glared at each other a moment, then the tension broke. "If it's any help," Molly said with a rueful smile, "I never really felt as though I was in danger. Trevor was still working his charm offensive."

"*Offensive* is the word," replied Michael, but ceased and desisted while she told him about Dunhill's lies, and Trevor coming to Blackpool to begin with because Willie had e-mailed him.

She finished, "Willie could have used one of the public terminals at the Jade Dragon to search for coin collectors and then sent the message. Or maybe, when he showed his coins to Charlotte, she said something about Hopewell wanting to buy the one Alfie Lochridge borrowed from the British Museum."

"Just because Hopewell admitted he lied about the coins doesn't mean he's not the murderer. If he isn't, then who is?"

Molly looked around to see Trevor walking out onto the deck of the *Pearl* in his full Francis Drake outfit. Martin Dunhill slouched toward him.

"You said yourself…" Michael murmured, working

it out the way he'd run through a game scenario. "You said that every bit of evidence pointing to Hopewell also points to Dunhill. We've even got the photo of Hopewell angry with him over the lost knife, just as we thought."

"But Martin can't have been in two places at once. Rebecca saw him at the festival at the time of the murder. I saw him buying a pie from Thomas Clough with my own eyes. And he was right in front of us, talking to Trevor. Wasn't he? By now I'm wondering if I know my own maiden name."

"Sullivan," Michael said.

"Well, yeah…" Molly had the distinct feeling a thread was dangling before her, if only she could grasp it.

On the yacht, Martin answered Hopewell's query by silently pointing out Molly standing beside Michael on the pier. Trevor turned and waved.

The thread whisked through her fingers. "Uh-oh. I'd better come up with some excuse for running out on him."

"There's one just there," said Michael, pointing to D.I. Ross.

The detective was working his way through yet another Other Syde tour, a raven in a drift of confetti. As he strode down the pier, he glanced up at the Elizabethan apparition on the deck of the *Pearl* and for a fraction of a second his pace faltered.

Molly thought she detected a smile playing at the corners of his mouth, but all he said was, "Good afternoon, Mr. Graham, Mrs. Graham. You've recovered the murder weapon, I believe?"

"Yes," Michael said.

Molly motioned to Trevor, pointing to Ross and spreading her hands in a gesture of, *Sorry, something's come up.* He offered her a conciliatory wave. Beside him, Martin offered nothing but a black look. It didn't matter whether either man remembered Ross from yesterday's Scene of Crimes operations. Events were moving along too fast to dissemble now.

Michael escorted Molly and Ross to the Grahams' own cruiser and sat them down in the tiny cabin, where Rohan was faithfully guarding the two plastic bags.

Ross lifted one, then the other, and questioned the men about where they'd found the contents. "The medical examiner dug out a bit of granular gold, a tiny bead, from Daisy Coffey's wound, just as he did from Willie Myners's. There's no doubt this is the weapon that killed them both. As for that neckerchief…" His thin lips curved downward, boding a hard time for the dive team that *didn't* notice it, high tide or no high tide.

Molly chimed in with the story of Trevor and Francis Drake, of Martin and his alibi. "At least, it looked like him buying a pie at Clough's, the navy blue suit, the white shirt, the neckerchief. Though he was wearing a hat when he came up to us and Trevor. But it was a sunny day."

Ross considered the bag holding the damp, stained red scarf. "How many of these are about, do you reckon?"

"Quite a few," said Rohan.

Michael added, "Hopewell's got his men dressed as seafaring clichés, but then, that's why they're clichés. Everyone recognizes them."

"Recognizes them," said Molly. Her thread of thought flittered across her senses and then knotted.

"That's it! That's why poor Daisy used her own blood to write a number two on the wood beside her!"

"You saw that 2, as well, did you?" Ross asked. "I've been wondering what that means."

"It means there are two murderers?" hazarded Rohan.

"No, two *men*. There was a guy walking along behind Holly McKenna earlier today," Molly said, "wearing one of Trevor's seaman's uniforms, a dark blue jacket and a neckerchief. I thought at first I recognized Martin Dunhill, but then realized he only looked like him."

"I saw him on the tour, too," Michael said. "I was trying to remember where I'd seen him before. He was standing with Martin when we left the yacht Saturday afternoon."

And I thought you were looking at Holly. Molly said, "That's right. They don't resemble each other that much when you put them side by side, but if you dressed the second one in clothes like Martin's and put a baseball cap on him to hide his features…"

"Hang on," said Rohan. "You're sayin' this second guy is the murderer?"

"No, no, no. I'm saying he's the decoy. *He* was the man buying the pie. He's the one who was wearing a neckerchief while reminding Trevor of his phone call. At the same time, Martin was on the yacht cleaning himself up after murdering Willie with the knife he stole from Hopewell."

"Meaning to fit Hopewell up?" Ross's face was tight with thought. "Or perhaps Dunhill simply didn't care if Hopewell was blamed."

"Either way," Michael said, "that's why there was a neckerchief in the water by Willie's boat, when Hopewell doesn't wear one. Dunhill used his to wipe his hands or the knife—or both—but the wind probably blew it away from him."

"But how did Daisy Coffey figure it out?" asked Ross.

"Daisy was always watching Willie's flat—it was her telly—maybe she saw both men in the flat."

"This other chap needs locating." Ross stood up. "The drugs trade must have been their motivation, since Martin didn't seem to know about the coins—at least at first."

"No, he didn't," Molly confirmed. "Hopewell ordered the yacht to Blackpool for Seafaring Days, but he neglected to tell Martin why."

"Also it's a wee bit counterproductive to kill a man who knows where a treasure is hidden," Ross added. "So the coins were another diversion. This was about the drugs all along." He swung his attention to Molly. "Where's this pie seller of yours?"

Molly said, "He was at his stall an hour ago."

Tucking the evidence bags under his arm, Ross led them off the Grahams' small boat, past Trevor's large one—Molly scanned the railing, but saw no one she recognized—and into the square.

Thomas Clough was still dispensing his crusty, gravy-soaked meat pies, although his stainless-steel trays were now almost empty. Silently, stern-faced, he handed a customer his change and without shifting expression turned to Ross, Michael, Molly and Rohan. "Can I help you?"

Ross held up his warrant card. "D.I. Jason Ross, investigating the murders of Willie Myners and Daisy Coffey. You were at this stall Sunday morning round half past ten?"

"Yes."

"Did you see one of Trevor Hopewell's crew members walking about the area? Did he buy a pie from you?"

Clough gazed at the masts of the *Black Sea Pearl* rising above all the others, then back at Ross. "Yes."

Michael produced his phone. After a moment fingering the screen, he angled it so Clough could see. From the side, Molly glimpsed the photo of Trevor having words with Martin over the disappearance of the knife. "Was it this man?"

Clough considered. Finally, he said, "No. He was like to this one, right enough, but no. That's never the same one."

"Gotcha!" exclaimed Molly beneath her breath.

Michael pocketed the phone.

"Thank you. We'll be taking a statement soon as may be." Ross started toward the *Pearl* again. His hand that wasn't securing the knife and the neckerchief held his phone to his face as he laid out orders in full outline form.

Clough returned to his trays, but not without casting an eye at the transparent mistiness gathering over the harbor and blotting out the remaining daylight. "We're in for a fret, I reckon."

Rohan grinned at Michael and Molly. "It's not that Martin Dunhill was in two places at the same time. It's that there were two of him. Good going!"

Ross stowed his phone and looked over his shoulder. "Well done, the pair of you."

But Molly wasn't about to breathe a sigh of relief, not yet. As Ross increased his pace, she pulled Michael into a fast trot after him.

CHAPTER TWENTY

TAKING MOLLY'S HAND and checking to make sure Rohan was still with them, Michael hurried after Ross. Well done, yes, but they had yet to actually apprehend either man.

What had Clough said? *We're in for a fret.* He wasn't joking. A mist was rising off the water and clotting into cloud. Already the horizon was matted with fog.

The two uniformed officers from the Ripon team ran past them to Ross's side, Luann Krebs on their heels. Ross handed the evidence bags to Krebs and sent her back to the station to bring Paddington up to speed. She opened her mouth as though to protest at the task, but one cool glare sent her scurrying away.

He told the other officers to accompany them up the gangplank and onto the deck of the *Black Sea Pearl*.

Trevor Hopewell popped out of a hatchway like a genie out of a bottle, still dressed in the doublet, hose and off-the-shoulder cloak. His golden head resting on the white ruff reminded Michael of a roast suckling pig on a platter. All Trevor needed was an apple in his mouth, which went from the crescent of an affable smile to an O of astonishment when Ross displayed his warrant card.

"D.I. Ross, Mr. Hopewell, investigating the murders of Willie Myners and Daisy Coffey."

"Ah—I've already spoken with the authorities about—"

"You have a man named Martin Dunhill in your employ."

"Yes, I do. If you wish to speak with him—"

"Are you employing another man as well, one who looks a great deal like him?"

"Dark hair," Molly interjected. "Black beady eyes. Heavy jowls. We've seen him wearing Martin's uniform."

"Have you now?" Trevor replied. "Whyever would he be doing that?"

"To pose as Martin," answered Michael.

"So he could alibi Dunhill for Willie Myners's murder," Molly went on.

Ross waited.

Trevor's already fair complexion went ashen. "My word, if that isn't a turn up! You must be referring to Gary Dunhill, Martin's brother from Newcastle. Martin asked if he could spend his holiday weekend here on the yacht. He's swanking it, I expect. Martin, that is. Not everyone's as fortunate to have as good a position as he does. Some cheek, though, dressing Gary in one of my uniforms!"

"Where are these men?" asked Ross.

"Um, well…" Trevor looked from bow to stern and back again. "Martin was here a few moments ago—you saw him yourselves, Molly, Michael—and, Rohan, is it?"

Rohan nodded politely.

"As for Gary…"

Voices rang out from a nearby doorway, and a man plunged through it, knocking two more aside. *Gary.*

Everyone rushed forward, piling into a small chart room. Gary stood behind a table, cornered. The two constables seized him and, after a brisk scuffle, subdued him. Ross began the official caution, "Gary Dunhill, I arrest you for the murder of Willie Myners and Daisy Coffey…"

Gary's stubbled jowls quivered, his eyes bugged out like ripe blackberries. "I didn't murder no one," he whined. "That was Martin. I didn't know he meant to kill the bloke. It wasn't me, I tell you."

"Nothing like a little brotherly love," said Molly.

Trevor stepped up, his features set in cold indignation. He tugged the neckerchief from Gary's throat. If Gary had had a sword, Michael thought, Trevor would have broken it over his knee.

"Now, Martin," Ross said. He left Gary in the custody of the constables and led them back onto the deck.

"The presumption of the man! With his references, as well!" Trevor called to a passing seaman, "Here, have you seen Martin?"

The man gestured toward the town, its roofs and walls indistinct in the gathering gloom. "You've just missed him, Guv'nor. He legged it off the ship while you were tussling with Gary, there."

"Damn!" said Rohan, and started for the gangplank.

Michael was just behind, Molly on his heels, but Ross passed them both. "Adams," he shouted to a constable at the foot of the gangplank, "call for assistance. Put out a description." Leaving Hopewell watching, mouth agape, Ross sped off the ship and up the pier, and only stopped when he came to the cobblestoned square.

Michael and the others pounded up behind him. "Which way did he go?" Molly shouted. "Is he trying to lose himself in the crowd?"

Her answer came from Dockside Avenue. A shout and a sudden squeal of tires sent seagulls squawking into the sky. A woman screamed. Passersby scattered to the winds. A silver car sped away from Coffey's Garage toward the road out of town, bouncing off a curb and knocking over a rubbish bin.

Ross sprinted in the opposite direction, toward the police station and his own vehicles, aiming to break an Olympic record with his speed. Michael ran for Coffey's, Rohan at his side.

Randall Coffey lay sprawled on the cracked and stained cement in front of the garage, his long, gray hair and his gray beard framing a face the same color. "Who the hell was that? He pulled me out of the car and off he went. Maniac!"

Grasping Randall's bare arms, Rohan and Michael hauled him to his feet. Molly pushed through the gaping onlookers, none of whom had cameras. This time around, Fred Purnell and Tim Jenkins had missed their cue.

"Was that Aleister's Alfa Romeo?" Molly asked.

"That it was," said Randall. "He'll have my guts for losing it, and it not repaired yet."

"We'll never catch up," Rohan told Michael. "It's a saloon, not a sportier model, but it's fast. Once he gets past the switchbacks and onto the road west…"

Randall was still talking. "The thermostat's buggered. I'd just drained the coolant. He'll not get two miles out of town without it overheating, and if he doesn't switch it off it'll ruin the car. How will I explain this to Aleister?"

Laughing, he said, "Tell him to just lie back and think of England." Then Michael took off again. He heard Rohan's boots and Molly's farther back, and his own labored breathing—you could create another sort of Ironman competition out of his day's activities—spelunking, diving, running.

Logically, they should let the police chase Martin down. Or radio ahead for a roadblock, come to that. But logic had nothing to do with it. There was still a chance

the villain would escape. Michael was determined to deny
him that chance.

There was the train station and the packed parking
lot—please, let no one be parked behind him—no, the
Land Rover was in the clear. Michael leaped into the
driver's seat and Rohan into the passenger side. Even as
he found his keys and started the engine, he looked back
to see Molly climbing into her MINI Cooper. Now he
cursed his earlier practicality of taking two cars so he
could go home for his tunnel gear.

"Stay here," he shouted.

She didn't hear him. Or else she ignored him. Her car
started up just as his did. Her headlamps pierced the twilight.
So did his. But it wasn't exhaust that was thickening the air.
Michael had time for one quick glance behind him.

The harbor had disappeared behind the fog, a vaporous
wave front tinted a muddy pink by the setting sun. One
by one Blackpool's red pantiled roofs vanished into the
fog. Tendrils reached over the top of the cliffs and spread
across the moorland and forest. Its cold breath raised the
hair on Michael's arms.

The sound of a siren rose and fell at the far end of town,
and another, not quite in rhythm. Michael peeled out of
the car park, accelerating onto the moor road heading
west, the only one connecting Blackpool to the rest of
the world.

Before him, the sunset flared across a crimson sky.
Behind him, the remorseless fog flowed onward, draining
the landscape of color and definition.

Would Dunhill try to leave the road? The moorlands
rolled like a green-and-gold sea dotted with thick stands of
trees, but peat bogs hid in the hollows. While it would be
amusing to see Aleister's silver Alfa Romeo covered with
black peat, he'd just as soon Dunhill took the straight—

"Look there!" shouted Rohan.

Taillamps gleamed through the thickening air to his left. Michael waved his arm out of his window, pointing over the top of the Land Rover—and made an expert skid-and-turn onto a narrow blacktopped road while Rohan hung on for dear life.

In his mirrors Michael saw the MINI Cooper just behind him, lights smearing in the creeping fog. He held his breath as the dim shape of the vehicle swung around. Good, Molly hadn't run off the road.

Michael slowed as the asphalt beneath his tires disintegrated and the Land Rover bucked and jerked. The dilapidated barbed-wire fence beside the track, tufted with bits of wool from passing sheep, disappeared into scrubby heather and prickly gorse.

He knew where he was. He was driving up to Ravenhearst's front door.

There was the iron fence, a row of spears planted in the muddy soil. And there were the charred ruins of the mansion, the serrated edge of broken walls and shattered chimneys outlined briefly against the sky and then fading into the mist as though they were no more than evil memory.

The stolen Alfa Romeo sat before the gates, no lights, no engine, just a thin cloud of steam escaping from beneath the hood to mingle with the fog. Dunhill must have realized the car was overheating and turned off onto the first byroad he reached, hoping to lie low.

Michael drove up beside the other car and parked. Where was Martin, then? If he was still in the car, he was hunkered down. If he'd gotten out, he could be anywhere.

With a growl of its engine, the MINI Cooper stopped behind the Land Rover. Then it fell silent. Michael heard nothing but the clicking of his own cooling engine. He saw nothing but the headlamps focused on Ravenhearst's gates.

Their iron was wrought in sinuous shapes—branches, perhaps, or serpents. The stone gateposts were topped with stone beasts and half-concealed by clinging weeds and vines. Beyond the fence, trees loomed in the fog, each branch as sinister as a gallows. A faded no trespassing sign was mounted on a gatepost. Two padlocks secured the gate itself.

Those still, humanoid shapes on the other side—those were the infamous stone gargoyles. But the humanoid shape slipping along the fence beyond the far gatepost, bent in a low crouch, that had to be Dunhill… The figure vanished into the curtain of fog.

Michael scrambled from the car and ran toward where he'd last seen Dunhill. Rohan jumped out and made a flanking movement. Then Molly screamed.

Michael spun around to see Dunhill rush from the murk and jerk open the door of the MINI Cooper. Seizing Molly's arm, he started pulling her out of the car. Michael and Rohan doubled back, their hoarse cries echoing eerily.

Instead of resisting, Molly slid forward, got a foot on the ground and lunged. Her elbow landed in Dunhill's stomach and his breath escaped in an *oof.* But he still held her.

Michael wrapped an arm around Dunhill's chest and hauled him backward. Molly jerked free and staggered against the side of the car.

Dunhill turned and knocked Michael to the ground.

Michael had a split second to wonder if the man had armed himself with another knife. Then the soft turf gave beneath his back and water splashed on his neck. Dunhill's hands groped for his throat and he caught at the wiry wrists.

Rohan's forearm slammed up under Dunhill's chin and pulled him off Michael, while Molly tugged at his forearm.

Sirens, echoing like a banshee's wail, drew closer. Lights flared. Voices shouted. Footsteps thudded forward and Dunhill was seemingly plucked into the air.

Michael sat up, shook himself, then stood. Another set of hands touched his shoulders, but he recognized them. Molly. He coughed, cleared his throat and inhaled the moist fog enshrouding them. "I'm all right."

She slipped her arms around him. "You'd better be."

He returned her squeeze.

One of the Ripon constables was holding Dunhill's right arm, his face a businesslike mask. Luann Krebs, her lean features contorted by a grimace of triumph, held the other. Ross stepped forward, Paddington not far behind, his chest puffed, his moustache curling in glee. He thrust his face close to Dunhill's. "Thought you could cause trouble in Blackpool, did you, my lad? D.I. Ross, you may do the honors."

"My pleasure, sir," said Ross. "Martin Dunhill, I arrest you in connection with the murders of Willie Myners and Daisy Coffey. You do not have to say anything, but it may harm your defense if you do not mention, when questioned, something which you later rely on in court. Anything you do say may be given in evidence."

Dunhill cursed Ross. He cursed Paddington. He glared at the Grahams and cursed them, too, along with everyone else in Blackpool. "I didn't kill him. I didn't have anything to do with what's happened. You're fitting me up because I'm not a local."

"Yeah, right." Molly shifted against Michael's side. The lighted screen from her iPhone swam into his peripheral vision and her fingertip moved across it.

A ring tone erupted into the fog, the theme from

Rocky. Krebs dived for Dunhill's pocket and pulled out a phone.

"He tried to kill me," Molly explained. "Then he threatened us both. He imitated Trevor's voice."

"After stealing our phone numbers from Trevor, the way he stole Trevor's dagger," concluded Michael. He looked at Molly. "I heard that ring tone while I was standing at the gangplank trying to talk Dunhill into letting me onto the *Pearl*. Was that you, trying to prove the call came from Trevor's phone?"

"Yes, that was me."

"May I see that?" Ross took Molly's phone from her hand. "Mmm, just as I thought. This is the last number Willie phoned Sunday morning. What was he after, Dunhill?"

"Filthy sod wanted to deal with me. Threatened me. It was self-defense, Inspector."

"Oh, so now you're admitting to knifing him?"

Martin's thick features curdled.

Paddington said, "Willie threatened to expose you to your boss, was that it? Reveal that you'd been using Hopewell Transport as a vehicle for your drugs?"

"Blackmail," said Molly. "There's your motive. Blackmail and the coins added later for good measure."

"It's all about money," Michael remarked.

"What of Daisy?" asked Rohan. "Did she see Gary as well as you? Were you afraid she'd literally put together two and two?"

"And she'd tell everyone in town about it, until it got back to me," Paddington finished.

Martin didn't speak.

Molly said to Michael, "I can just hear him—Trevor, that is—carrying on about nurturing a viper in his bosom or whatever the verse is."

Michael nodded.

For half a tick he let himself wonder just who or what he and Rohan had seen slipping away along the fence, right before Dunhill leaped on Molly. A sheep, no doubt, its shape distorted by the fog.

After all, he didn't believe in ghosts.

"Take him away," Paddington said.

And with one last wary look onto the grounds of Ravenhearst, a place that had already absorbed so many curses, they hauled him off.

MOLLY DRAINED THE LAST bit of delicious, sweet, milky tea from her cup and sat back. The morning sun sent a bright glow across the floor of the breakfast nook. Iris had strutted her stuff with breakfast—even Ross had chowed down.

Michael had bruises on his throat, and she had bruises on her arm, but...

It was all over but the shouting, and she and Michael didn't have to shout.

She glanced across at Irwin and Iris, enjoying the last of the tea with the Grahams and their guest. "I felt like an extra in *The Hound of the Baskervilles*," she told them.

"That may be just about the only story not told about Ravenhearst," Iris said, "a spectral hound dripping phosphorescence from its jaws."

"Was that your forensics chaps who phoned earlier?" Irwin asked Ross.

The detective patted his lips with his napkin and folded it beside his empty plate. "They found Martin Dunhill's fingerprints on the dagger, and shreds from the rope tying Myners's boat to the dock on his jacket as well as curly gray hairs that match Daisy's. Analysis of the bloodstains on the neckerchief will take a while longer, but they look to be Myners's."

"Has he confessed?" Michael asked.

"Yes. I'll spare you the details, though—it was hard going getting useful information from the bragging and the bravado. Gary was a bit more forthcoming, but then, he's the sailor. Martin's the captain."

Iris placed the lid on the butter dish and started collecting the plates. "And Trevor Hopewell?"

"Eager to please," said Ross. "He was shocked that the Dunhills were running a drugs operation from the depths of his own corporation. We'll investigate further, of course. I expect some of his collecting activities would bear scrutiny, as well, but..."

"They're not your brief," said Molly.

Ross nodded acknowledgment. "Dunhill bribed Hopewell's secretary not to check his references. The man's been sacked."

"I should hope so," Irwin remarked.

"Martin Dunhill and Myners did meet in prison. Dunhill drew Myners into his family's drugs operation—had no problem adding one more port in case of a storm in Newcastle, so to speak. Here you are—cheers." Ross handed his plate to Iris. "Dunhill never expected Willie to have anything valuable, which is why he wouldn't at first let him through to see Hopewell."

Molly said, "He didn't know Willie had already contacted Trevor."

"Right. But it was only a matter of time until both Dunhills learned about Willie's gold coins."

"And both of them turned over Willie's flat?" Irwin asked.

"Yes, but the lad, Addison Headerly, scared them away before they found the coins."

Michael shook his head. "They weren't well hidden—I turned them up quick smart. If I'd known I was playing into Dunhill's plans, and putting Daisy in jeopardy..." Molly took his hand beneath the table.

"By finding the coins, you helped expose P.C. Fotherby," Ross told him.

"Well, yes."

"The break-in was also meant to put the frighteners on Willie," Ross went on, "showing him that as an agent for the Dunhills, he'd best cooperate."

"That's why he called Naomi," said Molly with a sigh. "He was going to take his windfall—the coins—and run, and he wasn't about to saddle himself with Michelle and her child. What a rotter, as Geoffrey said. And yet, I feel sorry for him."

Iris lifted the tea cozy off the pot and shook it. "Another pot?"

"No, thank you." Glancing at his watch—a rather posh model for a policeman, Molly noted—Ross scooted his chair back. "If the Dunhills had left well enough alone, the Dunhills would have had their drugs trade. But they wanted the gold, too."

"Treasure," said Michael. "There's a grand motive for all sorts of crime."

"Myners phoned Dunhill on the Sunday morning, said he was willing to deal. But when Dunhill arrived, the *deal* Myners suggested was blackmail—that was his last, desperate gamble. If Dunhill paid him the worth of the coins, then he wouldn't tell Hopewell about Dunhill's past, let alone Dunhill's present, which would cost him his access to the inner working of Hopewell Transport. They argued. Myners lost his temper and pulled his pocket knife on Dunhill."

"But Dunhill's knife was bigger," Molly said.

"Quite so, yes. As a villain himself, Dunhill sensed villainy, and armed himself with a handy weapon when he left the yacht."

"The fact he set Gary up as an alibi indicates he expected there to be trouble. After he killed Myners, he texted Gary to talk briefly with Trevor—albeit with a hat—to solidify that alibi further. I suspect we'll discover more about whether Dunhill meant to frame Hopewell by using that distinctive knife, giving his boss yet one more reason to be distracted from the internal affairs of his corporation."

No one offered an answer to that.

Ross went on, "After hearing about town that Naomi had been on the boat as well, he and Gary followed her, and sniffed round the bicycle shop. They thought Naomi might know where Myners found the coins. They figured she might have seen Martin stab Myners, come to that. If they'd managed to kidnap her, well…" His smile was tight as a high-tension wire. "Dylan was looking after her."

Michael exhaled loudly. "And thank goodness for that."

"No kidding," said Molly, "even if they never patch things up. Now, that's beyond *our* brief."

"The Dunhills also heard about town that the coins were missing," Iris suggested.

"They heard quite a bit, I reckon, not least from—and about—Willie's neighbor, Daisy," Irwin stated. "Who knew too much and told even more."

"Poor old soul," said Iris, "using her last breath to write down that number two. Using her last breath to spread one more bit of information about the folk around her."

Molly sighed.

"Was it Martin or Gary who lobbed the rock through our window?" Michael asked. "He wasn't actually meaning to break in, was he?"

"It was Gary. He and Martin only meant to intimidate you. Your security system has a reputation. But then, you and your wife have a bit of a reputation, as well." Ross's smile crisped at the corners. "I don't need to tell you, Mr. and Mrs. Graham, to mind how you go. You might see investigating crimes as an extreme sport, but…"

"No. We don't see it as sport at all. We don't go looking for these things. They just happen." Michael squeezed Molly's hand beneath the table.

Ross got to his feet. "Thank you for the five-star bed-and-breakfast. I must be off, though. The paperwork always takes longer than investigating the crime. To say nothing of the interaction with folk like your Fred Purnell and Tim Jenkins."

Laughing ruefully, everyone else stood up. In a flurry of activity they helped Ross collect his gear and saw him into his car and down the driveway off to Ripon.

Iris and Irwin went to attend to other duties, leaving Michael and Molly alone on the front step. "Seafaring Days are over," she said. "But it will take a while for the Blackpool Gold Rush to slack off."

"Autumn's coming soon. More fog, rain, cold—that will calm things down." Michael held the door open for her. "What are you planning for the morning, love?"

"To start working on a grant for a local drug rehab program."

"Good," he said, but he'd already pulled his phone from his pocket and was thumbing through the screens.

"Gold, treasure, edged weapons, pirates, ships, fog on the moors—you have more than enough material for your new game," Molly told him with a smile, and craned around his arm to get a glimpse at what had caught his attention.

His photos of Charles Crowe's model of Blackpool slipped one by one across the screen. "If Blackpool's haunted by anyone, it's Charles Crowe."

"If?" With a cautious glance over her shoulder, as though the man's ghost threatened to walk up the driveway, Molly pushed Michael into the house and shut the door.

* * * * *

REQUEST YOUR FREE BOOKS!

2 FREE NOVELS
PLUS 2 FREE GIFTS!

MYSTERY ™ W⊕RLDWIDE LIBRARY®

Your Partner in Crime

WWLI0

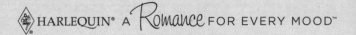